**Suddenly, she was entirely too aware
of how close they were.**

His scent surrounded her, warm and masculine, amber and spice, with just a hint of the kitchen and his cooking lingering in the air. The sound of his laughter mixing with that of her sisters echoed in her ears, and time seemed to disappear. It could have been thirteen years ago.

They could have been something so much more to each other than just old friends.

As if he was feeling the same powerful sense of nostalgia, he turned his head to look at her. His gaze and mouth soft, he curled up one corner of his lips. "It's nice. You know. Seeing you and your family like that."

Again, the defensiveness she would usually feel about that sort of comment failed to materialize. "Yeah?"

"Yeah. Feels like old times."

"I guess..."

He wasn't wrong.

But as pleasant as it was, drifting along in ancient memories, strengthening connections she'd neglected over time, it somehow didn't feel like enough.

She broke their gaze, shifting to look forward through the window. "I don't know about you," she said. "But I'm ready to go explore something new."

D1007847

# RETURN TO CHERRY BLOSSOM WAY

ALSO BY JEANNIE CHIN

*The Inn on Sweetbriar Lane*

*Only Home With You* (novella)

# RETURN TO CHERRY BLOSSOM WAY

## JEANNIE CHIN

FOREVER
New York  Boston

This book is a work of fiction. Names, characters, places, and incidents are the product of the author's imagination or are used fictitiously. Any resemblance to actual events, locales, or persons, living or dead, is coincidental.

Copyright © 2022 by Jeannie Chin

Cover design by Daniela Medina. Cover photographs © Shutterstock. Cover © 2022 Hachette Book Group, Inc.

Hachette Book Group supports the right to free expression and the value of copyright. The purpose of copyright is to encourage writers and artists to produce the creative works that enrich our culture.

The scanning, uploading, and distribution of this book without permission is a theft of the author's intellectual property. If you would like permission to use material from the book (other than for review purposes), please contact permissions@hbgusa.com. Thank you for your support of the author's rights.

Forever
Hachette Book Group
1290 Avenue of the Americas, New York, NY 10104
read-forever.com
twitter.com/readforeverpub

First Edition: August 2022

Forever is an imprint of Grand Central Publishing. The Forever name and logo are trademarks of Hachette Book Group, Inc.

The publisher is not responsible for websites (or their content) that are not owned by the publisher.

The Hachette Speakers Bureau provides a wide range of authors for speaking events. To find out more, go to www.hachettespeakersbureau.com or call (866) 376-6591.

ISBNs: 978-1-5387-5362-0 (mass market); 9781538753637 (ebook)

Printed in the United States of America

OPM

10  9  8  7  6  5  4  3  2  1

**ATTENTION CORPORATIONS AND ORGANIZATIONS:**
Most Hachette Book Group books are available at quantity discounts with bulk purchase for educational, business, or sales promotional use. For information, please call or write:
*Special Markets Department, Hachette Book Group*
*1290 Avenue of the Americas, New York, NY 10104*
*Telephone: 1-800-222-6747 Fax: 1-800-477-5925*

*For anyone who's ever felt like they didn't belong. This one's for you.*

# Acknowledgments

Thanks as always to my incredible agent, Emily Sylvan Kim, and my editor Madeleine Colavita, as well as Amy Pierpont and Sam Brody, all of whom helped shape this book into the story it is.

None of this would be possible without my family, especially my husband, Scott, who remains a source of endless support, and my beloved Tiny Human, who might make it hard to write sometimes, but who makes life a joy worth writing about.

Thank you also to my writing community, my Tea Ladies, and the organizations formerly known as CR-RWA and the Bad Girlz. I am eternally grateful to Knit Net Night for being a voice of reason during these long, tough couple of years.

Finally, thank you to everyone in my elementary, middle, and high school classes who made me feel like I belonged. You know who you are.

# CHAPTER ONE

❄ ❄ ❄ ❄ ❄ ❄ ❄ ❄ ❄ ❄ ❄ ❄

I have to hand it to you, May." May Wu's best friend Ruby shook her head before passing May's phone back across the table to her. "I didn't think it could be done, but you managed it."

"Story of my life," May said dryly.

She always had been an overachiever, but even she wasn't particularly impressed with this accomplishment.

"How exactly does a person run out of options on a dating site?" Ruby held up her hands and gestured around them in bewilderment. "In *New York*? It's like hitting the end of Netflix."

May shrugged. "I just have high standards, I guess."

They were about forty-five minutes into their "weekly" catch-up lunch, squeezed in amid both their busy workdays. Weekly was probably a stretch at this point, though. May traveled so much for her job she was lucky if she managed once a month.

Which meant Ruby had to cram all of her marveling about May's lack of a personal life into a mere fraction of the time.

Ruby picked up her chopsticks again and laughed.

"That's one way of putting it. What was wrong with the last guy you got matched with?"

"He carried a picture of his mother in his wallet, Ru. His *mother*."

"So?"

"So?" May didn't have anything against a healthy parent-child relationship, but she'd seen a guy get too attached to his mom before, and she wasn't going there again. Besides... "It was cut in the shape of a heart."

Ruby pulled a face. "Okay, yeah, that's kind of weird. But what about the guy before him?"

"You mean twelve-bottles-of-mustard-in-his-fridge guy?"

"Right." Ruby rolled her eyes. "How could I have forgotten."

"Fine, fine, so maybe I was little picky on that one," May conceded—though she still maintained that a man who owned more condiments than food was a bad bet. "But remember his predecessor? The one who brought baggies to an all-you-can-eat place?"

Scrunching up her mouth, Ruby brushed her dark hair back from her face. She was half Chinese and half white, and the slight wave to her hair still made May envious. "Yeah, you were right to pass on him."

With a dramatic sigh, May pocketed her phone and snagged a piece of mango tuna roll off the little boat of sushi they were sharing.

After giving the roll a quick dip in the soy sauce, she popped it in her mouth. Yum.

There was a sour note to the bite, though, and it had nothing to do with the flavor of the food. This was her favorite sushi place in Midtown, but she should know better than to order anything with fruit in it. More than a decade had passed, but mango and soy would never not bring up old memories.

She chewed and swallowed, dark eyes and a soft smile floating through her mind.

There was a reason she had high standards, after all.

Taking a sip of water, she frowned at herself in her head. She was a grown woman. At thirty years old, she'd achieved every one of her goals. She lived in New York. She had a great job that paid well, writing for a travel magazine. She got to visit incredible places all over the world.

And she still got mushy, thinking about her high school sweetheart whenever she ate something that reminded her of his cooking.

"Seriously, though," Ruby said, continuing as if one bite of sushi hadn't sent May on an unwelcome jaunt down memory lane. She tipped her head toward where May had stashed her phone. "You reject a *lot* of guys."

"All for good reasons."

Reasons that had nothing to do with said high school sweetheart.

Ruby narrowed her eyes. "You said that back in college, too."

Okay, maybe Ruby wasn't as oblivious as she seemed.

May had met Ruby their first semester together at NYU. May had been born in New York—Queens, to be specific—but her mom and sisters had relocated to a tiny dot in the middle of nowhere, North Carolina, when May was in middle school. She'd spent every day after that trying to find a way back. Upon her triumphant return, May had been desperate to experience everything life and the big city had to offer. She would have, too, if the afore-mentioned high school sweetheart hadn't been an anchor wrapped around her heart.

A fact that Ruby knew entirely too well.

May sighed. "What? You think I should have married the first guy to hit on me at a frat party?"

"No. But I think you've been avoiding commitments for about thirteen years now."

"Hardly." She had commitments. Her job, for one. Her pet tortoise, Todd, for another. Those things could live for thirty years.

"When's the last time you went on more than three dates with a guy?"

"It's been a while," May admitted.

"You and Josh broke up, what? Five years ago."

"Something like that." Her one and only real adult relationship should probably be more of a milestone in her mind, but it wasn't. They'd spent just shy of a year together, and she'd liked him. Maybe she'd even loved him, a little.

But there'd been no fire. No passion.

And in the end, no compatibility about what they really wanted from their lives.

Turned out Josh had loved having a stay-at-home mom when he was a kid. He expected his children to have the same.

Which meant he was going to need to find somebody else to have them with.

May wasn't against having kids. But if she'd wanted to quit her job and stay in one place for the rest of her life, she could have done it thirteen years ago—and with a guy she actually cared about.

Something in Ruby's expression softened. "Look, you know I support you all the way. But I worry about you sometimes."

May let out a long breath. "I know."

"Do you want to be single forever? Because if you do, that's fine—totally a valid life choice. But if you don't…"

May's insides squirmed, and she looked toward the window.

She didn't *like* being alone, exactly. But she hadn't been joking earlier. She had a great life, so she had high standards for letting anyone into it. Work was her priority. It always had been, ever since she was a nerdy kid, concentrating on her homework instead of paying attention to what the mean girls were saying about her at school.

Looking back at her friend, she reached across the table and squeezed her hand. "I'll loosen up my filters a little, okay?"

"Promise?"

"Promise." She pulled her hand back to snag the last of the shrimp tempura. "Just as soon as I get through this next round of layoffs at work."

Ruby scoffed. "They'd be fools to let you go."

Darn right they would, but ever since her magazine had been acquired by a bigger publisher back in the fall, the threat of the chopping block had been hanging over them all.

Speaking of which…

Catching the look in May's eyes, Ruby let out a put-upon sigh. "Fine, fine, you have to get back, I know." She lifted a hand to get the server's attention. "Check, please!"

Ten minutes later, May emerged from the elevator at her office. *Passage* magazine's headquarters was a clean, modern space, decorated with giant prints of photographs from all over the world. It had an open layout with writers, editors, and researchers at their desks focused on their screens, while assistants flitted from one station to the next.

She smiled to herself. It wasn't for everybody, but the hustle and bustle of the place filled her with energy.

Right until one of the interns stopped her some ten feet in the door. "Boss is looking for you."

"Oh?"

"Uh-huh." The intern nodded in the direction of the chief editor's office. "She's in a mood, too, so watch out."

May's pulse ticked up. That was never good. She cursed herself and her hubris in her head. What had she been thinking, agreeing with Ruby that her job should be safe? The fates could always hear that kind of thing and find a way to put you back in your place.

She kept her smile bright, though. "Thanks for the tip."

After stashing her jacket and purse at her desk and checking her lipstick, she headed straight for the big open door in the southwest corner—no point prolonging the agony.

May knocked on the glass without hesitation.

Zahra Thorne was a middle-aged Black woman with dark brown skin and short hair, buzzed on the sides, with longer, natural curls on top. At May's approach, she held up a single finger, her gaze glued to her screen through her chunky black reading glasses. She lowered her hand to tap rapidly at her keyboard for a second. Then she lifted her head.

Her crimson lips curled into a smile. "May, just the person I was hoping to see. Come on in."

Relief flooded May's nervous system. Whatever kind of "mood" Zahra might be in today, her wrath wasn't directed at May.

May settled into the chair on the other side of Zahra's desk. "What's up?"

"You unpacked from Costa Rica yet?"

"Does it matter?"

"Nope." Zahra clicked her mouse a couple of times, then turned her screen so May could see.

May's stomach just about dropped into her toes.

"You're from North Carolina, right?" Zahra asked.

"Uh-huh," May said numbly.

"You seen this?"

Of course she had.

She'd seen it when her younger sister, Elizabeth, had sent it to her.

"And why exactly have you been holding out on me?"

May jerked her gaze to the side to meet her editor's. "I mean, I..."

"There a lot of Wus in Blue Cedar Falls?"

"No, ma'am. No, there are not."

"Didn't think so."

There were three, in fact. Once upon a time, there had been four, but that was before May had run screaming from the place.

Now it was just her mom and her sisters. They weren't the only Asian people in the tiny little tourist town in the Carolina mountains, but they were close.

A fact May had been reminded of over and over again.

"So your mom's cat becomes an internet celebrity." Zahra tapped a pink-polished fingernail against the screen right over Sunny's face. "Bringing tons of tourists to a town where your sister launched a giant fall festival and helped a local vet open a bar. And you didn't think that was worthy of my attention?"

May just about swallowed her tongue.

She stared at the photo Zahra had brought up for a long second, trying to figure out how to get her mouth to work. In the shot, her mom was holding Sunny, the mean, three-legged calico that had basically become her fourth child since she'd had her stroke a year and a half ago. Beside her stood May's older sister, June, looking annoyingly perfect, as usual, with soft curls in her hair and wearing a red and black flowery dress. The guy with his arm around June was the aforementioned army veteran, a big, muscular white guy covered in tattoos named Clay—aka June's new boyfriend—and didn't that still make May's head spin.

"Look." Zahra turned her monitor back around, breaking the spell May had been under. "I know you have some issues with your hometown."

"Understatement," May said under her breath.

"But this is literally your family being highlighted in our competitor's magazine."

Could May's stomach sink any lower than her toes? At this point it was buried in the carpet.

Because her sister June had asked her to come to the Pumpkin Festival she'd revived back home in Blue Cedar Falls. May had wanted to go, even, but Zahra had handed her a last-minute assignment to write a story on the maiden voyage of a hot new luxury cruise liner, and sure, she could have begged off. But with *Passage* magazine's new owners looking for places to make cuts, she'd been afraid to miss the boat—literally.

Deep down, she had to admit that wasn't the only thing she'd been afraid of.

"I can send somebody else." Zahra gestured at the busy office beyond the glass wall. "But for a cover feature, an insider perspective is what's going to sell copies."

May sat up straighter. "A cover feature?"

"Local driving tours are the new staycation. People may not be able to afford to go to Costa Rica, but they can put the top down and head a few states over. I'm thinking we do the whole region. Lots of little towns in the area."

"There sure are." Despite herself, she started listing them in her head. All her information was a decade or so out of date, but June would be happy to catch her up. Running their family's inn had basically turned her into a walking, talking travel encyclopedia. And then, when June was done, their baby sister Elizabeth could give May the real scoop on where all the cool people were hanging out.

Zahra smiled and leaned back in her chair. "So what do you say?"

May bit her lip and calculated for all of ten seconds. She hadn't been back to Blue Cedar Falls outside of Christmas and family emergencies in thirteen years. She had good reason, too.

Heading back there to research a cover feature on the region would be a weeklong assignment. Her family would be happy to have her, and she'd be happy to see them, of course.

But June would give her that *look*. The guilt-tripping one she pulled out every time May showed her face. Her mom and stepdad would give her a gentler one, but it would still turn her inside out.

And being there that long, touring around, finding hidden treasures to spotlight for the story . . .

Who knew who she'd run into. A dozen faces flashed through her thoughts. Ones that made her blood boil.

And one that squeezed at her heart.

She pushed them all aside. This was a cover feature they were talking about.

"When do I leave?" she asked.

Zahra's smile only grew. "How fast can you repack your bags?"

———

"Still can't believe how fast you pack that stuff up."

Han Leung chuckled as he fit the last container of hot and sour soup into one of the cut-open liquor boxes the Jade Garden used to package up pretty much all of their takeout orders.

"Decades of practice." He tapped a couple of keys on the register, waited for it to print the sales slip, then stapled it to a fresh menu and slotted it into the front of the box. "Plus, I played a ton of Tetris on Uncle Arthur's old Nintendo."

"Don't remind me." Han's buddy Devin shook his head and kept slowly folding menus over on the other side of the counter.

"You're just mad I always beat you."

"Neither of you ever touched *my* high score." Han's mom reached past him to place a neat packet of napkins, chopsticks, and fortune cookies on top of the smallest of the containers.

"To be fair, you haven't given us a shot at a rematch in twenty years," Han said.

His mom made a disapproving sound in the back of her throat. "The queen does not need to prove her right to the throne."

She retreated into the back of the restaurant as the front door opened, probably off to go get ready for her bridge club.

Han greeted their customer with a smile. It was an out-of-towner with a coupon from the new visitor guide that had been circulating this spring. Asking about their stay, Han applied the discount.

The Jade Garden was his family's restaurant, started

by his uncle Arthur and continued by his folks and now mostly by him. Tourism in Blue Cedar Falls had been on the decline the past few years, and it had just about gone off a cliff when the freeway outside of town had opened. For a while there, business at the restaurant had been eighty percent locals.

But ever since the previous fall, when June Wu had relaunched the Pumpkin Festival and her mom had gone viral with her cat photos, tourists had started coming back. June had used her success with the festival to introduce a bunch of other promotions, including a coupon book that advertised all the Main Street businesses, and Han was grateful for the extra traffic.

Even if he didn't love being constantly reminded about the Wus.

Never mind that half of his social circle seemed to revolve around their family these days, despite his best efforts to avoid them for the past decade or so.

Putting on a smile, he finished the transaction just in time to catch the phone for the next incoming order.

"Want me to get this started?" his mom asked. She already had her jacket on and her purse slung over her shoulder, but she never made offers she didn't mean.

The lunch rush was just about over, though. He shook his head. "Nah, I got it. Say hi to the ladies for me."

One corner of his mom's lips tilted up, and she fussed with her scarf. "There are some gentlemen at bridge club, too."

Han tried not to vomit in his mouth.

He wanted his mom to be happy, after all. She'd been alone for over a dozen years now, ever since Han's father had died.

"Have fun, Mrs. Leung," Devin called.

Han's mom shot him a look that probably seemed friendly, but there was a chill underneath it.

Devin had been hanging out with Han since they were kids, so he reacted properly—by dropping his gaze and shutting his mouth.

Satisfied, his mom headed out the back.

As soon as she was gone, Devin scrubbed a hand over his face. "Think she's ever going to get over me dating your sister?"

"I am literally the last person you should be asking about that, you realize."

"Yeah, yeah."

The thing between Devin and Han's youngest sister Zoe was a few months old now, and Han tried not to act weird about it, but it was still taking some getting used to.

He wasn't willing to lose either of them over it, though, and at least he trusted Devin to treat Zoe well. So in the end, his own feelings about the relationship didn't matter.

"How's construction going on the new house?" he asked as he got a pan heating. He was interrupted by another order coming in online, and he grabbed a second wok down from the shelf.

Handling everything himself was hectic, but at least it meant he got to cook.

"It's good," Devin said, not missing a beat. "Framing's just about done."

He kept on folding menus. Beyond that, he didn't offer to help; Han had trained him out of that ages ago. Devin was his friend, and Han appreciated the company during long shifts behind the counter. He didn't want him here out of any kind of obligation or duty, though.

"Nice. You still hoping to be in there this fall?"

"I'd move in tomorrow if it weren't a code violation." He frowned. "Or if I thought there was any chance Zoe would go for it."

Han laughed. He could see it. Devin had been saving up to build his own place on the outskirts of town forever, and now that it was finally under way, he was champing at the bit.

"Just you, a sleeping bag, and a concrete slab?"

"I've had worse." Devin shrugged, a hint of darkness to his gaze. It disappeared quickly, though. Faster than it had before he and Zoe had gotten together, Han had to begrudgingly admit. "Anyway, you know me. Home is anywhere you feel like you belong."

"Home is my bed in my house with my dog in my hometown," Han countered. He'd tried it elsewhere, and it had felt like his skin was itching the entire time.

Sure, he would've liked to finish culinary school. Some days, he idly daydreamed about going back. But even if he hadn't gotten the call about his father a few months into his first term, he wasn't sure he would have stuck with it.

This was where he belonged.

Anything—or anyone—trying to lure him elsewhere didn't have his best interests at heart.

Too bad he'd had to learn that the hard way.

Han and Devin lapsed into quiet as Han focused on cooking, multitasking like mad to get six different dishes going. He rolled his eyes as he made yet another General Tso's, but someone in the second group had picked a new pomegranate shrimp dish off his experimental menu, so at least that was fun.

The bells over the front door chimed, and he looked up from the stove to spot their mail carrier Amy coming in. "Hey," he called out.

"Afternoon, Han."

"Here, I can grab that." Devin took the bundle of bills and junk mail and started skimming through it.

"Isn't opening someone else's mail a felony, Amy?" Han asked.

"Sure is. Want me to ring Officer Dwight?"

"You guys are hilarious."

"Have a good one, boys." Amy turned to the door, waving at them over their shoulder.

"Just leave it," Han told Devin, gesturing for him to put the mail on the counter as he stirred the sauce for the shrimp.

"You got something from the AARP. Want me to set it aside for you?"

"Ha-ha. Seriously, you don't have to—"

"What's this?"

Han squeezed some lemon over the shrimp and looked up. He squinted at the big manila envelope in Devin's hand. "I don't know. You're holding it—you tell me."

"It's hand-addressed from town hall."

Han dropped the lemon, flicked off all the burners, and strode over to snatch the envelope away.

"Well, excuse you." Devin rolled his eyes but he backed off.

Han glanced around before tearing open the envelope. His mom had left a while ago now, but she was like a cat. She snuck up out of nowhere sometimes. Lucky thing, this arriving on bridge club day.

He took a deep breath. The stack of papers he found inside was thick—that was a good sign, right?

"Seriously, what is it?" Devin asked.

Han shooed him away.

His heartbeat quickened. The logo at the top of the

letter was a familiar one, blue and yellow set on a white background.

Taste of Blue Cedar Falls.

It was another of June's brainchildren. She'd sold it as a festival for foodies. Fancy, gourmet, upscale, refined, blah, blah, blah. Tourists ate that stuff up.

Well, tourists ate up Chinese takeout, too.

Han had put in his application on the first day. He hadn't told June. They weren't particularly close, outside of her being attached at the hip to his buddy Clay, but he hadn't wanted any possibility of favoritism. He was already a long shot for a festival like this.

But his proposal for a booth serving upscale Asian fusion street food had been good enough to get him an interview. It had been a pain in the rear preparing for it without his mother finding out. She already thought his "secret" experimental menu was an indulgence. He wasn't going to tell her he was wasting time developing a menu for a specialty food festival unless he got in. He'd had to wait forever—the committee made its decisions about out-of-town vendors first, leaving locals until just a few weeks before the event.

And now it was the moment of truth.

The judges who had tried his samples at the interview had seemed impressed. He was pretty sure he'd even managed to sound coherent when he'd talked to them about his "unique perspective on the culinary arts."

He swallowed and scanned the opening paragraph of the letter.

*Dear Mr. Leung,*

*The selection committee for the first annual Taste of Blue Cedar Falls received an overwhelming number*

*of entries, from both restaurant professionals and
creative home cooks. After a very competitive review
process, we are pleased to offer you a booth…*

Han whooped out loud.

Holy crap. Like, holy *crap*, holy crap.

"What?" Devin crowded him, trying to read over his
shoulder.

Han passed the letter over and dove into the rest of the
paperwork. Details and terms and important dates were
laid out with excruciating specificity, and he'd take the
time to go through it soon.

For the moment, though, he set the entire stack aside.

He was going to have a booth at Taste of Blue
Cedar Falls.

He might not have any real interest in going back to
culinary school, but he still had a dream.

Back before he died, his father used to tell Han he
could have anything he wanted if he worked hard enough.
The sky was the limit, and the family restaurant was just
a jumping-off point.

Han didn't know about all that. He loved the family
restaurant. Fulfilling his duty and stepping into his old
man's shoes behind the counter had been fun, for the
most part.

But that didn't mean he didn't also want something
more. Something that was *his*.

If the booth was a success at Taste, who knew?

It might be his chance to move up in the world.

# CHAPTER TWO

❊ ❊ ❊ ❊ ❊ ❊ ❊ ❊ ❊ ❊ ❊ ❊

Well, this was certainly a step down in the world.

As May rolled her suitcase through the tiny airport in Asheville, she sighed. One week ago, she'd been at a deluxe resort twelve feet from the ocean in Costa Rica.

Now she was getting ready to do battle with a rental car company about getting a vehicle with four-wheel drive instead of the compact sedan the magazine's travel agency had secured for her.

Even as she grumbled to herself about the hassles, though, a bubble of anticipation grew behind her ribs. Part of it was dread, of course. There was a reason she had left western North Carolina in her rearview mirror over a decade ago.

But there was a lightness to her step, too.

Costa Rica had been beautiful, but May had been doing solo trips around the world nonstop for years now, researching spectacular destinations for *Passage*. Once upon a time, when she'd been dating Josh, he'd gone on a couple of her adventures with her, and it had been fun, having somebody to talk to. Even if he was kind of boring.

She rolled her eyes at herself and chuckled.

One thing she could say about her family was that they were never boring. She hadn't been home for more than three days since she was eighteen. Having a full week to spend with her mom and stepdad and sisters would undoubtedly be too much.

But it might be nice, too.

Negotiations with small-town car rental agency supervisors complete, she slotted the key into the ignition of a sensible little SUV. She took a second to get her phone paired with the Bluetooth. She'd need it for the directions, if nothing else.

She hesitated, her phone still in her hand for a minute.

In the rush of heading out here, she might have accidentally forgotten to let her family know she was coming. She'd told herself it was because she didn't want to disappoint them. If anything had gone wrong, or if Zahra had changed her mind about May's assignment at the last minute...May couldn't have handled letting her family down again. Not after the way June had practically pleaded with her to come for the Pumpkin Festival last fall, only for May to have to cancel on her with barely two weeks to go.

At this point, nothing short of a head-on collision was going to keep her away. But she wavered, anyway. Nerves stole over her, making her heart jangle.

She set her phone down and put the car into drive.

Surprising them would be more fun than giving them a heads-up. She wasn't chickening out. She was just excited to see their looks of shock when she walked in the door.

It was a gorgeous spring afternoon as she merged onto the new freeway heading out of town. She rolled her windows down, and the breeze poured in. The scent of it took her back, crisp pine and warm sunshine, and for a second, she was sixteen again, riding around with Han and Devin and their friends on the back roads. Careless and happy.

Only had she ever really been careless? Or happy?

The warmth of sitting next to Han as he drove his parents' Jeep receded from her memory, and hot, skittering flashes of humiliation swept in to replace it. Instead of fresh mountain air, she smelled the teenage sweat and industrial cleaners of Blue Cedar Falls High.

She remembered Jenny Sullivan knocking her books out of her arms. Getting a finger stepped on when she bent to pick them up. Taunts about her glasses, her lunches, her grades, her clothes.

One of Jenny's hangers-on asking her if she wore a kimono at home. A teacher wanting to know what China was like.

The word "CHINK" spray-painted in red across her locker door.

Her vision went a little blurry for a fraction of a second before she righted herself. Stupid, letting herself get distracted thinking about ancient history when she was on unfamiliar roads.

The closer she got to Blue Cedar Falls, the harder it became to keep her emotions in check. Nervous energy buzzed around under her skin. Her thoughts flitted from her family to her work to Han to Jenny and back again.

When her GPS told her to get off the highway, it was a relief just to have something else to concentrate on.

Another forty-five minutes of steep, winding roads lay in front of her, though, and she groaned. June had told her that the highway commission's decision to cut south through the mountains without any exits near Blue Cedar Falls had been a death knell, and she had to admit her sister might have been right. May made a couple of voice memos to herself to refer back to when it came time to write her story about the region for *Passage*. There were all kinds of ways to make "in the middle of bleeping nowhere" sound appealing. "Off the beaten path," for example. "Remote," "secluded," "worth the trip." She could spin this.

Finally, familiar sights began to crop up. The farm where her stepdad used to drag the family to go apple picking in the fall, the art center where her little sister Elizabeth went to fire her abstract pottery creations.

The secluded outlook off the road where she and Han used to sometimes go park.

A whole different kind of memory swept through her, thinking about the stolen kisses they would share up there. The first experimental touches, the overwhelming flushes of blossoming desire.

Something inside her fell.

And then there was the last time they'd gone to the outlook together.

After he'd decided not to follow her to New York for college, and after he told her they should see other people while they were apart.

After his father died, smack-dab in the middle of their freshman semesters, and she'd flown to his side.

Only for him to bring her up here and tell her he needed her. He needed her to come home—forever.

And she...*couldn't*. She couldn't abandon her dreams or drop out of school. She couldn't spend the rest of her life in this town she'd put all her energy into trying to escape.

The town he was never, ever going to leave.

And so they'd said goodbye for good.

Tightening her grip on the steering wheel, she exhaled long and slow. What was wrong with her? She'd been back to Blue Cedar Falls for holidays in the past, and sure, she'd gotten a little emotional from time to time. But something about this longer, unplanned trip, with spring in the air and no snow on the trees…It was making it hard to stay in the present.

Her thoughts were pulled even deeper into the past as she turned onto Main Street. This was the part of town where the tourists flocked. Most of the shops and restaurants she passed had been there since she was a kid. She averted her eyes as she drove past the Jade Garden, focusing instead on the new sign at Sprinkles ice cream shop and the handful of folks sitting at tables outside Gracie's Café. There was the record store that defied expectations by somehow staying in business all these years. Patty Boyd's snooty art gallery and old Dottie Gallagher's florist shop.

And then there were places she'd never seen before. What looked like a little bistro, and a wine bar, and a café with its name spelled out in giant Scrabble tiles on the roof. She'd have to check them out as part of her research.

Finally, the Sweetbriar Inn came into view.

Her family's bed-and-breakfast was a grand old place, three stories tall with bright white siding and balconies that peeked over the magnolia trees just coming into bloom. In her article, she'd call it refined, but with plenty of southern charm.

She frowned as she glanced across the street. That charm looked different with the new bar that had taken over Susie's Quilts and More pumping faint strains of classic rock into the dusky air.

Well, she'd always said Main Street could use some shaking up. Looked like it had gotten plenty.

Curious about what other new discoveries awaited her, she found a spot to park in back of the inn. She grabbed her suitcase and rolled it around to the front.

Standing on the blue painted porch, she sucked in a deep breath.

Then she put on her best confident New Yorker face and marched right on in.

The warm, comforting scents of apple pie and roses greeted her in the lobby. The local artist whose work was on display this month was an oil painter. Pretty still life canvases dotted the walls. The pillows on the off-white couches were immaculately fluffed. Not a speck of dust was to be found on any of the lamps or tables.

For a second, May swore she was transported back in time. Things had changed, but she could have been the one behind the counter, working on a paper for school while standing ready to help any wayward guests.

Instead, it was her older sister June.

And when June caught sight of May, she gave the Saturday morning cartoons they used to watch a run for their money, her eyes bugged out of her head so hard.

Grinning, May strode across the lobby. Memories of the last time she came home rose to her mind. June had met her at the airport with a box of cookies from the bakery next door and a bouquet of balloons. The two of them weren't as tight as they used to be when they were kids, but they'd talked the entire drive home, about anything and everything, falling back into their rhythm as if no time had passed at all.

As she reached the counter, shivers of nervous excitement raced up and down her spine.

A lot had changed since that last, planned visit. This meeting was on May's terms, not June's, and June hated that.

Then there was the small matter of her standing June up last fall.

In her most casual tone possible, she announced, "I'm looking for a room."

"May?" June rose to her feet.

Her heart doing flip-flops, May lifted one hand and wiggled her fingers in a wave. Ugh, where was that New York confidence she'd been projecting? "Um, hi. So I was just in the neighborhood."

June shook her head. "You were— Wait." She blinked. "I mean, *What?*"

This wasn't quite the greeting May had been hoping for. It wasn't the one a part of her had feared she'd deserved, either, but could she get a little excitement?

"Are you okay?"

"I'm fine," June answered automatically. Then she seemed to check herself, and her deer-in-the-headlights act changed. "Oh my gosh, what am I doing? May!"

She darted around the desk, and May's chest squeezed as she released the handle of her suitcase and let her sister wrap her up in a hug. The embrace didn't linger as June pulled away.

"What are you doing here?" June asked. She was still smiling, but her posture was stiff.

"Glad to see you, too," May teased, but she wasn't quite sure what to do with the tension in the air.

A sinking feeling opened up in her abdomen.

Last fall, when she'd had to cancel on coming in for the

Pumpkin Festival, there'd been a franticness to June's tone. May had asked their mom if things were going okay the next time they'd spoken, and Mom had waved it off, saying June was just stressed, but that was nothing new. Her younger sister, Elizabeth, had said more or less the same thing when May had brought it up during their weekly texts about the trashy show they were watching together. But May still hadn't been so sure.

Then she'd gotten stuck in a blizzard in Norway for Christmas.

After going almost a solid year without seeing each other, she thought she'd get a little warmer of a welcome.

But maybe that was presumptuous. "Sorry," she said instinctively, and she hated how being back in this town made her revert to being mousy. "I should have called."

"I mean, it would have been nice."

"Things just happened so fast. My editor came up with this story idea out of the blue yesterday—"

"Your editor?" June's voice rose.

More nerves jangled around in May's stomach. "Yeah. She saw the piece you did for one of the other magazines and recognized the name."

"So this was her idea."

May couldn't read her sister's tone. "Sort of."

"Oh." June swallowed. The new smile that took over her face left May all turned around. It was half annoying-older-sister June and half working-the-front-desk June, and crap, was May screwing this up? "Well, that's great."

"If nothing else, it means I have the corporate credit card." May plucked the AmEx from her purse and wiggled it around. That should raise her sister's spirits. "So stick me with your highest rate."

June's mouth pulled to the side, and she darted her gaze to the desk behind her. "You see, the thing is…"

———

"Love what you've done with the place," May muttered beneath her breath.

She glanced around her childhood bedroom in the back section of the inn where her family lived. Her sister Elizabeth's room had been converted into her mother's craft studio ages ago. May should have known her room would be next.

She didn't begrudge it, even. She only came home once a year.

Still, she eyed the treadmill folded up against the pale pink wall with suspicion. She raised an even more skeptical eyebrow at the way the handles of the elliptical machine had been turned into what appeared to be a laundry rack.

"Sorry about this." June fluttered about, tugging a couple of bras down off a clothesline that ran across the ceiling. "If I'd known you were coming..."

"It's fine, it's fine."

Again, May fantasized about the deluxe suite they'd upgraded her to in Puerto Viejo.

Apparently, all the guest rooms at the Sweetbriar Inn were occupied, which was great for her family's bank account, but not so great for May. Her *Passage* magazine press credential and her corporate AmEx could get her in a lot of doors, but not this one.

June waved a hand at the rack of weights set up in front of May's old bookshelf. "The doctor said that now that Mom's feeling better she should really be exercising more. Ned's doctor's been telling him the same thing, so..."

"Seriously, it's not a problem."

June stood there for a minute, gazing at May. May

fought not to squirm. "It's great to have you here, May. Really."

"It's great to be here," May assured her.

In her head, she was calculating how long it would take her to finish the research she would need to do so she could get the heck out of here and back to New York.

It wasn't just the room. June was being weird. The only upside of having to come back to Blue Cedar Falls was getting to see her family. So where were the rest of them?

May had texted Elizabeth with a selfie of herself in the lobby, captioned, "Surprise!" In reply, she'd gotten fifteen emojis, and then something about being stuck running a paint and sip at the wine bar down the road, along with some promises to catch up tomorrow.

"So are Mom and Ned around?" May asked.

"They were supposed to be having dinner with Bobbi's folks tonight, but I texted them and—"

As if on cue, the door between the family residence and the rest of the inn slammed open, and footsteps rang through the hall.

"Brace yourself," June warned.

May grabbed on to the edge of the treadmill for good measure.

Her mother appeared in the doorway a few moments later. "May!"

"Hey, Mom." May smiled. Now there was the enthusiasm she'd been looking for.

"What are you doing here?"

Why did everyone keep asking her that? "Work trip. I was hoping you and Sunny would give me an exclusive."

Her mother narrowed her eyes.

Well, maybe her eye.

May scanned her mother up and down, her smile fading slightly as she did.

And the thing was that she knew her mother was still only a year and a half out from a major stroke. To hear June tell it, their mom had practically been on her deathbed, though everyone from Elizabeth to their mother herself had said June was blowing things out of proportion.

May had managed to come down for a couple of days right after to see for herself. She'd found their mom in rough shape, but the doctors had said she was young and strong and likely to make a full recovery. May had still felt guilty about having to take off again so soon to get back to her assignment, but she'd left reassured that everything would be all right. In their monthly phone calls, her mother always swore she was fine, and okay, yes, the partial paralysis on her one side had been evident in the handful of video chats they'd done.

But May had still been completely unprepared for how severe it would be in real life.

May's mom leaned heavily into her cane as she crossed the room. Her smile was lopsided, and when she leaned in for a hug, her right arm didn't lift all the way to reach May's shoulder.

May wrapped her arms around her mom anyway, looking over her head at June. Her sister shrugged, her gaze defensive.

"We talk about work later," her mother said. "Just glad to have you home."

"Me, too."

"Ned," her mom shouted. "Ned, it's May!"

May's stepfather, Ned, lumbered into the doorway. In his southern drawl, he said, "Figured I'd give you girls a minute. Not much room in here, you know."

May's mom made a disapproving tutting sound behind her teeth as she backed off. "Plenty of room."

"I should head back to the desk anyway," June said.

May kind of wanted to chase after her. She had questions, but before she could, Ned came forward and slipped an arm around her. He pressed a kiss to the top of her head, and good grief. Her mom may have changed, but at least her stepdad hadn't. Like, at all.

"Hey there, sweetie."

"Hey." She looked to her mom, then down, her gaze drawn by motion on the ground. Sunny, her mom's internet-famous, grumpy, three-legged cat had slipped in at some point. As Ned gave her a little space, May crouched down and held out a hand. "Hey to you, too. Remember me?"

The cat literally turned up her nose, which wasn't exactly a definitive response.

"Of course she remembers you," Mom said. "Just give her a minute to warm up."

I feel you, Sunny, May thought.

She rose again. "June said you were at the Moores' place. You didn't have to—"

"Nonsense," her mom scolded. "They live here. How long you staying this time? Couple days?"

"A week is the plan."

Her mom let out a sigh of relief. "I'm so glad June finally convinced you to come. She's been trying to get you to write a story about this place for months!"

"Wait." May scrunched up her brows. Sure, June had floated the idea once or twice, but her mom was making it sound like there had been some sort of a campaign.

"Doesn't matter now," her mom admonished. "Come on, I don't have much in the kitchen—you should have let me know you were coming."

"I know, I know—"

"But I manage. Tomorrow, I make your favorite."

Oh, wow—a hot plate of her mom's lasagna sounded incredible. But then May's heart sank. Preparing the meal was a whole day, whole family affair.

May shook her head. "I have to tour a bunch of restaurants for research."

Ned put his hand on May's shoulder. "Give her this, will you?"

Her mother's expression was carefully neutral. Like she was expecting May to refuse again.

Or to disappear.

May kind of wanted to, but only to sink into a hole in the ground.

She managed to summon a smile. "Lasagna tomorrow sounds great."

"That's my girl." Her mom led the way into the kitchen, listing everything they could do together while May was in town, and May carefully bit her tongue. They could discuss how to fit all the social calls and shopping trips and cooking in around the tasks May had set for herself for researching her article later.

Out in the living room, Ned stayed one step ahead of her mother, pulling out her chair, getting her a drink. Fluffing a pillow.

Her stepfather had always doted on her mother. But this was on an entirely new level.

As she perched on the edge of the couch, May snuck a peek through the open door to where June was doing something on the office computer. She tried to catch her sister's eye, but June studiously kept her gaze pointed straight ahead.

May frowned.

Discussions with her mom about her schedule might be able to wait.

Discussions with her sister about what on earth was going on here?

Now, those couldn't wait at all.

———

Of course, leave it to June to hide behind a combination of work and their mother's skirts. May tried to catch her half a dozen times, but it was just like it had been back when they were kids. Whenever May had needed something, June was always busy, busy, busy, busy, busy.

Finally, after a mapo tofu dinner their mother had "just thrown together," June bustled Mom and Ned out of the kitchen so she could do the dishes.

May pounced.

"What the hell, June," May accused, her voice low. *Jeopardy!* was on in the living room; between that, the sound of the running water, and their mom and stepdad being near-future candidates for hearing aids, she probably didn't need to keep it down, but it was instinct.

"Excuse you?"

"What's going on?"

"I don't know what you mean." June pointed at one of the lower cabinet drawers with her foot. "Towels are still in there if you want to make yourself useful."

"Drying dishes is stupid. That's what the air is for." May still bent down and got a towel out. "Seriously, though."

"Seriously what?" June asked, turning to face May for what felt like the first time all night.

May sucked in a deep breath. Gripping the towel,

she exhaled slowly. "Why didn't you tell me how bad things were?"

June laughed, but it wasn't a funny laugh. She faced the water again and started aggressively scrubbing pans. "This? This is fine."

"Mom—"

"Mom is *healthy*." June shoved a pot at May. "Her doctors say she's doing great, considering."

"I thought she was supposed to make a full recovery."

"She basically has."

"Have you seen her?" May still couldn't get over how much worse her mother's health seemed, now that she was seeing it with her own eyes, as opposed to on a pixelated screen.

"Every day." June whipped her head around, daggers in her eyes. "Every day, while I've been here taking care of her and running the inn. The better question is, have *you* seen her?" She pursed her lips and scrunched up her brow. "Oh right, you haven't, because you've been in New York."

"That's not fair."

"You know what's not fair? Last year, I needed you." June's voice suddenly caught. "The inn was barely staying afloat, the town was dying, and I asked you to come."

May took a step back. Crap, she'd known June wanted her to come down for the Pumpkin Festival, but where was this anger coming from? "You said you wanted me to see the festival."

"And would I have done that if it wasn't important?"

"You didn't say—"

"I shouldn't have had to." June dropped the pan she'd been washing into the sink with a *clang*.

"You girls okay in there?" Ned called.

"We're fine," June and May replied as one.

June huffed out a breath and dropped her gaze. "Look, it all worked out okay, May. I found people who could help me. Elizabeth, Mom, Ned, Bobbi, Han." She swallowed when she said that last name, darting a glance at May and then away. "Clay. They all rallied, and we got through it."

The cracks in June's voice—not to mention the name of May's ex—rattled May. She'd had no idea things were so bad.

May forced herself to speak softly. "I just wish I had known there was something to get through."

June sighed. Her hands flexed and released before she picked up the pot and a sponge again. "I wish you had, too." She ran the sponge over a stuck-on bit of rice. "I wish you'd been here."

"June…" They'd had this conversation a hundred times, back when May was in college, and then a few hundred more after she accepted her first job and elected to stay in New York.

May had thought they'd gotten past this. That her sister had accepted her decision.

"But you weren't," June said quietly. "I've been the one here, working my rear end off. So you don't get to question the choices I had to make. You don't get to imply that I'm not taking good enough care of Mom."

"I didn't mean—"

June's voice turned sharp. "Really?"

May rubbed at her eyes until she saw stars.

How did this always happen? How did June twist her words? May had been taken aback by the lingering symptoms of their mother's stroke. And yes, maybe she'd come on a little strong, asking why she'd been left in the dark, but she hadn't been trying to pick a fight.

June held out the clean pot a little less violently this time. May took it, dried it—even though it was stupid—and put it away.

May opened her mouth a dozen times, but she couldn't think of anything to say that wouldn't make things worse. This was part of why she and June had stopped talking about anything that mattered. Random funny memes and jokes about shows they were watching were fun, but at the end of the day, June was never going to forgive May for making a life for herself outside of this tiny, small-minded, suffocating town.

And May was done apologizing for it. June knew why May had left. She'd dealt with some of the same crap from bigots and bullies herself, if never to so severe of an extent.

She'd watched her cry her eyes out over Han.

May could explain it all again and again. She could explain the pressure she felt at work, and how precarious her position always seemed. How difficult it was to hold on to what she'd always considered to be a dream job. How even if she'd wanted to come home more often, she rarely could.

But what would be the point?

They finished washing the dishes together in silence.

Drying her hands, June gestured at the front desk. "I'm going to go take care of some paperwork. You should spend some time with Mom and Ned. You know. While you're here."

Wow. Passive-aggressive much?

May sank her nails into her palms to keep herself from saying something she'd regret and smiled tightly.

As June took off to go be a martyr somewhere else, May found her mom and stepdad in the living room.

Her mom patted the couch cushion. Sunny glared at May from her perch on her mother's lap, but then went back to licking her own butt, so May wasn't going to put too much stock in her opinion.

May sat down next to her mom, and her mom reached for her hand. "Give her time."

May made a dark sound in the back of her throat. A century wouldn't be enough. All May had was a week— and that was with a ton of work to fit in, too.

She put her sister out of her mind the best she could, but between the crappy things June had said and the too-happy looks her mom kept giving her, guilt rolled around in her gut.

The air felt too heavy, and the walls too close. She put on a good face through the rest of *Jeopardy!* and then a few games of euchre, but the restless itch under her skin was back.

By the time her mom and Ned decided to turn in for the night, she was buzzing with the need to get out; she probably should have never come. A sneaky voice inside told her to wait for them to fall asleep and then grab her suitcase and head straight back to the airport, but she couldn't.

She couldn't stay here in this silent apartment, either, though.

Unsure of what else to do, she snagged her jacket from where she'd hung it on the arm of the elliptical and headed out.

But even the fresh spring air of the courtyard couldn't settle her. It was too quiet; it always had been. Hugging her arms around herself, she walked down the path toward the gate.

In New York, it wouldn't matter that it was nine o'clock

at night. The streets would be full. There'd be bars and bookstores and weird avant-garde theater performances.

While here there was...

She emerged out onto the sidewalk, only to hear the faint strains of eighties hair metal on the air. She looked across the street.

And, well. It might still be tiny, sleepy, backward Blue Cedar Falls.

But at least now it had a bar.

# CHAPTER THREE

❋ ❋ ❋ ❋ ❋ ❋ ❋ ❋ ❋ ❋ ❋ ❋ ❋

Looked like you guys could use another round."

Han's little sister Zoe approached the table where Han, Devin, and Clay were sitting. She balanced her tray of drinks seemingly effortlessly, even when Devin gave her those obnoxious moon eyes he always shone on her.

Barf.

Han didn't want to go back to the days when they were trying to hide their relationship from him, but did they have to rub it in his face?

"Thanks," Han said as she placed a fresh pint in front of him.

"No problem." She raised a brow at Clay. "You planning on getting back to the register at some point or should I start trying to teach Kenny how to use it?"

"What do I pay you for again?" Clay asked, accepting the glass of stout she passed him.

"Um, being the best waitress you have, closing three nights a week while you're off canoodling with your girl-friend, and doing all of your accounting for you."

"Right." Clay shook his head. "I'll be there in five."

"Whatever you say, boss."

Zoe gave Devin both a fresh drink and a kiss on the cheek before heading off to a different table.

It was a decent night at the Junebug, with just enough people for it to feel lively but not so many that it was overcrowded.

Clay had opened the bar the previous fall. Despite being a newcomer to town—and despite a bunch of the senior residents on Main Street giving him a ton of crap—he'd really made something of the place. It was homey and fun, classy without being pretentious. Locals and tourists alike came for a beer or a burger or the chef's special cheese fries—which even Han could admit were pretty genius.

Clay had also managed to become one of Han's best friends.

To prove it, he raised his glass. "To the breakout hit at Taste of Blue Cedar Falls."

"To Han Solo," Devin agreed.

Han groaned. "I told you to stop calling it that."

"You come up with a better name for your new restaurant, and I'll consider it. Until then…"

"You guys are the worst." Han still clinked his glass against both of theirs.

As much grief as he gave them, he was secretly pleased they were there, celebrating his acceptance into the festival with him. Devin had been encouraging his quiet ambition forever, and a bunch of his other friends were happy to show up at his house for the occasional informal dinner party where he used them as guinea pigs for his new recipes.

But he hadn't really acted on his dreams of creating his own business in years. Not since his father had died and all his plans had gone out the window. He'd been too busy running the family restaurant and taking care of his sisters and his mom to focus on anything he might want for himself.

With the exception of Devin, no one had really questioned his need to put his duty to his family above his own desires. No one had really taken his back-burner pipe dream of opening a high-end restaurant seriously. No one since...

He took a deep swallow of his beer and set it down.

Nope. He wasn't going to think about—

"May," Devin said.

Han just about choked on his beer. As Han coughed, Clay scrunched up his brows.

"What?" Clay asked.

No way Devin could read Han's mind. They'd been friends for a long time, but that was just weird.

"May," Devin repeated, more urgently this time. He clapped Han on the back, and with his other hand, he pointed at the door.

Han turned around.

And for a second, time stood still.

He hadn't seen May Wu in thirteen years. Not since that awful night and their even more awful fight, but for a second all of that faded.

If it was possible, she was even more stunning at thirty than she'd been at seventeen. May had been beautiful forever, but back in high school, she'd hidden behind chunky glasses and boxy clothes. Underneath, she'd been soft, though, and when she'd fixed her brilliant, dark eyes on him, he'd turned into a bumbling mess.

She wasn't hiding anything now, and he was still a mess. She must have gotten contacts or Lasik or something. Her liquid eyes shone, framed by dark lashes.

Her lips shimmered, and her skinny jeans and tailored jacket showed off a figure that brought something inside him to life.

Only it wasn't really her figure—attractive as she undeniably was.

It was her.

May had been *it* for Han. Even after she'd left, he'd thought of her that way. The goodbyes they'd said after his father's funeral had been heartbreaking and final, but he'd never fully believed they were *final* final.

Years had passed. But deep in the back of his mind, he'd always thought they'd run into each other again. She'd come home, and he'd spot her, or she'd spot him.

He'd had fantasies, back in those first few months, that she'd come running into his arms, apologies spilling from her lips.

Here in the present, he stood up. Dully, he felt himself putting down his beer.

As if she could feel his dumbstruck stare, May turned. Their gazes connected, and lightning shot through Han's chest. This was it. The moment he'd forgotten he was even waiting for.

May ran all right. But not into his arms.

Instead, she whipped right back around and ran straight out the door.

"May," he called out, the word escaping him before he'd so much as thought it. He lumbered forward, only to have Devin grab him by the arm.

"Dude." Devin yanked harder when Han tried to pull away. "What are you doing?"

The door slammed closed behind May. The sudden vacuum in Han's chest made his rib cage want to crumple.

"Maybe she didn't hear me."

"She definitely heard you," Devin said.

"Wait." Clay shook his head. "Was that *that* May?"

Devin didn't let go of Han, who was starting to feel like one of those cartoon characters, his legs spinning in midair. What was he still doing here?

To Clay, Devin said, "You mean your girlfriend's sister, aka the girl who smashed Han here's heart into a billion pieces May? Uh, yeah."

"I'll be right back," Han swore.

"No, you won't."

Clay backed away slowly. "Uh, I'm going to go check on the register." Before he could get too far, he paused, looking at Han. "Unless you need me."

His sincerity pulled at Han—almost as hard as the instinct to follow May.

"All he needs is a knock on the head." Devin gave him one for good measure, a gentle tap of his closed fist against Han's temple. Then with a sigh, he let him go. To Clay, he said, "Guess I better settle up with you."

Devin moved to follow Clay, casting a backward glance at Han that was full of warning and concern.

Han rolled his eyes at both.

He had to follow May. Every fiber of his being compelled him to.

But he wasn't completely oblivious. May turning tail at the very sight of him spoke loud and clear.

He was just going to say hi. Make sure she was okay. Then walk away. Head home and take his dog out before his mother could give him grief about it.

He'd be fine.

With a nod to his friends, he took off. Only a minute had passed, but it felt like an age. He got outside, and for a second, his heart thudded around in his chest.

Then he caught sight of her.

He ran after her, calling her name again, then once more when he was close enough to grab her, only he kept his hands to himself.

She finally stopped. She turned to face him.

Han sucked in a rough breath. The power of seeing her again after so long just about bowled him over. Up close, she was even more beautiful.

"May," he said again, but then he stopped himself.

She was gorgeous, all right, but her eyes shone, and her cheeks were pink. She bit her lip with enough force it looked like it hurt.

Like she was trying to keep from bursting into tears.

"What—" he started.

"Can we just—" she spat out, and her voice was a vise around his heart. She looked away, the wet gleam to her eyes only growing. "I'm sorry. I know I'm the worst, and you probably have plenty of things you want to tell me about how I've screwed up."

Han flinched. Okay, maybe fantasizing about her running into his arms had been a little deluded, but did she really think he'd followed her out here to lay into her? "May, I—"

"I got stuck coming here on some stupid assignment that I should have turned down, okay? I've been here for five hours, and I've already had enough emotional reunions to last the rest of my life, and I can't do another one. So can we just *not*?" She finally met his gaze again. "Please?"

He studied her for a long minute.

So many things had changed. But he'd heard that tone of voice before. Back a dozen years ago, it hadn't been one she'd been willing to reveal to many people. She hadn't been willing to reveal much of anything to much of anyone outside her circle.

She was clearly less of a wallflower than she used to be, but was she any less guarded? Did it mean any less that she was willing to tell him how she really felt?

Did he want to get a chance to find out?

Making a snap decision, he said, "You need a drink."

She scrunched up her brows. "I'm not an alcoholic, Han."

"Didn't say you were. Look." He jerked a thumb in the direction of the bar they'd left behind. "The Junebug is the only decent place to get a drink on Main Street."

He wanted to offer to take her back there and buy her one, but something in her eyes told him that would be a mistake.

Instead, he softened his voice. "Don't let me chase you out of there, okay? My buddies were just leaving anyway."

She let out a little snuffling snort. "Devin got one glimpse of me and took off, you mean."

"Stop putting words in my mouth." It came out more raw than he intended. But he meant it.

No, Devin wasn't May's biggest fan after everything that had happened, but back before then, before graduation and the mess of the following summer and fall, they'd been friends.

May chewed on her bottom lip. "I wouldn't be chasing you away?"

"Would it make you feel better if I went back, too?" His pulse ticked up a notch. This was skirting a line. To make it clearer what he was offering, he promised, "No emotional reunions." He flicked his finger in an X over his chest. "Cross my heart."

She shook her head, but her chuckle of laughter was gentler this time. "Well, when you put it that way..."

He raised his brow. He wasn't going to be any more presumptuous than he'd already been tonight.

Rolling her eyes, she waved her arm back in the direction of the Junebug. "Lead on."

"Okay."

And it was like he'd told both Clay and Devin when they'd shot him glances of concern. This was no big deal. He wasn't going to need them for emotional support afterward. He was a grown man.

He could handle one drink. With May Wu.

This was totally going to be fine.

———

This was a terrible idea.

Still, as May sat at the bar, nursing a glass of reasonably priced but surprisingly decent chardonnay, she couldn't help but admit that Han had been right. She had needed to sit down and relax.

She'd been the one to come up with the idea of walking into this bar first, of course. But his conviction in marching her back in after she'd run for the hills had been spot on.

Laughing to herself and mentally shaking her head, she took another sip before putting her glass down.

Hadn't that always been the way with them, though? She was perfectly capable of handling herself, of knowing what she needed. But he'd been the one with the confidence—some would even say the recklessness—to see things through. When she'd been ready to back out of giving the big speech at graduation, he'd gotten a crew of her safest, least judgmental friends together to listen to her rehearse. When she'd wanted to put a sweatshirt on over the strapless dress Elizabeth had talked her into picking out for prom, he'd been the one to take her into his arms and kiss her senseless, to cup her face and tell her she'd never looked more beautiful.

And tonight, when she'd been halfway down the street, no plan and no place to go except back to the airport, he'd chased her down and convinced her to come inside and have a drink.

"Ahem."

May looked up from her nearly empty glass to find Han's little sister Zoe standing behind the bar. Time flashed before May's eyes again. When she had left for college, Zoe had been in middle school. Now she was all grown up and waitressing, apparently. How on earth their mom had let that come to pass, May hadn't a clue.

Zoe passed a fresh glass of wine across the polished wood. "Some guy sent this over to you." She leaned in conspiratorially. "He seems kind of sus, though, so I don't know." Shrugging, she tipped her head dramatically to the other end of the bar.

"I can hear you, you know," Han called.

Looking to Zoe, May agreed, "Definitely sus."

When she'd taken her seat, he'd made a big show of selecting a stool several feet down, giving her plenty of space. And there he'd remained. Like a really annoying, conspicuous houseplant. A really annoying, conspicuous houseplant with whom she had an unreasonably large amount of history.

She huffed out a sigh and accepted the new glass, then downed the remainder of her old one. Zoe plucked the empty glass off the bar and walked away.

May tried to ignore the houseplant for another few minutes, but now that he'd gone and drawn attention to himself, it was really hard to tune him out. She couldn't seem to help the way her entire body—and maybe an old, achy, tender little piece of her heart—remained constantly aware of him.

Finally, the tension got to be too much. She called to him, "You realize you're making this weird, right?"

He held up his hands in front of himself. "I promised no emotional reunions."

Right, because that was what she'd asked him for, but she hadn't realized what she was getting herself into. Having him right there while also so far away was the worst of all worlds somehow.

She may not have been ready to have some big confrontation with him earlier, but she was as drawn to him now as she had been when she was twelve.

In a moment of weakness, the tender part of her heart that had always wondered *What if?* seized control. "And I said I'm not an alcoholic." She nudged the stool beside hers with her foot. "I don't like to drink alone."

He considered her for a moment, his gaze too intense. She looked away, down at her drink. After all that, if he turned down her attempt at an invitation, she really was going to go pack her bags and head back to the airport.

He let out a deep breath before draining the rest of his beer. He raised his brows at Zoe, who was doing something with the register. When he held up his empty pint glass, she nodded.

She met him at the stool next to May's, sliding another beer toward him. May didn't miss the careful distance he kept from her as he sat down, and that was good. The last thing she wanted was to get too close to the ex she still compared all other guys to.

So what if she could feel the warmth of him beside her? Or if it felt weirdly right to be sitting next to him, even after all these years.

"Okay." Han drew a little design in the condensation on his glass. "So we're *not* emotionally reuniting here."

"Definitely not."

"Just two people each having a drink near each other."

"Like bros," she said. She sipped at her wine. Forget that "brotherly" was the last way she'd ever describe the way she felt about him.

Even when they were too young to have any ideas about romance. Looking at him had made her stomach squirm in a way that scared her and excited her at the same time.

Once they hit high school and she realized he was sneaking glances at her the same way she was at him... Any thoughts of regarding each other as siblings had gone flying out the window, never to return.

Even now.

He scrunched up his mouth. "Bros where one of us has boobs."

She just about did a spit take. After swallowing her wine, she mock-glared at him. "Really?"

He shrugged, like everything he was saying was completely normal and not weird. "There is no word less emotional in this world than 'boobs.'"

"The way I remember it, you had a lot of emotions about them back in the day." Heat flared on her cheeks the instant she'd said it. Good grief, what were these words coming out of her mouth?

But instead of giving her a hard time about it, he tossed back his head and laughed. "Okay, fair enough."

"And there are plenty of other less emotional words." She dug around in her brain. "Like... 'turnip.'"

He pulled a face. "Is revulsion an emotion?"

"They aren't that bad."

"You remember that new cook my uncle Arthur hired back when we were in—what—tenth grade?"

Han's uncle ran a food pantry and soup kitchen on the north end of town. They'd both volunteered there all the time.

"Oh, gosh. I'd forgotten about him. Was it Vlad?"

"Something like that. He was only there for two weeks, but wow did he leave an impression." He grimaced. "Or at least his turnip casserole did."

The memory suddenly came back to her, and she cringed. "Yikes, yeah, okay, that was pretty revolting."

"Right?"

"And Arthur kept him on for two entire weeks?"

"You know how he is." Han shook his head fondly. "Too nice for his own good."

"Yeah." May's chest gave a little squeeze. Han's family had always been so kind to her. Losing them had been salt in the wound after she and Han had broken up. She got updates here and there through the familial grapevine, but that was about it. "How's he doing, anyway? Bouncing back okay?"

He'd had a heart attack not that long ago that had scared everybody out of their minds. Her mom said he was fine now, but apparently she wasn't that reliable of a narrator, considering how much of her own condition she'd hidden.

"Good. Having a hard time staying away from work." Han glanced toward his sister. "But Zoe's keeping him in line."

"Darn right," Zoe said, not looking up.

"Oh?"

"She's practically running Harvest Home these days."

Zoe waved him off. "Just parts of it."

"Wow." So May had totally misjudged that situation. She raised a glass to Han's sister. "That's awesome."

"It is," Zoe agreed, smiling.

"She's also shacking up with Devin."

May whipped around toward him. His baby sister and his best friend? "Wait. *Devin* Devin?"

"Yup."

"You should have seen Han's face when he found out." Zoe waved a hand at her own features. "He turned purple."

"I bet."

It was hard to wrap her head around the idea of little Zoe Leung, all grown up, running Uncle Arthur's place, and in a committed relationship. How much else had changed while May had been gone?

Zoe finished up whatever she was doing at the register, grabbed a tray, and headed off to bus some tables on the other side of the room. May and Han lapsed into silence for a minute. As she took a sip of her wine, she snuck a peek at him.

In so many ways, he looked the same as ever. Handsome, with golden skin and dark eyes. His jaw had sharpened over the years, and he'd put on some muscle, too, if she did say so herself. His hair was still short on the sides, but it was longer on top. Would it still feel the same if she ran her fingers through it?

Setting down her glass, she sat on her hands just to be safe.

Around them, the evening seemed to be winding down. While there were still other people hanging out and eating or drinking, it was just the two of them over here at the bar, and the air around them felt charged. Intimate, almost.

She glanced at him again. Softly, she asked, "And how are you? The restaurant?"

"Good." A wry note colored his tone, and that was new. "Pretty much the same as ever, for better or worse."

"Oh?"

"You know Blue Cedar Falls. Not much changes."

"Really? I feel like I hardly recognize the place." On some level, she hardly recognized him.

He smiled, but it didn't reach his eyes. "That's just because you've been gone so long."

"You make it sound like I've been away for decades." She meant to say them jokingly, but the words got stuck in her throat.

As far as he was concerned, that was exactly how long she'd been gone.

Avoiding him for thirteen years hadn't been the plan. Okay, fine, it kind of had been, at least at the beginning. Her first couple of years at college, she'd missed him like a limb. Between semesters, when she'd had to come home, she'd gone out of her way to make sure they wouldn't cross paths. She couldn't have handled seeing him and not being able to hug him or hold his hand or tell him all the things she'd been keeping inside.

By the time the sharpness of the hurt had dulled, she was coming home less and less, and for shorter and shorter stretches at a time. She'd stopped actively trying to stay away from him, but she didn't happen across his path, either. Not until tonight.

Talk about ripping off the Band-Aid.

Gently, he nudged her elbow with his, and she had to fight to hide the shiver of electricity that buzzed through her arm.

"How've you been?" he asked quietly. His gaze was so open as he regarded her.

This wasn't some acquaintance asking out of courtesy, expecting her to automatically reply that she was fine. This was Han, the guy she'd been closest with in the world, once upon a time, genuinely wanting to know how she'd been doing.

"I'm all right." She breathed out long and slow. "Work is good. Stressful but good."

"You like New York?"

"I love it." She snuffed out a little chuckle. "If only I ever got to spend any time there."

He hummed, encouraging her to go on, and this whole conversation wasn't supposed to be emotional. So why did it feel safe to say the things she never really admitted to anyone?

"I love traveling. There's so much to see out there. Different people, different cultures. Really puts small-town life in perspective, you know?"

"Not really." He shook his head.

Right. Because he'd stayed here. After he'd decided not to come with her to New York—after he'd announced, out of absolutely freaking nowhere, just weeks before she was set to leave for college, that he thought they should consider seeing other people—she'd told anybody who would listen that he was determined to die here if it killed him.

But that wasn't what they were talking about right now.

She traced the base of her glass with her fingertip. "All the times people here made me feel small for looking different. And there's this big wide world they've never had the chance to experience."

"Sounds like their loss."

"It is." But deep down, sometimes, she wondered if it wasn't her loss, too.

What she didn't say—maybe couldn't, not to him—was that traveling was great. But as much as she loved New York, her tiny studio apartment would never really be a home. She was there so little, occasionally she wondered if she should let it go. Just put her stuff in a storage unit upstate and live out of a suitcase for real.

A thoughtful silence descended on them for a minute. It was as comfortable as ever; they'd never had a problem spending time together without saying much of anything at all. The big difference was that once upon a time, she would have been able to read him like a book. When she gazed at him now, the book wasn't exactly shut. But he wasn't showing the pages to her, either. Behind his serious eyes, was he mulling over what she'd said?

Considering his own life choices of the past decade? Ready to admit all his mistakes?

Probably too much to hope for.

Finally, he tipped back the rest of his beer. When he turned to her again, the solemnity of his expression was gone. A sparkle returned to his eyes. "Remember when we used to play Never Have I Ever?"

May couldn't hold in the snort that came out with her laugh. "Oh jeez, yes. But none of us had done anything! Ever!"

"Bet your answers would be an awful lot different now."

"Darn right." And this was wading into dangerous waters. But she cocked a brow regardless, her breath going tight. "Would yours?"

A flicker of heat raced through her body. Teenagers playing Never Have I Ever covered a wide range of ridiculous topics. But there were always some dirty ones, too.

Was he thinking about those? About the time they'd played it at that party in his uncle Arthur's basement?

When his buddy Devin had knowingly smirked at them both and said, "Never have I ever had sex in a car."

She'd been mortified at the time—and not a tiny bit pissed at Han for spilling the beans about them finally going all the way.

Han's eyes darkened. "Want to find out?"

"Zoe?" Not looking away from Han, May lifted her hand.

"Yeah?" Zoe called from the other end of the bar.

May's heart raced, and if this entire evening had been a bad idea, then this one was the worst of them all.

She let one corner of her lips curl up. "I think we're going to need another round."

# CHAPTER FOUR

❖ ❖ ❖ ❖ ❖ ❖ ❖ ❖ ❖ ❖ ❖ ❖

N ever have I ever…" May swung her gaze around, fumbling wildly in her increasingly fuzzy brain, trying to come up with something to finish out that sentence with. Inspiration struck when she spotted the EXIT sign above the door. "Ooh, I got it—never have I ever dined and dashed."

"One time," Han groaned. He thumped the table before taking a gulp of his beer.

After a couple of not-so-subtle hints from Zoe, the two of them had moved their game to the booth in the far corner of the bar. That was probably for the best. They weren't bothering anybody over here.

But they were also all squished in together, it felt like. Maybe it was the beer she'd switched to after her glass of wine had run out, or maybe it really was that cramped, but her knees kept bumping his. She'd stopped counting the number of times their hands had brushed. An amber-shaded light hung above them, casting everything in a soft glow, but beyond their little bubble, everything was dark. It was so easy to imagine they were alone.

That thirteen years and a big, fat, irreparable heart-break didn't lie between them.

She forced herself to sit up straighter. She was well past the point of tipsy, thanks to Han's uncanny ability to pick out things she'd have to drink to, but she could at least pretend that she was keeping her act together.

"Really?" she asked. "You never did it again?"

He put his hand over his heart. "I barely did it the once. How was I supposed to know that Devin forgot his wallet?"

"Sure, sure, blame it on the guy who isn't here."

"It's the truth! He admitted it, back when we hashed this out *in 2008*."

She could remember it like it was yesterday. They'd both been red-faced from running as they'd taken refuge at the Sweetbriar Inn. Giggling, May had hidden them behind the front desk, and she got a shiver even now, remembering how Han had risen out from under there the instant the coast was clear. He'd kissed her breathless in gratitude—or so he'd said. Devin had felt no need to thank her so ardently, thank goodness.

Fat lot of good any of it had done them. This was a small town. The instant Han's mom had gotten wind of what her boy had been up to, she'd marched on over, taken him and Devin both by the ears, and hauled them back to Fran's Diner to apologize and settle up. With interest.

"How long did it take you to pay that off?"

"Monetarily?" Han asked. "About a month. Emotionally? Pretty sure I'm still paying."

"Your mother always was the master of the guilt trip."

"Reigning title holder." Han shook his head, his smile fading. It didn't stay gone for long, though. A sly grin stole across his mouth. "Never have I ever forgotten Mother's Day."

She shot him a dirty look. "That's not fair. I was in Japan. The time zones screwed me up."

"Excuses, excuses. My mom still got an earful about it from your mom."

He made a motion to her glass, and she begrudgingly drank up.

Well, fine, if that was how he wanted to play. "Never have I ever..."

She cast about again. They'd been sitting here for long enough that they'd already covered all the easy ground. She'd discovered he had eaten puffer fish but had not tried haggis; that he'd been to a Taylor Swift concert but never set foot at Disney World. That he'd finally gone out and gotten himself the rescue mutt he'd always dreamed about adopting; her name was Ling-Ling, she was a shepherd mix, and she was a very, very, very good girl.

And that was all interesting. It was stuff she wanted to know.

So why did it feel as if they'd barely scratched the surface? Why did it bother her, when she'd been the one to dictate that they wouldn't get emotional?

Before she could think about it, she blurted out, "Been engaged."

He narrowed his jaw and tapped his glass. When he pulled his hand away from it, she let out a quiet sigh of relief.

"Never have I ever had an adult relationship that lasted longer than a year," he said.

Never, ever had she been so glad that she and Josh had broken up when they had. Another few weeks and she'd have had to take a drink.

Shaking his head, Han drummed his finger on the table. "I'm not sure if that's supposed to make me feel better or worse."

"It's not supposed to make you feel anything at all."

She bumped his knee under the table. She maybe let it linger there for a second longer than she would have, half a pitcher of beer ago. "Remember?"

Like she was one to talk. She was having all kinds of feelings.

Wasn't it bad enough that he was the one who got away? Did he also still have to be the best-looking guy she'd ever met? The funniest and the easiest to talk to?

Finding out he'd had as meandering and as unsuccessful of a romantic life as she had made her want to reach across the table and shake him.

He could have followed her to New York. Their entire junior year of high school and most of their senior one, too, he'd told her he would. She'd be a reporter and he'd be head chef at the fanciest place in Midtown, and it was going to be great.

It would have been.

Only he'd made his choice. Out of the blue, mere months before graduation, he'd decided to stay in state instead. Long before his father died, he was married to this town and to his family.

And to think—stupid May had thought he might be thinking about marrying her.

As if he could read her mind, he looked at her with those soulful eyes. His deep voice dropped even lower. "Never have I ever stopped regretting..."

"Han." Her heart was in her throat.

Suddenly, a dozen warning signs all started flashing in her head. Whatever he was about to say—she couldn't let him say it. Best-case scenario, it'd be exactly what she'd been dreaming of him saying for more than a decade now, and it would be too late.

Or it would be... well, anything else. And her disappointment would break her heart all over again.

He searched her eyes for a long moment. His throat bobbed as he swallowed.

He raised a brow. This time, when he spoke, there was no confession to his tone. "Never have I ever stopped regretting not breaking into the mini golf course one last time before we left for school."

And just like that, the iron bands around her heart dissolved. She broke out laughing. "Oh wow, I'd almost forgotten about that."

How many times had they snuck in there after hours? Sometimes it had been their entire group of friends.

Other times, it had been just the two of them, itching for a quiet place to be alone.

"I still have the flag for the eighteenth hole," Han said.

"Seriously?"

"Like I could ever part with a treasure like that." He grinned. "Remember the time Mr. Sullivan caught us?"

She scowled. "Only because Jenny ratted us out."

"You still don't know it was her." There was an odd note to his voice that made her pause.

But not for long. She was dead certain about this. Bitterness crept into her throat as she told him, "Believe me, it was her."

Jenny herself had confessed. Bragged, really.

As if she and her mean girl squad hadn't had enough material to torture May with.

Pulling his knee away from hers, Han reached for his drink. It wasn't his turn to take a swig, but he finished it off all the same. He set it back down on the table with a *thunk*.

"Well, I promise you, there's no way she could rat us out now."

"Wait—"

Han stood. Looking down at May, he held out his hand. "What do you say? Want to go knock off one regret?"

And here May had thought that playing Never Have I Ever with Han was the most terrible idea of the night. Of course he would manage to come up with one that was even worse.

But as she stared at his outstretched hand, her heart pounding inside her chest, she couldn't help herself. She slipped her palm into his, and for a dizzying fraction of a second, it felt just a little bit like coming home.

They might be about to go cross an old regret off their lists.

All she could do was hope they didn't manage to create a dozen more.

———

Hands down, this was the best idea Han had ever had.

Sun & Fun Mini Golf and Go-Karts was a half mile walk from the Main Street strip, and he and May kept laughing and reminiscing the entire way. Neither of them was stumbling, but they were definitely tipsy, and it didn't do things to his heart to see the girl he'd loved since he was sixteen all loose and smiling and happy.

His heart contracted, and he shut down that line of thought.

No emotions. That was the rule.

And he was doing a really crummy job of following it.

What was he supposed to do, though? They'd skipped the heartfelt reunion, and yeah, he was maybe a little salty about that. But the truth remained that he had never gotten over her, and now she was here, her arm brushing his as she walked, her soft, sweet orange blossom and honey scent in the air, her face and hair lit by the warm glow of the streetlamps and the light of the moon. He wasn't a robot. He had feelings.

He just had to do a better job of ignoring them, was all.

When they hit the end of the street, he steered them around toward the back of the course. The Sullivan house stood on the corner, and no way he was taking May past that place. Jenny Sullivan might not be around to rat them out tonight, but Han had his own reasons for not wanting to run into her, either.

With exaggerated movements, he led May tiptoeing along the big wooden fence until he hit...

"Jackpot," he whispered, tugging on the old loose couple of boards. They swung forward, leaving a gap just big enough for a bunch of teenagers to sneak through.

Or a couple of fully grown adults, if they were determined enough.

May giggled and crawled under and into the row of hedges on the other side. She let out a muffled yelp when her hair got caught on one of the branches. He leaned forward, struggling to see, and their hands touched as he helped get her free. She turned back to look at him. Their gazes met through the darkness, and yeah. Feelings. They were the worst.

He hadn't snuck in here since the summer after high school, though he had been back to actually pay and play once or twice—most recently just a month ago when Clay's friend Lisa had come to visit with her five-year-old. Not much had changed since he and May were kids themselves. He skirted around the giant alligator and past the big mushroom house.

"Oh yikes." May cringed, pointing. "The creepy gnomes are still here."

Han chuckled and resisted the urge to pull her into him the way he would have back in the day. "Never understood why they wigged you out so bad."

"It's their beady, little eyes." She shuddered.

"Here." The admittedly creepy gnome figurines were lined up outside the mushroom house. Han stepped onto the green and reached over, grabbing the first one by its pointy blue hat, picking it up, and turning it around.

May smacked the heel of her hand into her forehead as he spun the rest of them, too. "Why didn't we ever think to do that back when we were teenagers?"

"We thought we were daring enough just being in here after hours. Couldn't possibly mess with the gnomes." He finished and stepped back to admire his work. Mr. Sullivan was going to have a fit.

"Funny how that goes," May mused.

"Oh?"

"There are all kinds of things like that. When you're a kid you don't realize what you have control over."

He glanced down at her. "How so?"

"All the rules we followed." She gestured between them. "With our families, especially."

Okay, she had a point there. He'd been wide-eyed, visiting his friends' houses when he was a kid. Their parents would do all these weird things, like expressing affection openly when nobody was dying, or telling their kids "good job" for doing completely normal, simple human tasks. Word on the street was that they also told their kids directly what they wanted instead of just laying on the crushing pressure of expectation.

It was one of the things they'd bonded over, after the Wu girls had moved to town. Mrs. Wu and Han's mom had become instant friends, so the kids had been thrown together, and it felt so easy when they came over. They didn't think his food was weird or go all quiet when his mom lit into him. At ten years old, with two little sisters, he'd had no choice but to act annoyed at the three new girls who were suddenly always hanging around, but the truth was that the Wus understood his life in a way that none of his other friends ever could. Even Devin, who practically lived at the Leung house, didn't quite seem to get it sometimes.

"It's like the optional ingredient fallacy," May said.

Han scrunched up his face. "The what now?"

"You know how recipes are always putting a star next to the last few ingredients, then it says at the bottom how they're 'optional'?"

"Tell me more about these 'recipe' things."

She jabbed her pointy elbow into his side, and he pretended like it hurt.

"Yes, yes," she said, "you're a fancy chef who doesn't need recipes. You still know what one looks like."

"I have a vague idea."

She shot him a look that said *Humor me*, and he motioned for her to go on.

"It's just a pet peeve of mine, okay? Recipes tell you some ingredients are optional, but think about it. You're the one making the recipe. No one is *making* you put anything in it. Literally every single ingredient in the recipe is optional."

"Huh." He'd never looked at it that way. Though, again, it wasn't like he really followed recipes for anything except fancy *Great British Bake Off* cakes anyway.

She cast her arms toward the horizon, and had she ever looked so free before? Smiling, she declared, "The world is your oyster."

"Just so long as you don't put that oyster in a brownie."

"Why?" She dropped her hands and looked over at him like he was the one with two heads. "No one's going to stop you."

"Yeah, but they should."

"But they can't." She pointed a finger at him. "It will be a terrible, terrible brownie."

"Not to mention a waste of a perfectly good oyster."

"But that's your choice. If you're willing to live with the consequences, you can do anything."

Their gazes met, and all of a sudden, it felt like she was talking about something else entirely. Choices. Consequences. What a person felt like they had to do versus what someone could actually make them do.

His throat tightened, and he cleared it, taking a single step back.

She looked down and away, like maybe she was hearing the echoes of arguments they'd already had a long, long time ago, too.

"Well." He moved back onto the path and off the green, motioning with his hand toward the mushroom house. "I'm willing to live with the consequences for gnome rotation."

"Dangerous." A spark twinkled in her eyes as she lifted her gaze. "Never have I ever..." She paused for dramatic effect. "Stolen a gnome."

"Wait—"

She darted forward and snagged one off the ground. "Oops, never mind, I guess I have now."

He laughed as she tucked the gnome into her jacket and took off at a sprint down the path, toward the center of the course. He chased after her. "I thought you hated those things."

"Oh, I do." She glanced back at him. "This is for you to help you keep an eye on that eighteenth-hole flag."

"How thoughtful."

"You know me, always thinking of others."

Han just about tripped over a gap in the sidewalk.

Was that really how she thought of herself?

He didn't hold it against her that she'd chosen her great life out in the world over the one they could have had together, here. Not much, in any case. It was her choice to follow her dreams, and he was happy for her.

That didn't make it any easier to be one of the ones she'd left behind.

Before he could stop himself, he said, "Like when you skipped out on Pumpkin Festival and Christmas last year?"

He still remembered the look on her big sister June's face after May canceled her plans to come out the previous fall. June had tried to act like it didn't bother her, but she had been devastated.

May slowed to a stop beside hole thirteen. "Not you, too."

"I know, I know, no feelings." He kicked the stones that lined the path and shoved his hands into his pockets, glancing at her out of the corner of his eye. "You broke your sister's heart, though."

He cursed himself in his head. It wasn't his job to be yelling at May for June, but it felt like something he was allowed to give her grief about. While the rest he had to keep buried inside, or she'd just run again.

Lifting her gaze to the sky, May let out a harsh breath. When she spoke again, her voice was softer. More measured. "I know." She looked to him. "And if she'd told me that at the time, maybe I could've tried harder not to."

Han swallowed thickly. "The people you love don't always tell you what they need."

She hadn't told him what she needed, that whole last year of high school, but he knew. Every moment of every day, she was studying or filling out applications, talking about what she'd do when she got out. Like this place was a jail.

For Han, though, it had always been home.

So he hadn't told her what he needed, either. Not until it was too late for either of them to change course. He'd shredded all the applications he'd collected for schools in New York and quietly accepted a spot at the Culinary Institute in Raleigh, and she'd been mad enough about that, but she'd recovered. As she'd been packing up to go to school, she kept talking about how often they could visit each other, though, and he'd seen it all playing out. She couldn't really have the freedom she wanted if she was still tied to him.

So right before she'd left, he'd told her they should play it loose, that first year apart. See other people. He'd said it so casually. Like it was nothing at all to break his own heart. For a bit there, he was pretty sure he'd broken hers, too. But that was the thing. With people you really loved...

You did what you had to do. Even when they couldn't find a way to ask it of you.

May's eyes shone in the darkness as she stared at him. She lifted her chin. "Well, maybe they should."

He couldn't quite find a way to agree with her. "Maybe."

Their gazes held for too long. Time went all strange on him. It was like he was eighteen and thirty at the same time, standing in front of the girl he'd had to let go and the woman he'd always imagined would come back. Only she never had—not until now, and forget no feelings. He had every single one of them, burning so hot in his chest he could barely open his mouth for fear they'd all come spilling out.

"May...," he started, no concept of where he could be going with it.

She looked away. Still cradling the bundle of stolen gnome under her jacket with one hand, she gestured to the side with the other. "Is it still there?"

A whole new bubble of emotion formed in his throat. His voice scratched as he said, "Probably. It's not like I've checked."

She raised her brows, and then she was off again. Her pace was more sedate, at least. He walked alongside her, past the awful clown and over the bridge. At the ninth hole, she glanced back at him before stepping onto the green and through the gap between the blades of the windmill. He sucked in a deep breath before heading in, too.

And there it was. Tucked away back here, behind the obstacles at the far west corner of the course, where nobody would ever see it except them.

"Well, would you look at that." May reached out a hand to trace the heart in the trunk of the tree. MW + HL.

He flashed back to the night they'd carved it into the wood. They'd used his pen knife, and he'd almost cut off his finger, but it had been worth it. They'd been kids, barely eighteen, and leaving a permanent mark of their love on the world had felt monumental. They might not have lasted—he might have even known, back then, that they couldn't last. But this was still right here.

She turned her head toward him, but it was so cramped—just a foot or so of space between the windmill and the tree line. She bumped into him, and heat flared all along his front. His skin prickled with awareness through his clothes, and she smelled so good. Just like she used to, only different, and he wanted to know if she still liked the same shampoo, or if there was some new lotion, or if they'd just grown up. Thirteen years apart.

"Oh." Her red lips parted, her gaze darting from his mouth to his eyes and back. Did she feel the same electric force, pulling them together?

Every instinct in his body told him to lean forward. Curl his arms around her and press his mouth to hers, but no.

That wasn't what either of them needed.

So he did what he had to do. He tugged himself away.

Out on the green, on the right side of the windmill again, the night air felt cooler and clearer, and he drew in deep gulps of it.

She brushed past him, erasing any clarity he might have gained. She sat down, right there in the center of the green. Putting down the gnome, she hugged her knees into her chest and turned her face up to the stars.

He stood there, drinking in the sight of her. In profile against the darkness, she was so beautiful it hurt.

After a minute, he sat beside her. It was easier out here, where there was room to breathe. He left a few inches of space between their bodies, except it wasn't enough. Sending her five hundred miles away had been the only way to make it enough.

They rested there in silence together. Overhead, the Big Dipper shone, bright points spread out across the vastness of the sky. Everything was still.

"Han," she said quietly.

He turned his head to face her, and yeah. They were too close. Their hands were almost touching on the ground, and tingles zipped along his arm.

write about the Sweetbriar Inn and the Jade Garden just fine, y'all. It's not like anything has changed."

"You might be surprised," her mom said.

"I doubt it." May picked up her now-empty mug. "But I won't say no to brunch. Then it's off to try a few places where I didn't grow up."

"And then lasagna for dinner tonight, right?" her mom prodded.

May smiled. "Definitely."

Seemingly satisfied with that, May's mom walked her friends to the door, and May waved goodbye to them. Mrs. Leung reached out and gave her hand a little squeeze that definitely didn't make May's throat go tight.

"Speaking of places you have to try," Elizabeth said, "you checked out the Junebug yet?"

It was May's turn to cough suspiciously. "Uh, yeah. Briefly."

She and Han had only been there for a couple of hours. Compared with the age of the universe, that was brief.

If Elizabeth noticed May being weird in her response, she was kind enough to keep it to herself. "Me and Graham and a bunch of other people are heading there tonight, if you want to join. Two for one chef's special cheese fries."

May pursed her lips in thought. She had a lot of work to do, and after last night's questionable decisions, she should probably beg off. But she'd been working so hard for so long. Sure, she had fun catching up with Ruby when she was home in New York or having drinks with Zahra and the folks from the office—or just staying in and hanging out with her pet tortoise. But she hadn't been back to Blue Cedar Falls in forever. It felt good, making plans. Reconnecting with the people she cared about.

May smiled. "Who could resist a deal like that?"

———

"How am I supposed to resist a face like that?" Han's shepherd mix, Ling-Ling, bounded out of the car the instant they arrived at the dog park. She looked up at him with pleading eyes, reminding him of their bargain. Poor girl hated the back seat. He gave her a good, rough rub along her neck. "Fine, fine."

She panted and wagged her tail like a helicopter about to take off, nosing at his pocket. He reached in and pulled out a treat.

"Sit."

She did so obediently, tongue lolling out of her mouth. When he tossed her the biscuit—his own recipe—she barked, caught it, and wolfed it down.

"I'd say that dog has you eating out of the palm of her hand, but I'm pretty sure she's the one eating out of yours."

He turned to find his friend Caitlin already inside the fenced-in area. She was a Black woman with long locs she kept tied back, and she was dressed casually in a gray and maroon baseball tee and jeans. Her girlfriend Bobbi stood beside her, her wavy blond hair and white dress blowing in the breeze.

Han grinned and nodded at the tiny Maltese the two of them had adopted to celebrate moving in together last fall. "Like Vlad is any better."

"Vlad the Impaler is a well-disciplined military man," Caitlin said dryly, but her smile cracked as the pup tugged at the leg of her pants.

"Fetch," Bobbi called, and every one of the half dozen dogs in the park perked up at once. She tossed a pink ball toward the corner, and Vlad raced after it, all the other bigger beasts on his tail.

Ling-Ling barked, and Han patted her side, leading her to the gate and letting her in. She happily joined the fray.

Han closed the fence behind himself and wandered over toward Bobbi and Caitlin, nodding across the yard to some other regulars he recognized standing by the giant fire hydrant.

It was midafternoon—Han's best opportunity to sneak away from the restaurant and give Ling-Ling some exercise and love. He'd already been on a good long walk with her that morning, but he liked to keep her decently socialized, too.

Honestly, he wished he could just let her hang out in the back room at the restaurant, but apparently there were "health codes" or something. Stupid health codes.

Bobbi felt the same way about Vlad and her bakery café, which was why she was often here around this time as well.

Caitlin, on the other hand, was a building contractor who was usually at work until five.

"Didn't expect to see you here today," he commented to her.

"Took the day off," Caitlin said.

"Because we're celebrating," Bobbi chimed in. She practically vibrated as she grabbed Caitlin's hand.

"Oh?" Han raised a brow, bracing himself. There were only a couple of options for what was about to come out of their mouths, and he had a pretty good guess at which one it was going to be, considering Bobbi had been obsessing about it for months.

Caitlin gazed down at Bobbi with hearts in her eyes. "Yup."

"We got engaged!" Bobbi held out her hand, confirming

his suspicions. The platinum band and its big square diamond sparkled.

Caitlin wiggled her own hand with its more subtle gold ring.

"I wanted to buy her a giant rock, too, but she said she couldn't wear it on the jobsite," Bobbi pouted.

He beamed, genuinely happy for them. Bobbi had been planning this for ages, but something had always gotten in the way. First coming out to her parents, then finding out Caitlin was opposed to getting married before at least living together. But it was finally happening for them.

So what if his genuine happiness held a twist of envy? He was thirty. Everyone he knew was settling down. Sure, his love life was nonexistent—a fact that had become even harder to ignore after hanging out with his ex last night—but that didn't matter.

"It's gorgeous," Han assured them. "They both are. Congratulations!"

"Thanks," Caitlin said.

"I asked," Bobbi volunteered.

Caitlin rolled her eyes fondly. "You beat me by a week. I had the ring and everything."

"I cooked."

"I was going to cook."

Ah. Han grinned. "So that's why you asked me for my tenderloin recipe."

"Ooh!" Bobbi's eyes lit up. "I didn't know that. Are you still going to make it?" she asked Caitlin. "Because if not I will totally give you back this ring and let you ask me next week."

"I'll still make it," Caitlin promised.

Bobbi clutched her hand to her chest. "Cool, because I was definitely not going to give this back."

Ling-Ling bounded over, Vlad's ball in her mouth, and she set it at Han's feet. Han patted her head, grabbed the ball, and lobbed it toward Vlad, who barked and took off at a sprint, Ling-Ling hot on his heels.

"So you discussed plans yet?" Han phrased the question carefully, not wanting to put any pressure on them. They deserved the chance to bask. "For the wedding?"

"So many plans," Bobbi confirmed. "We don't want to wait at all."

"Never know when we're going to get outlawed again, you know," Caitlin said, only half joking.

"I don't think—"

Bobbi's voice went all dreamy. "And a June wedding just has such a nice ring to it, don't you think?"

"June? Like a-few-weeks-from-now June?"

"We're not going to make a big deal of it," Caitlin said.

"We're going to make *kind of* a big deal of it." Bobbi started rattling off details. "Simple ceremony in my parents' backyard. Caitlin's cousin Robbie will officiate, her brother Matthias can deejay. I'll do the cake, of course."

"Who else?" Han agreed.

"But we were actually going to ask you." Caitlin smiled hopefully. "Any chance you'd be available to cater?"

"Of course," Han said automatically. In his head, though, he was doing three-dimensional calculus. "Wait, when in June?"

"Second Saturday? We're not sure yet."

Crud, that was only a week after Taste Of Blue Cedar Falls. Pulling off a wedding so soon after what had the potential to be the biggest night of his career so far was going to be tight.

But for friends, he'd find a way to make it work.

"As long as it's not any earlier than that, I've got you."

"Yay!" Bobbi leaned in and gave him a hug. He wrapped his arms around her in return.

"Thanks, man." Caitlin held out her hand in a loose fist, and he tapped his knuckles against hers.

"No problem."

Two of his favorite people getting married, two giant events to prep for.

What kinds of problems could there possibly be?

# CHAPTER SIX

"You came!" Elizabeth held up both hands as May made her way through the crowd at the Junebug that night.

Exhausted as she was after a day of research—and full to the brim with both lasagna and her mother's hovering—her mouth curled into a genuine smile at her little sister's enthusiasm.

"Of course." She had to raise her voice to be heard. Joining Elizabeth and her friends at a set of high-tops in the rear section of the bar, she leaned in for a quick hug, then looked around. "It's really hopping tonight."

"Such is the power of cheese fries."

Sure enough, little baskets of saturated fat sat in front of pretty nearly everybody here. May had just downed a full serving of pasta and cheese—on top of sampling dishes from half a dozen places earlier in the day—so she wasn't exactly starved, but she reached forward anyway. "May I?"

"Please."

She grabbed a fry. Strands of melty cheese stretched for the better part of a foot before snapping. She popped the thing in her mouth, and her eyes lit up. Salty, tangy, maybe the tiniest hint of spice. "Oh, wow."

"Right?" Elizabeth passed her a much-needed napkin, then gestured around. "You remember all these weirdos?"

"How could I forget?"

Elizabeth's crew of artists, goths, and slackers had grown up in the past dozen years. Half of them were dressed in business casual, though even they still displayed signs of their rebel pasts, be it edgy haircuts, chunky jewelry, or peekaboo tattoos. Elizabeth reminded her of all their names again.

Standing out as always was Graham. May would never quite understand how such a straitlaced guy had fallen in with this bunch. He'd been high school salutatorian, for goodness' sake, and he still wore a pair of unironic—if well-fitted—khakis and a button-down shirt. He'd traded slicking back his dark hair for leaving it tousled, and his glasses were cooler, but his wide-open smile hadn't changed a bit.

"Hey." He held out his hand.

May slapped his fingers with her own, then they took turns bumping the tops of their fists together before each making the gesture for the right-hand rule from AP calculus at each other. She grinned.

Elizabeth groaned, but she was smiling. "You guys are such *nerds*."

"Always have been," Graham agreed.

May chimed in, "Always will be."

Elizabeth shooed her toward the bar. "Go get a drink. And another couple baskets of fries."

"On it." She glanced around. "Anybody else need a refill?"

She took a couple of orders from Elizabeth's friends, then turned around.

And stopped cold in her tracks.

A lot had changed in thirteen years, and a lot had stayed the same, and in no way was that more exemplified than by her body's visceral reaction to the sight of Jenny Sullivan and her swarm of girlfriends buzzing around the bar. Her knees locked, and her throat went dry, fire bursting across her cheeks and chest while ice poured down her spine.

Her shoulder slamming into a locker, her books falling, a foot coming down on her hand. *Go back to where you came from—*

Only this time, no one was telling her to go back to China.

It was just every fiber of her being telling her to go back to New York.

The instant panic in her body simmered over into something stronger. As a teen, she'd been an easy target: quiet and shy and different. But she'd been to every corner of the globe now. She'd lived in a city where the population of her neighborhood was bigger than the population of this town.

She'd made it. She'd survived. She'd thrived.

And nobody was going to make her feel as if she hadn't.

Now all she had to do was tell her knees that.

"You okay?" Elizabeth asked.

"Fine." Apparently May's jaw was having a tough time unclenching, too.

Following May's gaze, Elizabeth groaned. "Oh, them."

"Yeah. Them."

Elizabeth glanced between Jenny and May. Slowly, she asked, "You want me to go get the drinks instead?"

May flexed her hands at her sides.

May's sisters had never had as much trouble with bullies at school as she had. June had been so busy trying to mother their mother and them that she didn't have time for adolescent social dynamics. Elizabeth fell in with—well, the people she was still hanging out with here—a bunch of iconoclasts who thought it was cooler not to fit in.

They knew what May was going through, though—or at least a toned-down version of it. June's advice had rarely been much help. "Just ignore them and they'll leave you alone" worked great for the girl who was above it all, and not so great for the awkward nerd who always felt alone. Sure, she'd had her family and Han and his friends, but none of them could follow her into the girls' locker room.

Elizabeth had helped her focus on the future. Someday May would show them all.

No reason someday couldn't be today.

May forced a tight smile. She bumped her shoulder against her sister's in silent thanks. "Nah. I got this."

Her legs finally obeyed her and consented to bend. Her lips and fingers and toes tingled as she made her way through the bar. She kept her gaze straight ahead, refusing to look at Jenny or any of the other girls who'd orbited her since middle school. Madison, Kelsey, Erika, Tori.

She made it to the bar without tripping over her own two feet or bursting into flames, so she counted that as a win. There was nowhere to stand except two feet away from the mean girl squad, but she refused to let that bother her. She caught Clay's eye, and he headed her way.

"Fancy seeing you here again." Clay smirked. "Have fun last night?"

Oh jeez, like she needed another reason to be a giant ball of unwelcome feelings. "Sure did."

"What can I get you?"

She rattled off her order, and he scribbled it on a pad.

"Kitchen'll send your fries out in a few. Drinks are coming right up." He grabbed a shaker and got to work.

As May waited, Jenny's girls went quiet. May's cheeks flashed even hotter when she heard one of them say, "Isn't that—?"

"Shh," another one said.

Between the music on the jukebox and the other threads of conversation floating around them, May couldn't make out anything more, but one of the girls laughed, and May's fight-or-flight instinct roared. Adrenaline surged through her all over again, and she was better than this. She was a successful, adult woman. She didn't give a rat's behind about these people anymore.

So why did she still care so much?

Just as her anger and shame threatened to boil over, a warm presence slotted itself in beside her.

"Hey!"

She turned to find Han looking down at her, a wide, easy smile on his face, but concern in his eyes.

"Uh—hey."

He leaned in for a hug, and oh no. Her body went into a different kind of lockdown as he loosely wrapped his arms around her, his spicy, amber scent clouding her brain. She returned the hug, trying not to let herself actually feel it. After last night, when they'd come so close to crossing the line between old friends and exes who apparently still kiss, she needed to be on her guard. Only she'd already been stripped of all her defenses.

Then he whispered in her ear, "Play along."

A bubble inside her popped. He pulled away, glancing meaningfully behind her.

Oh.

She'd never quite understand why she got so much crap from the bullies at school while Han seemed to float on by. Sure, they made the occasional slanty-eyed gesture or mumbled Asian-accented gibberish at him from time to time, but it had always stayed subtle. Maybe it was just that he was so cool, while she was an eternal dork. He'd stuck up for her whenever he'd seen people giving her a hard time, but since he wasn't there for most of it, that only helped so much.

She still instinctively took his lead now. She didn't want or need him to protect her, but it felt so right to let him try.

"It's great to see you again," he said, overly animated.

"Yeah. You, too."

"You're a writer now, right?"

She nodded. Where on earth was he going with this?

"That's so cool."

"I mean—"

His voice pitched even louder, his eyebrows rising, silently reminding her, again, *Play along*.

"I saw the award you got last year."

"Oh, yeah—" It was just some industry thing, no big deal, but—

"And that article you got in the *Times*?"

Her home publication, *Passage*, had set up that reprint. It had gotten a lot of attention, sure, but he was really overplaying this.

Which was exactly the point, she belatedly realized.

She smiled, the tension inside of her finally unwinding. "That was such a great opportunity. The magazine I work for does an amazing job promoting my stories."

"As they should." Han seemed to relax, too, now that she'd clued in to what he was doing. "I read the piece you did on ecotourism in the Maldives."

"Really?" Her voice squeaked, which was not cool,

but she couldn't help it. That story had been niche, to say the least.

He squeezed her wrist. Right. They were playing a game here, talking loudly about how great her career was so Jenny and her coven of witches would have no choice but to overhear.

"I had no idea green resorts could still be so gorgeous."

"Well, you know," she managed. "The Maldives never do anything halfway."

"You must be the envy of everybody, getting assignments like that."

And yeah. She kind of was. Her job had its downsides—did it ever—but the list of choice destinations she'd had the chance to cover was definitely a perk.

"I feel really lucky."

"You worked hard for it." Han's gaze caught hers and held, and an unspoken meaning passed between them.

She had worked hard. She'd earned her success.

And after everything he'd said to her, that last time, his acknowledging it now meant the world.

"Sounds like you've got everything you've ever wanted," Han said. It was still loud enough to be heard, but it was also quieter.

So why did her throat catch? Why did it feel like less than the entire truth to nod and say, "Yeah"?

A smile spread across his face, genuine for all that it was sad around the corners. Her expression felt like a perfect mirror.

"Hey, buddy." Clay set down the last of the drinks May had requested. "The usual?"

Han finally broke the staring contest they'd been having, but being able to look away didn't give May any relief. "Sure," he told Clay. "That'd be great."

Clay poured a pint glass of amber ale and passed it over.

They settled up. The entire time, May couldn't help but be aware of both the continued presence of the girls who used to make her life a living hell back in school and the nearness of the guy who'd made that all feel…somehow okay.

Han grabbed his beer then gestured with his free hand at the three martini glasses May was trying to figure out how to carry. "You want…?"

"If you don't mind."

Her heart fluttered as they made their way to the corner where Elizabeth and her friends were involved in a heated discussion about some animation studio. Elizabeth was seated so that she could see May's approach—probably so she could watch the entire conversation at the bar, too. She tilted her head and raised her brows. May rolled her eyes like it was no big deal that her ex-boyfriend had just come to her rescue, when deep down she was starting to worry it was a pretty big deal indeed.

May set down her own drink and passed out the other ones she'd ordered.

"Hey, man," Graham said to Han.

Han stood next to the table, exchanging pleasantries. It didn't seem like he was particularly close with any of Elizabeth's friends, but they all knew each other well enough to at least say hi. As the rest of them drifted back to whatever conversation they'd been having before, Han looked around.

May's heart gave a little squeeze. Han was here to meet someone else. He was just being nice to her—even after she'd quietly shut him down last night when he'd suggested they should hang out again.

She swallowed past the lump in her throat. "You want to join us?"

Dangerous. Really, really dangerous. They had chemistry and history, and spending more time together was a bad idea. So why did she hate the idea of him walking away?

One corner of his lips curled up. "The other guys will be here soon."

A bunch of tourists with midwestern accents had just vacated the next table over. She motioned toward it. "So snag that."

He cocked a brow. " 'The other guys' includes Devin."

"So?" She managed to keep her voice even. Forget the nerves fluttering around in her stomach along with the butterflies Han had put there. "We used to be friends."

That was before the breakup, of course. The last time she'd seen him, on her way out of town after Mr. Leung's funeral, she'd tried to be friendly and he'd told her in no uncertain terms what he thought of her waltzing in and breaking Han's heart *again*. As if Han hadn't broken hers first, and then asked the impossible of her.

Of course, Devin chose that moment to walk in the door. Han waved at him, and he smiled and headed over. A second later, his gaze caught on May, and his smile went flat.

May sucked in a breath and tilted her chin up. It was just like it was with Jenny and her brood. Show no weakness. Pretend she belonged here. Project the confidence she'd grown over the past thirteen years—and that Han himself had just reminded her of not ten whole minutes ago.

Devin slowed to a stop in front of them. "May."

"Devin."

His eyes narrowed slightly, but she just smiled pleasantly.

"You mind if we sit here?" Han moved toward the table right next to May's.

"You sure?"

Han looked to May, then back to Devin. "Yeah. I'm sure."

"Well, as long as everybody knows what they're getting themselves into..." There was no mistaking the warning in the glance he shot May.

But she kept her cool and stood her ground.

The way maybe she should have back a long, long time ago.

———

"You ready to head out?" Zoe came up behind Devin and put her hand on his shoulder. She had her apron slung over her other arm, a tired but happy expression on her face.

"Yeah." Devin downed the last couple sips of his beer and stood.

The rest of their group made motions to leave as well, and Han checked his watch. It was later than he would have expected. Devin, Tyrell, and a bunch of their other buddies all worked early shifts. Normally, Han would be happy enough to make his way home at this point, too.

Tonight, though, he glanced over at May. She sat at the end of the other table, laughing at something her sister Elizabeth had said. But as if she could feel his gaze, she looked up.

All night, it had been like this. They'd stuck to their own tables, Han shooting the breeze with his buddies, while May had hung out with Elizabeth and her friends. Countless times, though, Han had felt a prickle on the back of his neck, and he'd turned to find May looking in his direction, or vice versa.

In some ways it was kind of like old times. They'd

always had their own lives, their own friends and plans, but they'd also always been in each other's orbits. Aware of each other and eerily in sync.

Not that the old times were relevant anymore.

As Han's buddies drifted in the direction of the door, Devin cocked a brow at him. "You coming?"

Han fought the warmth that threatened to creep up his neck as he tipped his head toward the other table. "Just gonna say good night."

"That all you're planning on doing?"

Han rolled his eyes. "Yes, Mom. Did I give you this much grief about dating my sister?"

"Yes," said sister replied, and okay, fine, Han probably deserved that.

"I'll catch you later," he told them both, firm.

Devin was just looking out for him. He'd been there for Han through the mess when he and May had broken up over a decade ago. He had every right to be skeptical of them spending time together now, but he didn't need to be. Han had his head on straight. He and May had had a great time last night, but she was only here for a week. Nothing had changed. All he hoped was that maybe, by the time she headed back to New York, they might be friends again.

And that maybe she wouldn't feel like she had to avoid him for another thirteen years.

Shaking his head, Devin tucked Zoe under his arm, and they and the rest of the guys took off. A few of Elizabeth's friends were starting to drift away, too. Graham stood and yawned.

Elizabeth rolled her eyes, but got up with him. "Sorry," she told May, "but he's my ride."

"It's fine." May pushed back her own chair, but she still had her glass in her hand. She glanced to Han.

Han's heart beat harder. "I could stay for another round."

May nudged the seat beside hers with her foot, sliding it out in invitation.

"Have fun." Elizabeth's brows were high, her smile too smug, but May dismissed her just as readily as Han had Devin.

"I will."

And then, somehow, it was just May and Han again. Clay swung by and deposited a fresh beer in front of him, giving him yet another look of concern. Han internally groaned. Why was everybody making such a big deal about this?

May shook her head, laughing quietly. "It's a good thing Lady Whistledown is fictional."

"Lady who now?"

May waved him off. "Gossip columnist from this show Elizabeth and I got into. She would have had a field day with this." Sitting up straighter, she put on a high-class British accent. "All of society is aflutter at the reunion of one of Blue Cedar Falls's oldest couples."

"Aflutter, huh?"

"It's how they talk."

"Sure."

She raised a brow. "It's not exactly an inapt description."

Han supposed he could allow her that. "You know how it is around here. Everybody's always got an opinion about everybody else's business."

"That they do." The wry expression on her face bordered on fond. "I almost miss it, sometimes."

"Yeah?" That was a surprise to hear.

Back in high school, May never stopped talking about how she couldn't stand this town. He'd always thought it was normal teenage griping. She'd come around. Blue Cedar Falls wasn't perfect, but it was home.

Then she left and never came back, and in hindsight, all her complaining took on a darker, more bitter meaning.

"Sure," she said, shrugging. "I mean, I love New York and all the other places I get to go." Her tone softened, gaining a wistfulness he was going to work really hard not to read too much into. "But it's not like I ever bump into a stranger who has an opinion about my lack of a love life."

"And that's what you miss?"

"It's one of the things." She glanced at him, then immediately dropped her gaze. "Seems hard to believe, I know, but living the way I do…"

He kept his trap shut for a minute, waiting her out. Before long, it became clear she wasn't going to finish that thought, though, and he couldn't help himself.

When he'd spotted her at the bar earlier, bristling at whatever crap Jenny and her friends were saying, it had been second nature to swoop in. He knew better than to pretend May Wu could possibly need rescuing, but those girls always used to get under her skin. No way he was going to let them make her feel like crap about herself now, when she'd gone out in the world and created this amazing life for herself.

But there'd been something in the way she'd answered a few of his leading questions. She'd agreed she had everything she'd always wanted, but she'd been holding back.

Kind of like she was holding back now.

"Is it really so great?" he blurted out.

Her gaze jerked up to meet his. His question seemed to catch her by surprise, and a part of him wanted to take it back. What right did he have to go probing into her life?

The other part wanted to double down. He'd spent thirteen years trying not to think about her, but he'd never stopped wondering how she was. If she was happy out there, living her dream.

If things ever could have gone differently. Or if she ever even would have wanted them to.

When she blinked at him, her mouth opening only to close again, he let out a rough breath.

"Living the way you do," he clarified, repeating her words to her. "Having everything you wanted." His throat tightened, and he dropped his hands below the surface of the table to dig his knuckles into the meat of his own palm. "Is it what you hoped it would be?"

She studied him, and he felt like a butterfly under a magnifying glass, but he stood his ground.

"Yeah," she finally allowed. "I mean, it's good. It really is. I love what I do, and I like getting to see the world, but..."

His breathing caught. "But?"

May so rarely let her guard down, but before his eyes, he saw it happening. Her posture relaxed, and a genuine vulnerability turned down the corners of her smile.

"It can be lonely." She dragged a couple of fingers through the dampness on the sides of her glass. "Sometimes."

"Oh." His pulse ticked up.

She met his gaze again, but she was still allowing him to see behind the curtain of her relentless achievement. "It's all great on the surface, right? And I really am happy. But at the end of the day, I spend most of my time going on other people's dream vacations. Only instead of doing it with my family or my spouse or even my boyfriend—" Her voice cracked for a second, and seriously. Han was not reading *anything* into it. She shrugged, her mouth flat and her eyes defenseless. "I do it alone."

"Oh. I." He swallowed, trying to figure out how to respond to a confession like that. "I guess I never looked at it that way."

"I'm not fishing for sympathy or anything." She lifted her glass to her lips and took a sip. "I really do enjoy travel writing. It's fun—even when the places I visit start to blur together. I just wish sometimes that I got to live those experiences instead of documenting them for somebody else."

"It's okay." He shot her an understanding smile. "Even the best jobs have their downsides."

They were back in more comfortable territory now, and she leaned forward, putting her elbows on the table. "Even being head chef at your own restaurant?"

He rolled his eyes. "Please. It's my family's restaurant, and I'm a glorified cook."

"I doubt that." One side of her mouth lifted. "I hear your secret menu is pretty great."

Right. The special dishes he'd been working on these past few years, using his friends and a select group of adventurous regulars as guinea pigs. He still hadn't quite perfected the recipes, though with Taste of Blue Cedar Falls coming up, it was officially crunch time.

So why was he suddenly so nervous at the idea of debuting them for May?

"Hey." He shot her a playful scowl. "Who told you about that? The first rule of the Jade Garden secret menu is you don't talk about the Jade Garden secret menu."

"Pretty weird business model you got there."

"Everybody who needs to know knows."

"Well, Elizabeth says it's awesome, and I should write about it in a feature."

Han's heart pounded in his chest. Next to getting accepted into Taste of Blue Cedar Falls, having his passion project menu highlighted in a high-class travel magazine would be the biggest boost to his career prospects yet.

Uneasiness rolled around in the pit of his stomach, though. A restaurant of his own, with his own menu and his own vision, was his ultimate goal. But for now, the family business was his focus. If his mom knew he was encouraging May to write about his side hustle, she'd give him that *look*.

The same one she'd probably give him if he ever he got up his nerve to tell her about Taste of Blue Cedar Falls.

As far as she was concerned, he could run the Jade Garden until he retired. It was stable and safe. What else did he need?

With a self-deprecating shake of his head, he tapped his fingers against his glass. "You need me to remind you about the second rule of the Jade Garden secret menu?"

"Okay, now I'm really curious." Challenge sparkled in her eyes. "Guess I know where I'm heading for lunch tomorrow."

And okay, he could demur twice, but he wasn't going to be able to do it a third time. "Guess I'll have to bring my A game."

"Like you could bring anything else," she said, eyes soft. Affectionate, even, and heaven help him, how was a guy supposed to *not* read things into that?

They gazed at each other for a moment that dragged on. Finally, she looked away, and why did that disappoint him so much?

He recovered, though, taking a gulp of his beer. "So you've got lunch figured out. What else is on the agenda for tomorrow?"

"Staying in town, mostly, I think." She raked a hand through her long, dark hair. "June's got a whole list of the places I should visit."

Han chuckled. "I'm sure she does."

No one was a better cheerleader for Blue Cedar Falls and its tourist attractions than May's older sister.

"Eventually, I'm going to have to go a little farther afield, though. As *amazing* as this place is"—she rolled her eyes at her own impression of June—"the article's supposed to be highlighting the whole region."

"Well, if you need some suggestions. for where to start…"

"I'd love some, actually."

"I'll make up a list," he promised.

She arched a brow. "With footnotes and references?"

"Uh…"

"Kidding, kidding." Waving him off, she smiled. "Just saying. June's lists are pretty hard to top."

"I have no doubt."

An idea occurred to him. He hesitated for a second, warning lights flashing in his brain as he remembered how she basically shut him down the night before. But running into each other again tonight had changed things, right? She'd been the one to invite him to grab the table next to hers, after all.

"You know…," he started. He swallowed. "You were saying how it can get lonely going on all these research adventures by yourself." Screw it. He was in this now. "I may not be able to make as thorough of a list as June can, but I could always just show you around one of the other towns nearby. Lincoln. Or Harpersville."

She was looking at him like he'd sprouted another head, and he patted his shoulder real quick, just to make sure he hadn't. He was going out on one heck of a limb here.

"Han..."

"I'm just saying," he barreled on. "We kill two birds with one stone. You get to have some company. I don't embarrass myself making substandard lists."

As if that was the only way he could embarrass himself. Case in point, this conversation.

He had to give her credit—she faced him head-on. "You really think that's a good idea?"

"Of course not." He gestured around at the bar. "Like, ten people have already told me today that it's not."

He got it. They were exes. Things were awkward. But if he really wanted to get to a place where they could be friends, they had to get past some of it. The "no emotional reunions" rule hadn't been repealed, but there was some stuff they were going to have to talk through eventually, unless they wanted to go back to avoiding each other for another decade.

"Sorry." She dropped her gaze again. "It's just..."

She could have ended that sentence any number of ways.

"I know," he said, because no matter where she could have been going, he was pretty sure he'd considered it, too.

"We have all this history."

Understatement. So many of his happiest memories from his teenage years had been with her. She'd shaped what he thought of as a relationship. She was probably the reason he'd barely had another one since.

"Textbooks' worth," he agreed. "I just—I don't want things to be weird between us."

They'd already torn the Band-Aid off. Why not keep going?

"Me, neither," she allowed.

"It's been..." His throat was dry. Why was it so hard to put any of this into words? "It's been great. Catching up. Hanging out." He managed a smile. He was really putting it all out there now. "So I'd like to do more of it. What do you say?"

She pursed her lips. Carefully, she asked, "Like... friends?"

"Sure." He lifted one shoulder and put it back down. "Friends."

That was exactly what he'd been angling for. A better ending to their story instead of the bitter one he'd been left with.

So why could he hear Devin's voice in the back of his mind?

Friends with the girl he used to be in love with and who still made his whole body hum whenever they got close. What could go wrong?

Her lips curled into a crooked grin as she seemed to come to a decision. "All right, then, Person Who Is My Friend." Her tone was pointedly formal. "Some company while I explore the backwater small towns of the North Carolina mountains would be great."

He rolled his eyes. "'Backwater'? So glad you're going into this with such an open mind."

"Did you forget that I grew up here?"

"Never," he said, too fervently.

Mercifully, she ignored him. "I know what I'm getting into."

"I don't know." He tilted his head to the side, considering. "I'm not sure you do."

Honestly, he wasn't sure he did, either.

"Well, then." She raised her glass before bringing it to her lips. "Let's see if you can prove me wrong."

# CHAPTER SEVEN

* * * * * * * * * * * * * *

Well, look who the cat dragged in."

May narrowed her eyes at June as she passed her on the way toward the sweet, sweet lobby coffee. Her older sister was seated behind the front desk this morning, a spreadsheet open on the screen in front of her. May kind of wanted to be annoyed about her tone, but she wasn't caffeinated enough to summon the energy.

"Literally," she retorted instead. After all, their mom's cat and her internet following had been the ones to drag May back here.

June huffed out a little laugh. "Fair enough." She watched as May poured herself a mug of coffee, but as she reached for the creamer, June chided, "You know the good stuff is for the guests."

May shot her a disbelieving glare. How many times had they snuck generous splashes of hazelnut-flavored deliciousness into their cups back when they were teens?

Rolling her eyes, June shook her head. "Bring me one, too, would you?"

"That's more like it."

May fixed her sister a mug and brought them both over.

She set June's down next to the keyboard, then wavered for a second. She should probably head back into her family's living area and put herself together a bit, but she and June had barely interacted since she'd arrived, save May attacking June for keeping her in the dark, followed by June guilt-tripping her about being gone so long. Even the detailed, annotated list of new places to check out in town had been slipped under her door.

The two of them used to be so close. She hated this new tension between them.

She blew out a rough breath. Han's words from the night before floated back to her. He'd been so forthright. No hiding what he wanted or couching his invitation to spend more time together in veiled terms. That kind of boldness wasn't May's usual style, but she couldn't deny that it had worked.

Maybe she should give it a shot.

She grabbed another chair from the office behind the desk and plunked down in it. June started, looking at her in surprise, though she hid it well enough.

"So how are things going?" May asked.

"All right." June minimized the spreadsheet and swiveled her chair around to face May.

"Whatcha working on?"

June shrugged. "Just doing the books for the month."

"Wasn't that always Mom's job?"

"Used to be." June's jaw tightened.

Crap. Trying to start a conversation with her sister before she'd had her coffee hadn't been May's brightest idea. "Right."

"Lots of things have changed around here," June said carefully—like maybe she was actively trying not to start a fight. Would wonders never cease?

"I'm sure." She did her best to help steer them out of the awkwardness. "Speaking of which, thanks for the list. It's great to have a starting point for checking out new places in town."

They segued into talking about which restaurants and attractions May had visited the day before and which she planned to hit today. She avoided the topic of her lunch plans, and fortunately June didn't call her on it.

Chewing on her lip, June glanced toward the hall. "I think Mom was hoping you might be able to do dinner here again..."

"I don't know." Guilt tugged at her, but she was here for work. "I have a lot of restaurants to check out, and there are only so many meals in a day."

June's mouth tilted downward at the corners.

May braced herself for a lecture, only it didn't come. Somehow, the silence was almost worse.

Then an idea occurred to her. It was like Han had said the night before—two birds, one stone.

"Maybe we could all do dinner out." She could spend time with her family and feel less bad about ordering half the menu, since there would actually be enough people to eat the food.

"Oh." June still didn't quite sound happy. "I mean, sure. Mom would love that. Someone will have to stay behind, of course, but Elizabeth and I can just draw straws."

"What—to man the desk?"

June shrugged. "The only way to guarantee someone will lock themselves out of their room or blow a circuit is to leave the place unattended."

"What about Sally?"

The inn's old cleaning lady always used to pitch in with holding down the fort when they needed help.

"Sally?" June stifled a laugh. "She's eighty-five. She retired ages ago."

"No. She can't be—"

"She definitely is. I went to her birthday party at the senior center in March."

Now that May thought about it, Sally had been getting up there last she'd seen her.

"What about—"

"May, it's fine."

"Isn't there anybody?"

"I'll call around. But..."

"Wait." May blinked a few dozen times, realization dawning. "*Isn't* there anybody? Like, don't we have any staff?"

The number of people who worked at the inn had varied over the years. But they seriously had no one?

June's shoulders stiffened, and that was all the answer May needed.

"I told you money got tight," June said.

Holy crap. "I know, but..."

But running the inn was a huge undertaking. Their mom had been on light duty since her stroke—a fact she never failed to complain about on their monthly chats. That left just Ned, June, and Elizabeth.

No wonder June had been so stressed out.

"I have some favors I can call in," June assured her. "If Bobbi's free, she'll probably do it. I'd ask Clay, but I'm pretty sure he's shorthanded at the Junebug tonight." She put on a smile, but it was strained. "And seriously, if I can't find anybody, I'll take care of it. Mom and Ned would love it if you took them out."

May frowned. But they'd love it more if it was the whole gang. Like old times.

Usually, that kind of thought made her itchy under her skin, counting the days until she could leave again. She loved her family, but it always felt like there was so much pressure to make the most of her limited time with them. As a result, she probably came home even less often.

For some reason, today, though, the suffocating instinct didn't overwhelm her. Maybe it was that June wasn't laying the guilt on so thick. Maybe it was finally seeing how tough things had been here this entire time.

For once, she didn't want to run. She wanted to help.

Before she could begin to try to put that feeling into actual, verbal communication, June stood, smoothing out the skirt of her dress. "Either way," she said, "I'll let you know." She tipped her head toward the dining room. "I should go see if Ned needs any help. You know how the brunch crowd is."

"Right." May rose, too.

The phone for the inn rang. June held up a finger and reached for the receiver. She cast her gaze skyward. "Guess Ned'll have to wait a minute."

May set her coffee down. "You know what? No, he doesn't."

"What—?"

May waved a hand at the phone. "Go ahead. I'll check on Ned."

June's mouth scrunched up. "You sure?"

In a dry tone, May said, "I think I remember how to pour coffee and deliver plates."

The phone kept ringing, and June answered it. "Sweetbriar Inn, this is June speaking, how may I help you?"

May ducked out from behind the desk and made her way down the hall.

For a second, it was like she was eighteen again, working a shift on a busy Saturday morning before heading off to a speech and debate tournament or something. She ran her fingertips along the wainscoting and chuckled wryly at her former self. Back then, the itch to get out and start her life had been almost painful in its intensity.

She wished she could go back in time and tell that shy, lonely girl that they would make it out soon enough. The world beyond Blue Cedar Falls was big and exciting and accepting.

But this place wasn't so terrible, either.

Sure, Jenny Sullivan and her crew had turned May into a social outcast at school, but she'd always had her mom, her stepdad, her sisters. Han.

She didn't regret any of her choices when it came to flying the nest. But perhaps she could have appreciated what she had a bit more, too.

Perhaps she could have been there for the people she cared about more in the time since.

Standing up straighter, she grabbed the coffeepot and headed into the dining room. If she really thought that way, now was her chance to prove it.

Who knew? Between the plans she'd made with Han last night and her new idea to take her parents with her on a research trip tonight, she was turning over a whole new leaf. Balancing her work goals and her personal life had never panned out for her before.

But there was always hope. Right?

———

For the third time, Han checked the mangoes in the back of the restaurant's kitchen. The one he'd put in front had seemed like the ripest that morning, but what if it was overripe? The one behind it still seemed under.

Maybe he should come up with another backup plan. He paced across the room to rifle through his recipe notes again.

"Ai," his mother tutted. She was perched at the counter, reviewing the orders they were putting in to their suppliers, the ridiculous pink reading glasses she'd gotten at the dollar store resting on her nose. "Sit down. You're making me nervous."

"Someone has to do the lunch prep."

Their doors opened in a matter of minutes. May hadn't told him when he'd be coming by, exactly, but he was determined to have everything running like a well-oiled machine. It was what he'd do for any reviewer or food blogger coming through. The fact that it was *May*, and that they'd reached some kind of truce where they'd both admitted they'd like to try to figure out how to be friends was immaterial.

Mostly.

His mom made that annoyed sound again. "Lunch prep is done."

"Work is never done," he parroted at her. How many times had she herself drummed that into him? "Can't be too ready, right?"

"Ready for what?" she muttered, her voice pitched like she was talking to herself, but clearly he was meant to hear. "Beyoncé?"

"Hardly."

But if Queen Bey herself waltzed in right now, Han wasn't sure he could be any more wound up.

The clock ticked over to eleven thirty, and he strode toward the front of the restaurant to unlock the door, flip the sign to OPEN, and turn on the dining room lights.

On his way back to the kitchen to rearrange the

produce again, his mom shot him one last meaningful glare. Huffing out a breath, he planted himself on the stool beside hers.

She glanced at him out of the corner of her eye. After a second, she fluttered a hand in his direction. "Well, if you're just going to be sitting there, doing nothing, come look at these orders with me. Something's not adding up right."

Before he could protest that she'd been the one to tell him to take a load off, the bells over the front door jangled. A familiar figure poked her head in, and Han's whole body lit up.

May spotted him across the space and smiled. "Good morning!"

"Good morning," he greeted her, his voice too chipper, and his mom was going to give him such a hard time about this later. "Grab a seat anywhere, and I'll be right over with a menu." To his mom, he said, "The supply orders are fine—it's just some extra stuff I put in for a catering job I'm doing in a few weeks."

He grabbed a copy of both the regular menu and the secret one and headed to the table by the window where May was settling in.

His mom called after him, "Catering? We don't do catering."

Internally, he winced. Yeah, he probably should have mentioned agreeing to do Bobbi and Caitlin's wedding before now, but oh well.

"Later," he mouthed over his shoulder.

His mom rolled her eyes before fixing her gaze on May. Heat flashed across Han's face, because he was pretty sure his mother had started humming "Single Ladies," which was messed up on every possible level—not just for the Beyoncé reference but because of the fact that he never had put a ring on May's finger.

She'd left before he'd had a chance.

But now here she was, ready to eat his food and maybe promote it to the entire world, so he should probably get his hustle on.

Putting his mom's antics out of his mind, he crossed the space toward her, a broad smile on his face. "Welcome to the Jade Garden." His heart was racing faster than made sense, but he kept his composure the best he could. "My name is Han, and I'll be taking care of you today."

He presented both menus to her with a flourish, and she accepted them with a pleased curl to her lips. "Why thank you, Han."

"Can I start you out with a pot of tea—complimentary, of course—or can I tell you about our other beverage selections?"

"Tea would be great."

"Excellent."

"What's good here?" she asked, perusing the secret menu, which he'd printed a fresh copy of that very morning. He'd used the fancy faux-parchment paper and everything.

"I like the mango pork." That mango better be good. He knew he should have gone to the market to get a few more. "The basil shrimp might be to your liking, too."

She nodded. "I'll try them both. Plus…" She set the secret menu aside and grabbed the conventional one. "Some beef chow fun and…" She cringed. "Buddha's Delight."

He broke character to ask, "Why the face? You like fried bean curd."

"Love the tofu. Hate the name."

Okay, yeah, he could see her point. He shrugged. "It's what people expect."

"You always do things just because that's how people expect them to be done?" Her tone was friendly enough, but there was a hint of something pointed underneath.

His forehead furrowed. "What's that supposed to mean?"

"Nothing," she said, breezy.

He didn't buy that for a second. He kind of wanted to press, but she was here to review his restaurant, and he could actually feel his mom's gaze boring into his spine like a bright red sniper laser. This wasn't the time or the place.

"I'll go get your order started," he said slowly, unsure where exactly they stood with her making veiled comments and him trying to ignore them. Lunch was probably the safest territory he could retreat to. "And I'll be right back with that tea."

"Great, thanks."

He took the menus with him back to the kitchen. His mom met him with one brow arched. Holding his gaze, she called, "Hi, May. Nice to see you."

"Nice to see you, too, Mrs. Leung," she replied.

Han groaned internally and hissed, "Don't make it weird."

"Oh yes, I am definitely the one 'making it weird.'" His mom dropped down off her stool and headed to the kitchen. "I'll get the chow fun and Buddha's Delight going." Her glance was just as pointed as May's tone had been and forget Gang Up on Han Day—apparently it was a weeklong event now.

Ignoring her silent commentary, he nodded and made the pot of tea. Part of him wanted to do all the cooking for May's items, but he appreciated being able to focus on the special dishes.

Once the tea had been delivered, he returned to the kitchen and got out his ingredients. Moment of truth time; he sliced into the mango he'd selected and breathed a sigh of relief. It was basically perfect.

He and his mom worked side by side on the two separate sets of burners. She finished first.

"I'll take those over," he told her.

"No, no, you cook."

"Mom—"

But it was no use. She brought the two dishes over to May, and only the fear of overcooking the shrimp kept Han from thwacking his head into the counter. Whatever they said to each other, he couldn't hear it over the sizzle, which definitely didn't stress him out at all. Especially when they both looked in his direction and laughed.

Determined, he finished up the sauce and got down the good plates. Modern bone china with angular sides, like they used at the upscale fusion joints he'd visited out in Charlotte for research. He set out a molded dome of rice and surrounded it with mango pork on one plate, drizzled with a vivid orange mango reduction and fresh cilantro leaves—she'd always loved those. The other plate got saucy basil shrimp garnished with white and black sesame seeds and a dollop of spicy basil coulis. He decorated the edges of the plates with little swirls of extra sauce and flowers he'd crafted out of thinly sliced carrots and cucumbers earlier that morning, and if that didn't wow her, well.

He walked past his mother with his head held high.

*So fussy*, she always scolded when he got going with his original recipes. Today at least she stayed mum. Somehow, that didn't stop him from hearing her, though.

May had already gotten into the bean curd and beef dishes as he approached the table.

"You ready for more?" he asked, a smile on his face.

"Definitely. Though, wow." She gestured at the food spread out in front of her. "This stuff is even better than I remembered."

He brushed away a tickle of doubt. Everybody liked good old American Chinese takeout. Hopefully she'd enjoy his original fare just as much.

He set the plates down on what little space remained on the table.

She waved her chopsticks at the seat across from hers. "You want to join me?"

His heart did a little thumping thing behind his ribs. Of course he did. He shook his head, though. "I gotta get back to work." A couple of orders had come in while he'd been finishing up May's dishes, and his mom would need help. Besides, he didn't want to bias the jury, standing over her while she judged his food. "Enjoy."

He resisted the urge to look over his shoulder at her as he walked away.

His mom made no such effort. "She smiled when she tried the pork."

"Leave her be." Han studied the computer screen, glancing over at what his mom had going on the burners to see what he still needed to get started.

"Funny. I told her the other day she should come by for lunch, but she said she had to visit places she *didn't* grow up in." His mother's side-eye was palpable. "Guess she changed her mind."

His mom was leading him into a trap. He knew that, but he couldn't see it yet, so he didn't know where to step to go around it. "Guess so."

"You were pretty quick there with handing her your fancy menu."

He shrugged with one shoulder as he got a fresh wok heating. "It's what she came here for."

"She tell you that?"

Ah, and there the snare was, closing around his foot. "Actually, she did."

"Hmmm."

"'Hmmm' what?"

"Just 'hmmm.'"

Was everybody in his life—or at least in this restaurant—trying to make him paranoid? It was never "just hmmm" with his mother, and it was never "nothing" with May.

They cooked in silence for a minute, just the sizzle of onions and garlic hitting hot oil and the clank of the woks.

If his mother wanted to secretly judge him, she was welcome to. It wasn't as if it was anything new. She'd always communicated in unspoken expectations and subtle barbs, and yes—"just hmmm"s. It was part of why he tried to be forthright. Put what he wanted out there.

Mostly.

Right now, all he wanted was to finish up these couple of orders and go see how May was doing. So he did just that.

She glanced up at his approach, closing a tablet where it looked like she'd been taking notes.

His nerves rose. "So? What do you think?"

"You mean, 'How is everything?' 'Still working on that?' 'Anything else I can get you?'"

He tilted his head to the side and lifted his brows. "You want me to keep playing waiter after you giggled with my mom at me?"

"We weren't giggling." She smirked. "Just comparing notes."

"While giggling."

"While giggling."

"Seriously, though." The chair she'd offered him earlier was still pushed out a bit. He tugged it farther back and sank into it. Splaying his hands out to encompass the absolutely ridiculous amount of food she had arrayed in front of her, he asked, "What's the verdict?"

"It's good." Nodding, she smiled, but her expression wasn't as open as it had been when she'd been complimenting his mother's versions of the old standards.

"Good."

"Really good." She picked up her chopsticks again and pointed at the pork. "The mango is excellent."

Ha. All that squeezing and checking for ripeness hadn't been for nothing. There was still more she wasn't saying, though. "But the dish as a whole?" When she hesitated, his spirits fell. "Good. But not great."

That was fine. He didn't pour his whole heart and soul into this stuff or anything.

"It's really, really, really good," she promised. "Just..."

"Just what?"

She chewed at her lip for a second. "They're kind of...chef-y."

"Chef-y." Considering his goal in life had been to become a chef, was that a bad thing?

Pursing her lips together, she blew out a breath. "Like...Like you're cooking with your head instead of your heart."

"Is that a thing?"

"It can be."

"I've been working on those recipes for years."

Invented them, tweaked them, tested them on his friends, and tweaked them some more.

Her eyes softened, her fingers twitching beside her plate like she was going to reach out, but she stopped herself. Her voice kind but consoling, she said, "And it shows."

Okay, yeah. She definitely meant that as a bad thing.

He couldn't exactly say he felt betrayed. There'd never been any guarantee she'd like his new menu.

But back when they were kids, she'd hang out with him in his mom's kitchen while he tried out all the stuff he saw them make on his favorite cooking shows. She'd encouraged him to experiment.

At first, she was tentative with giving him anything other than glowing reviews, but over time she'd become more and more frank, and he'd loved that about her. It had both helped him improve, and it had helped him to better understand her tastes.

Maybe that was part of why this stung. When he'd picked his favorite things to recommend to her today, he'd thought they would be things she would love.

Apparently, he'd been wrong.

"Look," she said, even softer now, and it was a struggle to keep from getting defensive about her handling him with kid gloves. "They really were good. I liked them. And it doesn't matter if I loved them or not."

"Your opinion always matters to me." The comment came out too earnest.

He wasn't talking about her opinion as a reviewer, and they both knew it.

She was kind enough to pretend otherwise, though.

"It was probably just the pressure of having a media person here." Those twitchy fingers of hers finally gave in. She reached across the table and put her hand over his, brushing her thumb over his knuckles for a second. It was meant to be comforting, and it was.

But it was a whole lot more than that, too.

He shouldn't do this, but he turned his palm over, squeezing her fingers inside his own before letting her go. Her skin was warm and soft, and it felt better than it had any right to.

She pulled away and tucked her hair behind her ear.

"You know how it is," she said. The slight hitch in her voice was the only sign she was as affected by his touch as he was by hers. She looked out the window and shrugged. "Having a critic in always makes people get in their own heads."

He wasn't so sure about that.

Part of him felt like she was the first one to take him out of his head in so long.

She was certainly the first person to give him decent feedback in a while. No one else he'd tested his recipes on had told him he was overthinking things. As much as it smarted to hear that news from her, he valued her still being frank with him. Even when—maybe especially when—the truth hurt.

"So." She looked back at him, putting on a smile to defuse the tension. "That offer to show me around one of these other towns still hold?" Her voice pitched higher, like she was trying not to show her nerves. "Or you had entirely too much of my opinions now?"

"As if I could ever get enough of you." He flicked his gaze skyward self-effacingly. There he went again. Putting it all out there.

But she didn't give him crap about it or shoot him down. Instead, she waited for him to look at her again before asking, "So when's good for you?"

"Tomorrow?" He'd have to check the calendar. He normally worked six days a week, and he'd already taken a couple of evenings off in the past few days. But between his mom and the handful of employees they had, he was sure he could get the staffing figured out. It wasn't like this was going to be a regular thing.

"Tomorrow would be great." Her smile was broader this time. "Make a day of it?"

"Sure." He started running through the list of places he would take her in his head. "I'll pick you up around ten? Ten thirty?"

"You know where to find me."

That he did. At least for now.

He sent her on her way with four to-go containers to bring back to her folks. He held the door for her and tried not to think about all the times they'd done this basic routine before. Only then he would have sent her off with a kiss, too. Whispered promises of how they'd meet up again at the golf course or a friend's house or the overlook outside of town that night.

The past echoed in his ears as the door swung shut behind her. He watched her until she was out of sight.

"Don't," he said.

"What?" His mom stood a half dozen feet behind him.

"Don't say it."

"I wasn't going to say anything."

"Uh-huh." He turned and found her staring at him with the most carefully neutral expression he'd ever seen on her. "I'm going to need tomorrow off."

"What a shock," she said, deadpan.

"I'll get coverage sorted."

"I know you will."

He started back toward the kitchen, but his mom

clearly had something else to say, and she was going to make him drag it out of her.

"Fine," he burst. "Out with it."

"She seemed to have a lot to say about your food," his mom said.

Ouch. He hid the way that poked the bruise May had already left him with. "She's a travel writer. Having a lot to say about food is part of her job."

"You didn't look very happy about it."

Turning to check the online ordering system, he frowned. "She had some constructive criticism."

"Thought it was fussy." Her tone was way too knowing.

He clenched his hand into a fist before releasing it. He hated when his mom was right. "Basically."

"So what are you going to do about it?"

"I have no idea. Probably get the next few orders out the door, mostly."

"And then?"

"And then I'll figure it out."

What May said had stung, but it was possible she had a point. He had been painstakingly meticulous in his efforts to refine these recipes. He'd thought it was his artistry at work, but maybe it was just him dicking around. It was easier to keep tweaking than it was to decide he was ready and really strike out on his own.

It was easier to maintain the status quo.

The status quo being this dime-a-dozen takeout place that had been in his family for decades. Its winning formula would never blow anybody away, but it didn't have to. They sold good versions of familiar standards, and they made a decent living doing it.

So why had it started to feel like a cage these past few years?

And if it was a cage, why was he practically clinging to the bars?

Submitting his application to be part of Taste of Blue Cedar Falls had been his first step outside his comfort zone since his father had died almost thirteen years ago. May showing up out of nowhere with her feedback and her gently probing questions…On the one hand, it felt like a disaster. He didn't have time to be doubting himself now.

On the other hand…What if it was fate? What if she was here to shake him out of the rut he'd been in all this time? Professionally.

Personally.

He couldn't let on to his mom all the thoughts swirling around in his brain. But deep down, it felt like the earth beneath his feet was shifting. For the first time in ages, things were changing.

And it was going to turn out to be either the best thing to ever happen to him.

Or the worst.

# CHAPTER EIGHT

❋ ❋ ❋ ❋ ❋ ❋ ❋ ❋ ❋ ❋ ❋ ❋ ❋

*When are you getting back from NC again?*

May pursed her lips, her thumbs hovering over the keypad on her phone. She was seated at the empty kitchen table in her parents' apartment, her laptop in front of her as she nursed a cup of lobby coffee—heavy on the fancy creamer.

She and her editor Zahra had been texting about a few other pieces she'd been working on. Naturally, the conversation had turned to how her current research trip was shaping up—and how long it was going to take.

She'd originally budgeted a week. At the time, it had seemed like overkill, but now it scarcely seemed like enough. She debated in her head whether or not she should admit that to her editor. Writers for *Passage* maintained a fast-paced, jet-setting lifestyle. Dawdling in Blue Cedar Falls might not look good, especially with the threat of layoffs hanging over everybody's heads.

Despite herself, she'd been enjoying her time here, though. Sure, even distant glimpses of Jenny Sullivan still gave her the sweats, and her guilt reflex was getting a workout hanging out with June. But dinner with her parents and Elizabeth last night had been great.

And she still had the day to look forward to with Han. Little bubbles of anticipation formed in her chest, just thinking about it. She tried to tell herself it was the prospect of having some company for once that made her feel all fizzy inside. The fact that it was Han had nothing to do with it.

Right. And the Nile was just a river in Egypt.

*Return flight gets me back on Thursday*, she finally texted back. She sank her teeth into her lip. *But there's a chance I might try to extend a day or two. Lots of territory to cover.*

Zahra's reply didn't take long. *Keep me posted. Got something juicy for you when you're done.*

May sat up straighter. *Oh?*

*You know the deal. Send me your return ticket, and I'll send you details.*

May narrowed her eyes. *Tease.*

*Always . . .*

Shaking her head, May set her phone aside. She finished up the couple of work tasks she needed to check off her list. As she sent off the last of them, she picked up her mug, only to find it distressingly empty.

"Well, that's no good."

If she were going to be here longer, she'd buy her folks a new pod coffee maker. Her mom would hate the extravagance, but she'd also really like all the different flavors. May rolled her eyes at herself. Even with her days numbered here, maybe she should get them one anyway.

In the meantime, she trekked out to the lobby for her caffeine fix. The desk was unmanned, the little BACK IN 15 sign propped up next to the vase of flowers June still insisted on getting from old Dottie Gallagher's flower shop every couple of days.

As May doctored her coffee, voices rang out on the stairway. She glanced up to find a couple of men with suitcases heading down, one of them in cargo shorts and a band T-shirt, the other wearing a crisp, white button-down with a purple scarf May wouldn't have minded having in her own wardrobe.

"*Fifteen?*" the one with the good taste in scarves decried, picking up the sign. "We're already running late."

Cargo Shorts Guy rubbed his back. "You were the one who wanted 'the authentic small town, small business experience.'"

May glanced around. Down the hall, it sounded like brunch was in full swing, which meant Ned would have his hands full, and her mom probably had her usual crew of friends visiting. Was June supposed to be staffing the desk this morning or Elizabeth? She couldn't remember.

As the men grew more restless, May gave her coffee one final stir.

"Are you two checking out?" she finally asked.

"We'd certainly like to be," scarf guy said.

She chewed her lip as she slipped behind the desk. "This isn't usually my job," she told them. Understatement. "But let me see if there's anything I can do." She woke up the computer and put in the password, which she was both pleased and dismayed to discover hadn't changed in a decade.

The new reservation system bore only the most passing resemblance to the old one, but it didn't take long to figure out. She asked them for the last name and found their account.

As she got them checked out, she fell into the familiar rhythm of small talk. Turned out they were heading to Harpersville next, too, and they traded thoughts on itineraries.

Crossing her fingers that June would forgive her for any mistakes, she printed out their receipt and handed it over to them. "Hope you enjoyed your stay."

"Sure did," the man in cargo shorts replied. "Very authentic, small town, small business."

His partner fondly rolled his eyes before winking at May. "And the pancakes were to die for."

"I'll tell my stepdad you said so."

On their way out, they passed Elizabeth, who was rushing in. She spotted May behind the desk and let out an exaggerated sigh of relief. "I'm so sorry I'm late. Is June mad?"

"June is a ray of sunshine," June said, descending the stairs, the master key ring in her hand. She gestured up the way she'd come. "Room ten locked themselves out."

"I just checked out room twenty-two." May grabbed her coffee before stepping away from the computer. "Hope I didn't mess anything up."

June crinkled her brows as she slipped between May and Elizabeth to check the screen. She pursed her lips. "Looks okay to me."

May drew the back of her hand across her forehead. "Phew."

"Sorry again," Elizabeth said, nudging June out of the way to set her big, chunky boho bag down under the desk. "Graham tried to make breakfast."

May and June both winced in unison.

"Did you have to call the fire department?" June asked.

"Not this time."

"I guess that's something," May said with a chuckle.

Shaking her head, Elizabeth plunked down in the chair

behind the desk. "There are a lot of things I'll miss about the man, but his cooking is not one of them."

June furrowed her brows. "Wait…"

Elizabeth glanced at May and back. Ah, so the applications she'd been putting in to all those residencies were still a secret. She waved a hand. "I mean, like, theoretically."

May hid her wince. Her sister hadn't gotten any better at subterfuge in May's absence. There were two reasons Elizabeth had always been in trouble as a teen—one, she did ridiculous things. Two, she couldn't lie her way out of a paper bag.

"Okay…" June didn't look any more convinced.

Elizabeth blinked meaningfully at May, and May got the hint. Time for a distraction. To both of them, she asked, "You guys mind showing me how I'm supposed to do the checkout in the new reservation system? Just in case I missed anything."

Both her sisters blinked at her as if she'd asked them how to build a rocket ship to Mars, not use the computer.

A self-conscious flush warmed her cheeks. "I said, just in case." She shrugged as they both kept gawking at her. "Who knows? I might end up having to check somebody out again."

Was it that absurd of a request?

"I mean"—June's eyebrows pinched together—"sure, I guess."

More bluntly, Elizabeth said, "You really think you're going to be here long enough to make it worth the time?"

Ugh. Okay, yeah, May had walked right into that one. She couldn't pitch in without drawing attention to the fact she was never here and never pitched in.

"It doesn't matter," she started, backing away.

Before she could get too far, June stopped her. "I'd love to show you," she said. "It'll only take a minute."

And there was something about the openness to her expression. So many of their recent interactions had been shadowed by the silent guilt trips and the resentment June had been trying—barely, it seemed—to keep to herself. For once, though, all of that seemed to clear away. May had offered to learn how to help, and June was accepting it.

So that was how May ended up spending the next half hour getting a crash course on the new systems they were using. As June showed her the ropes, Elizabeth handled the controls and added color commentary, and it was...nice.

Really nice.

A point that was driven home when her mom and her brunch friends wandered past. Her mother bid her friends adieu, and May exchanged an awkward wave with Mrs. Leung. Then her mom came to stand on the other side of the desk, one arm propped on the counter, her gaze way too intense as she took in the three of them.

The back of May's neck went warm again. June's posture stiffened by a fraction, too.

Elizabeth outright squirmed. "Stop it, Mom."

"Stop what?" their mother asked. Like she could really be that oblivious.

Even Sunny the cat, who'd hopped up on the counter beside their mom, didn't seem impressed.

"Stop looking at us like a bunch of lost puppies who found their way home," Elizabeth groused.

Her description was over the top, but it wasn't too far off base, either.

As if she understood the word "puppies" and disapproved of it, Sunny flicked her tail, sending a couple of the inn's business cards flying in Elizabeth's direction. Their mom harrumphed, but placed a hand on the back of the cat's neck and gave her a good scratch, so the disapproving message may have gotten lost a bit.

"What do you want me to say?" their mother asked, petting Sunny—looking at the cat instead of at any of them. "I like to see my girls together, all in one place. Is that a crime?"

Something in May's chest squeezed. She couldn't help but be reminded that it was her ambition—and her bad experiences with this town—that had broken up their trio. But it was like when June had agreed to explain the new software. For once, there was no bite to her own self-recrimination. Yes, she was the reason they didn't get together often, but it didn't feel like anyone was blaming her right now. Instead, they were all just appreciating this pocket of time they had.

The pocket came to an abrupt end about five minutes later, of course.

At ten a.m. on the dot, the bell over the front door of the inn chimed. In strode Han, and May's heart constricted for a whole different sort of reason. He'd traded in his usual T-shirt for a black button-down, the sleeves of which he'd rolled up, showing off muscular forearms. His jeans were nicer, too. More fitted, and her throat went dry.

Was it possible he just kept getting hotter? Did he drink some magical potion every night?

Logically, she knew he didn't. But the only other explanation was that she was getting attached to him again, and she'd never forgive herself if she did that, so magical potion it must be.

"Good morning, ladies." He came right up to the desk and leaned against it like their mother.

"Han." May's mom glanced between him and May, one brow lifting. "So good to see you."

"You, too, Mrs. Wu."

There were some more raised brows from May's sisters—paired with a knowing smirk from Elizabeth, which May appreciated even less. Then again, inviting him and his friends to join them at the Junebug the other night hadn't been the most subtle move she'd ever made.

"Why yes, Han," Elizabeth said. "So great to see you. *Again.*"

Han nodded, one eye narrowing slightly. He directed his attention to May. "You about ready to head out? Or we can reschedule if you're busy . . ."

"No." May stood, shaking her head. She'd enjoyed this time catching up with her sisters, and it would be good to have a better understanding of the inn's reservation system, but she was here to work, and it was time she got to it. "Just let me grab my bag."

"Where are you two off to?" June asked as May extricated herself from the desk.

"Just helping her out with some research for her article," Han promised.

May missed whatever he said next as she slipped back into her family's apartment. She was basically dressed and ready for the day, but she took a second to check her lipstick. She was a professional and wanted to look the part. And if Han happened to do that thing where his eyes went dark as he took her in, well, that wouldn't exactly be bad for her ego, now would it?

She stuffed her notebook, tablet, and camera into her bag, and slung it over her shoulder. She reemerged into the lobby to find her mom and sisters laughing at something Han had said. All eyes went to her, and the laughter cut off, dispelling any illusions she might have had that they were talking about someone else.

Mentally rolling her eyes at them all, she tipped her head toward the door. "Shall we?"

She stepped out from behind the desk, and his gaze totally did that thing. Her skin tingled, and her breath and pulse ticked up. He lightly brushed a hand against the small of her back, and she really, really hated that her family was here to witness the casual touch. But the touch itself? She didn't hate that at all.

"After you," he said.

"Guessing you won't be home for dinner?" June called after them.

"Research," May reminded her.

Elizabeth muttered something, and June covered her mouth as she laughed.

"Ignore them," May told Han as he held the door.

"I don't know," Han mused. "It's sort of fun, watching them make you blush."

She cursed the telltale warmth on her cheeks. "I'm not blushing."

"Sure."

His car was parked right out front—a midsized hatchback, not exactly new but not old, either. A big blanket was spread across the back seat. He opened the rear door and folded it up. "Sorry, was out with the dog this morning."

"No worries."

Once they were in and buckled, he started the car, but then he paused, his hand on the gear shift. He glanced over at her, and it didn't matter that it was broad daylight, or that they were parked outside her family's home.

Suddenly, she was entirely too aware of how close they were. His scent surrounded her, warm and masculine, amber and spice, with just a hint of the kitchen and his cooking lingering in the air. The sound of his laughter mixing with that of her sisters' echoed in her ears, and time seemed to disappear. It could have been thirteen years ago.

They could have been something so much more to each other than just old friends.

As if he was feeling the same powerful sense of nostalgia, he turned his head to look at her. His gaze and mouth soft, he curled up one corner of his lips. "It's nice. You know. Seeing you and your family like that."

Again, the defensiveness she would usually feel about that sort of comment failed to materialize. "Yeah?"

"Yeah. Feels like old times."

"I guess..."

He wasn't wrong.

But as pleasant as it was, drifting along in ancient memories, strengthening connections she'd neglected over time, it somehow didn't feel like enough.

She broke their gaze, shifting to look forward through the window. "I don't know about you," she said. "But I'm ready to go explore something new."

———

Half an hour later, they were seated by the window at the Cricket Café in Harpersville. While the hostess got working on their drinks, Han opened his menu, glancing over its contents for half a second before closing it again. He'd been here a handful of times before, and he never ordered off the menu anyway. Mentally, he rolled his eyes at himself. His palms were sweating. What on earth was he so nervous for? It was just lunch with May. He'd done this a thousand times.

When he was seventeen.

"So." He set the menu aside. "Tell me how a big travel writer does a restaurant review?"

May shot her gaze to the side. Lifting her brows pointedly, she leaned in and lowered her voice. "The first rule of doing a restaurant review is don't talk about how you're doing a restaurant review."

"Oh." Great, so Han had messed up within two seconds of sitting down. He looked around, but if anyone had overheard his slip, at least they weren't being obvious about it.

"It's okay," May assured him, but she still seemed a little uneasy about the whole thing. "It's like I said yesterday at the Jade Garden. People act all weird when they know you're there to judge them. I want to be able to tell my readers how the average guest will be treated, so I have to pretend to be the average guest."

"Makes sense."

Not for the first time since he'd run into May again, he felt naïve and bumbling. He reminded himself that that was a good thing. He'd been too comfortable for too long. No, he hadn't been aware of how fancy travel writers operated. After all, it wasn't as if he'd ever met one before. But if he really wanted to make a go of it with his own restaurant, he was going to need to get used to this kind of thing.

Someday, maybe, if he got lucky, he'd be the guy in the kitchen eyeing the unfamiliar face in his dining room, hoping he could make a good enough impression to earn a glowing review, and with it, enough new customers to help keep his dreams afloat.

That was him getting way, way ahead of himself, though. As it was, even the reviewer he knew and at one point loved wasn't that impressed with his food.

Not that he'd been mulling *that* over for the last twenty-four hours or so.

Their server came by with their drinks and offered to take their orders. Han did his usual and just asked them to bring him whatever the chef thought was good today. May chose more carefully, picking a light salad for an appetizer and a heavier entrée.

After the server had gone, Han asked, careful and quiet this time, "Any rules of reviewing involved in your selection?"

"Mostly balance. Something fresh and something that takes some work. If they don't have the chops on either, hopefully it'll be clear." Shrugging, she took a sip of her iced tea—half sweet, half unsweet, just the way she'd always liked it. She gestured around. "This is cute, by the way."

It was—verging on twee, honestly, with vintage knick-knacks and pastel-colored walls, but the food was good. Or at least he'd always thought so. "I thought you might like it."

"How'd you find it?"

He chuckled and tapped his finger against his glass. He automatically pitched his voice lower. " 'Researching the competition.' "

"Oh?" Her brows pinched together. "That sounds like something your—"

"Dad would say?" He turned his head to look out the window. Without his permission, his mouth turned wry.

All of a sudden, he was regretting sticking with water to drink. How many times had he and May met up at bars? And now the one time he didn't have a drop of alcohol in him was the time he had to go ahead and bring up his father.

"Kind of," May said delicately.

He glanced back at her. She had the corner of her lip between her teeth, contrition in her eyes. Behind that, though, was also an invitation.

He took a big gulp of cold water before letting out a breath. "It was something we used to do. Just me and him."

"I remember."

So did Han. He never talked about his father—not really. Even among his family, his loss was this wound that everybody skirted around, like the world's worst game of The Floor Is Lava. Occasionally his mom brought him up, but even then, it was passing references. *Your father would have loved that.* Or, more frequently, it seemed, *Your father wouldn't have wanted that.*

Han wasn't so sure his mother had the market cornered on what his father would or wouldn't have wanted, though. He had his own memories. Great ones—ones he'd held on to.

His dad had been the one to teach him to cook, starting when he was just a kid. He'd taken to it like a duck to water. He loved the sizzle of the pan and the chemistry that made dishes sing. He loved re-creating and reinventing old standards, and he loved playing with new flavors, discovering unexpected combinations that brought out the best in ingredients, be they humble or hard to find.

His father had known it, too. He'd shown Han how to make every item on the menu at the Jade Garden by the time he was in middle school. Even as he was mastering those, learning the efficiencies that kept a commercial kitchen humming, he was riffing on them. His father gave him honest feedback, glowing and brutal by turns.

When Han made it clear he wanted to go to culinary school, his mother was skeptical. Even then, she worried about making ends meet. She already had her brother, Han's uncle Arthur, who'd drifted away from the family business to start a food pantry and soup kitchen. While Arthur had a nice nest egg he'd built through a series of wise real estate investments a couple of decades prior, the Leungs had invested all their time, energy, and resources into raising three kids.

Han's father had encouraged Han every step of the way, though.

"Those 'competitive research trips' were some of the best times we ever spent together," he said, swallowing past the lump in his throat. They'd traveled all over the western Carolinas, occasionally venturing as far as Charlotte and Raleigh, knocking out a few college visits along the way. The conversations they'd had over fusion dishes had ranged from food criticism to life ambitions. "He talked to me like an adult, you know? Even though in hindsight I was some dumb teenager."

His dad had never treated him like one.

After Han had floated the idea of following May to New York, his dad had even booked them tickets there.

Han had wandered around Chinatown with his father. His family had always prided themselves on being bilingual, but he'd discovered how basic his Mandarin was, surrounded by people who spoke it exclusively. They'd eaten their way uptown, and Han had never felt so backwards or naïve in his life. They'd only had to tour one culinary institute before he'd realized there was no way he could do this.

He felt lost, there among the big buildings and sneering chefs. His father had quietly listened to his burgeoning anxiety attack, and when Han was done, his father reminded him, with spare words, that Uncle Arthur had traveled south in search of a better life. Han's mom and dad had done the same, and while there was nothing wrong with New York—in fact there was quite a lot that was great about it—Blue Cedar Falls was their family's home for a reason. There was no shame in wanting a quiet life for himself, too.

But try telling that to May.

He turned away from the window and back toward her. His vision focused in and out as his brain tried to put the angry eighteen-year-old version of her together with the adult one sitting before him.

She was calmer now. She'd seen so much, experienced so many things—pretty much all of them without him— and he was happy for her and her success.

There was also this tender edge to his feelings, though. He wished he'd gotten to know all the versions of her that had come in between.

He wished he understood the bits of sadness and loneliness in her eyes.

He wished he didn't think he'd helped to put them there, a long, long time ago.

"My dad." He swallowed, glancing away and then back again. "He played a big part in my decision to stay here, you know. When I decided to go to school in Raleigh in the first place." Back before he had any inkling how precious and short his time with his father was.

May chewed on her lip, a flicker of a frown curling her mouth, only for it to straighten right back out. When she spoke, a new brittleness entered her tone. "I figured."

"Not like that." He wanted to go back in time and smack the iteration of himself that had tried to explain all this to her then.

He'd let her think it was all family pressure that had convinced him to stay behind, when the truth had been more nuanced. He'd been such a coward, blaming the decision on his folks.

"No?" she asked.

"Not entirely. I . . ." He scrubbed a hand through his hair. "I like it here. At home. In Blue Cedar Falls. I like being close to my family, and my dad—he didn't hold me back."

Maybe his mother would have, if push had come to shove. Only it never had.

"I held myself back." Only that wasn't quite right, either, was it? "I chose to stay close, because my family is my foundation. I didn't want to uproot myself."

He didn't want to lose them. Not the way May had. She'd been running from everybody else in their hometown, but there was no way to escape them without leaving behind the people who loved her.

He'd learned that the hard way. To hear June talk about it, the rest of her family had, too.

"I didn't like New York," he heard himself say.

May scoffed, and it brought him whipping right back to the present. "You never gave New York a shot."

"I saw enough. I knew that wasn't the life I wanted."

"Yeah, you made yourself plenty clear about that."

Impulsively, he reached across the table. When his hand covered hers, electricity shot through his arm, but he didn't shy away from it this time. "That didn't mean I didn't want a life with you."

"You just also wanted it to include seeing other

people." The hurt in her voice ripped into him, as fresh as it had been the day he'd told her that steaming pile of bull crap in the first place.

For a second he wavered. He could tell her he'd only pushed her away because he couldn't bear to be an anchor around her neck. She was set on leaving, and he loved her too much to try to stop her. She deserved better than some half measure of freedom, too.

If she wanted to go, she should do it free and clear.

Telling her that now would only make things worse, though. She'd be outraged—and rightfully so—if he basically told her he'd had to hurt her for her own good. Instead he settled for a partial truth. "It killed me. Telling you that."

"Seemed easy enough," she scoffed, pulling her hand away.

Really? Setting her free had been one of the hardest things he'd ever done in his life.

For better or worse, the server chose that moment to interrupt them with May's appetizer. Perhaps noticing the tension that threatened to rip apart the air between them, she put down the plate, smiled at them, gave them exactly two seconds to request anything else, and then hightailed it away.

He and May stared at each other over what looked like a really great baby greens, fruit, and feta salad, only neither of them touched it. He refused to squirm under the weight of her gaze, which didn't quite manage to come across as accusing but didn't quite manage not to, either.

He finally broke the silence with "I thought you said no emotional reunions."

"That was *days* ago, Han." She cracked a smile. "Keep up."

"So feelings are back on the table now?"

"In limited quantities."

May had always loved her rules.

He took a deep breath and let it out. "I'm sorry. What I said to you that last time…"

Neither of them had to specify which time he meant.

Even though she'd left, and he'd told her to make the most of her freedom while she was gone, they still stayed in touch that first year of school.

When he got the news about his father, May was the first person he called. He did it in the middle of the day, barely able to speak as he stuffed a few changes of clothes and a toothbrush into a duffel bag. She'd answered right away, and he still didn't know what she'd had to do to get herself back to Blue Cedar Falls the very next day, but she did.

She'd held his hand at the funeral. How would he have gotten through that awful day without her? He'd stood there at the cemetery, his sisters and his mom as numb and shell-shocked as he was. The first part of his life had ended with the sound of dirt on a casket, and he'd kept it together. He was the man of the family now, and yeah, that was some sexist nonsense, but he couldn't help feeling like it was true.

That night, he asked May to go for a drive. She went with him. She always did. He should have known better, but he was raw from swallowing all that grief and rage. He'd driven her to the spot, overlooking the falls, where they'd spent so much time. Shared such intimate moments.

And like the complete and total hunk of used-up trash he was that day, he let it all out. He told her his fears and his burdens, his desperation, because he had to give up culinary school. He had to come home and take care of his baby sisters and his mom and the restaurant. All his other plans would have to wait.

And then he asked her the one question he knew he couldn't.

He asked her to stay. He threw away his noble self-sacrifice, taking back everything he'd said in his attempt to set her free. He'd become the anchor around her neck he had sworn he'd never be. He asked her to give up her dreams and come home, where she belonged, and he'd known it was unforgivable. If anybody else had told her to drop out of school, he would have decked them. He kind of wanted to deck himself, only he was so far down in a hole.

She told him she couldn't. She'd always be there for him. Always love him, even, in some way. But her life was out there now.

So he told her to never come back. He lashed out. Told her it would be better if she weren't in his life at all than to have it halfway, there for him in spirit but from hundreds of miles away. And he hadn't been wrong. Their long-distance friendship filled with all that hurt and resentment had been torture for them both. He'd ignored her tears, and that had been easy enough, hadn't it? He'd been choking on so many unshed tears of his own.

After that night, she left. For good.

And he regretted being such a piece of crap to her for the rest of his life.

"Han…"

"I was hurting," he admitted, though it cost him something to do so. He tried to be forthright, but there was being open and then there was cutting a hole in your chest and asking the person you'd once loved the most in the world to take a look inside. "I shouldn't have told you—"

"It's okay." She reached across the table for him, curling a finger around his. "I knew you were upset."

He looked up, and their eyes met. "I just didn't think you'd actually do it." He swallowed, his throat closing up on him. "Disappear."

"Han," she said quietly. Her eyes shone, and she wrapped their hands together more tightly. "That wasn't your fault."

"You have some other explanation for being gone for thirteen years?"

"Life." She flung a hand around dramatically. "I mean—I'm not going to pretend it didn't hurt, you basically telling me to either drop out of school or never talk to you again." Her throat bobbed. "It hurt like you wouldn't believe."

"I know—"

"But we would have drifted apart anyway."

He flinched. "You think…"

"You were never going to leave. You made that clear." She pulled her hand back to her side of the table. "And everything was starting for me in New York. Classes, work-studies, internships, and then I got a job right out of school."

"I know."

"In some ways—" She paused. "In some ways, a part of me always thought it might have been for the best. As much as it sucked. Having a clean ending for you and me…"

That shouldn't be a knife to his gut, hearing her talking about this. They'd been over for more than a decade now. It still killed him, anyhow.

Maybe, deep down, a part of him had never given up hope on her coming back.

Any thoughts he might have had to that effect were annihilated now, though. She'd seen their ending as a clean break. And didn't that tell him everything he'd needed to know?

All that time he'd spent wondering...Holding her up as the standard every person in his life would have to live up to...

All the crappy decisions he made afterward, subconsciously trying to get back at her for abandoning him.

Meanwhile, she hadn't really been thinking of him at all.

He couldn't keep the bitterness out of his voice. "Right."

Only she wouldn't let it go. "Are you telling me it would have been better if we'd dragged it out forever?"

"No, just—"

"Just what?"

"I missed you," he blurted out. Pathetic. But it was true.

"Han." She waited until he looked at her again. "I missed you, too. More than I can say." Her smile faltered, and the softness in her eyes was a whole different kind of puncture wound inside him. "I thought about you all the time. Wondered..."

"Yeah?"

"Just..." She huffed out a breath. "Everything. How you were doing, what you were up to. Elizabeth told me some stuff, but it wasn't like she knew every detail. Besides, I think she was trying to protect me." One corner of her mouth tilted up. "Didn't want me mooning over you too much."

"Was there a danger of that?" he asked, like a freaking masochist.

"Of course there was." She gazed at him for a moment that seemed to go on and on. Tentatively, she stretched a hand toward him again. She brushed her fingertips over his knuckles once. "I really did think about you a lot. Your whole family. How you were doing, after your father..."

"We were a mess." Oh wow, what was he doing? He seriously never, ever talked about this stuff.

But May had always made him feel like it was safe to let her see the hidden parts of himself. His dating history might be limited, but he had had a few, brief relationships here and there over the last decade. No other woman had ever made him feel quite so open as May had.

Maybe that was a result of all their history together.

Maybe it was that she'd softened him up by making him rehash their breakup—the other most terrible thing that had ever happened to him. So why not go for broke and talk about his father dying, too?

"I mean, no one ever would have known it. My mom was stone-faced. Didn't even shut down the restaurant except the day of his funeral. But at night, behind closed doors..."

She locked herself in the room she'd shared with his dad. He could hear her crying, but the handful of times he tried to console her, she promised she was fine, just sentimental. Like that was a weakness.

"She got kind of neurotic for a while," he told May. "Fluttering about, obsessing over the finances. Dad had always taken care of that stuff, and she felt like she had to whip herself into shape or something."

"That sounds like your mom." May tentatively placed her fingertips over his again.

"Tell me about it." He turned his hand palm up and stroked his thumb across her skin. It was probably too intimate, but he was talking about this crap. If she was offering to hold his hand while he did, he wasn't going to turn that down.

His mom had always flown to extremes. She worried and she hounded, and she did every bit of it from a place of love. Right after Han's father died, though, she did a lot of it out of fear.

It was an awful, miserable first year.

"My sisters probably got the worst of it, my mom rode them so hard. They were still in high school."

"And you were all of eight months out of it."

"Totally a grown-up," he joked, only it wasn't entirely a joke.

He sat here, taking issue with his mom being closed off and paranoid, but he was just self-aware enough to recognize that he hadn't exactly been a whole lot better. Pushing all of his own feelings aside, he took up the mantle of man of the house. He was in charge of the restaurant now. He handled as much of the financial stuff as he could. Without his tuition or his housing to worry about it, the books balanced themselves a little better.

But there was still Lian and Zoe to get through college. They'd both had to take out some loans, but he'd covered the portion their father had promised them that the family would.

The day Zoe had graduated, one year ago this month, Han had celebrated by taking a three-hour long nap. After that, he'd started working on a whole new set of recipes for the secret menu. Dreams that had been collecting dust on the shelf for a decade remained on the shelf; he wasn't completely delusional. But he did give them a quick swabbing down with a metaphorical rag. They were still out of his reach, but without that coat of dust covering them, they shone with a different light.

He gave her fingers a final squeeze before releasing her hand and pulling his down into his lap. "In the end, though, we survived." Emotionally stunted and a little sadder than they used to be. But alive and well and doing their best. "Lian's got a great job teaching at Lincoln Elementary. Zoe's tending bar and bookkeeping and running Harvest Home."

"And shacking up with your best friend."

He groaned. "Don't remind me."

"Sorry."

"And I'm running the Jade Garden with Mom, and neither of us has murdered the other yet. So all around, I'd say we turned out okay."

Yeah, his father's memory haunted him sometimes— like when he went out on competitive research trips on his own. But more often than not these days, he could remember the good stuff, and be thankful he'd had eighteen great years with his old man. It was less than he'd wanted, but hey. It was more than some got.

"Well, I'm glad," May said. She gazed across the table at him, steady and soft. "That you're okay."

"You know me." He shrugged, and with that, he closed up the opening in his chest that he'd allowed her to peer through for a bit. To his surprise, the exposure to the light hadn't left the damaged parts inside him feeling worse. If anything, they felt...better. If only just a little. When he smiled, it hardly even seemed fake. "I'm always fine."

"Sure." May rolled her eyes, letting out a huff of a laugh, but she didn't call him on the lie, and for that much, at least, he could be grateful.

With an unusual lightness buoying him up, he unrolled

his silverware and pulled out his fork. He gestured at her untouched appetizer. "Well, if you're not going to try this..."

"Excuse me for thinking it would be disrespectful to start stuffing my face while you were rehashing a decade's worth of trauma." Laughing, she dug out her fork, too.

"Trauma always tastes better with a tart vinaigrette." Which this salad had in spades. He assembled a bite with just the right balance of ingredients—two young, green leaves, a strawberry slice, a blueberry, and a lump of feta cheese—and popped it in his mouth. Sweet, savory, bright flavor burst over his tongue.

"Wow," May agreed.

"Good, right?" He went back for more, just as their server returned with their entrées. To his delight, the chef had picked a duck and grits riff that looked amazing. May's chicken and waffles looked pretty great, too.

Before he could dig in with too much gusto, May held out a hand. She waited until their server had retreated an acceptable distance away. "Be forewarned—the second rule of being a restaurant reviewer is not one you are going to like."

"Oh?" He paused, fork in midair.

"Never eat more than a few bites of anything."

He might as well have shoved his lemon garnish into his mouth whole.

May laughed. "Or finish your whole lunch, if you want to. Just realize." She gestured out the window. "If we're going to do this town justice, we still have six more lunches to go."

# CHAPTER NINE

❋ ❋ ❋ ❋ ❋ ❋ ❋ ❋ ❋ ❋ ❋

This was a terrible idea," Han moaned, not ten yards from where they'd just parked the car at the botanical gardens outside Harpersville.

May's heart skipped a beat, but she kept her expression calm as she took another step along the path.

*This was a terrible idea.* Wasn't that the constant refrain of her thoughts this entire trip? Coming home, drinks with Han, helping at the inn, more drinks with Han, lunch with Han, more helping at the inn, and—oh right, even more lunch with Han. Every single step of the way, she'd kept thinking she was making yet another mistake.

And yet somehow, today, exploring Harpersville with him...she'd almost lost sight of her trepidation. Despite herself, she'd been having a great time.

Sure, there had been some intense conversations, especially at that first restaurant where they'd started their adventure. Difficult as it may have been, for both of them, those intense conversations had seemed to clear the air, though. Their subsequent stops had been lighthearted. She'd been able to focus on the food and decor and the article she was here to write.

And it had never turned into a slog. Her last few research trips had been to five-star resorts in luxury vacation destinations, and as pleasant as they'd all been, at some point one had started to bleed into the next. She'd had to work hard to keep her writing light and not let her own boredom color her impressions of the places.

Harpersville was a far, far, far stretch from the Maldives. But it didn't matter. Every place Han had taken her to had had its own unique charm. To her surprise, she'd enjoyed herself. Who knew? Maybe the quirkiness of small southern towns had been the secret to pulling her out of her funk all along.

Right. It definitely had nothing to do with having company for the first time in years.

Good company, too. Han was culinarily adventurous and knowledgeable. He offered context and commentary, and he was *funny*.

Handsome, to boot.

She'd caught herself, more than once, just staring at him across a booth, feeling exactly like that moon-eyed girl she'd been at fifteen. Lost in the depths of his dark eyes or mesmerized by that one bit of longer black hair he kept pushing off his brow. Entranced by the way his throat bobbed above the open collar of his shirt; her heart beating fast, her skin tingling with every casual touch of his hand or foot against hers.

So, yeah. For a minute there, she'd completely forgotten that this was a terrible idea. But maybe Han hadn't.

She dared a glance back at him, ready to laugh his comment off. It was just a quick walk around a garden. Compared with all the drinks and lunches, how terrible of an idea could that be?

Then she noticed how he was holding his stomach.

"I should not have eaten seven lunches," he complained.

Relief and amusement swirled inside her, and she laughed. "I warned you."

"I know. But it was all so good!"

"That it was."

"Except the turnip dish at Justine's."

"I warned you about that, too."

"Why don't I ever listen to you?"

Now that was a question she would never know the answer to.

Raising a brow, she gestured back toward the car. "You want to relax and have a little nap and digest?"

"No." He quickened his pace to catch up with her, and she ignored the prickle of warmth dancing across her skin as he slotted himself into place by her side. "I'm good, I'm good."

"Your funeral." Deep down, she was delighted.

Mentally, she kicked herself. Going back to doing research trips on her own was going to suck so hard. No way she should be allowing herself to get used this.

That was a problem for future her, though.

Present her was out for a walk on a beautiful spring day in the Carolina mountains, an attractive man by her side.

Their gentle teasing continued as they entered the garden proper. She grabbed a map from the kiosk and paid both of their admissions. Han grumbled about that the same way he had all their restaurant bills, but she waggled her corporate card at him again, and that quieted him down.

Beyond the big, sculptural hedges that surrounded the place lay neatly groomed grounds. Well-tended paths led them past fountains and topiaries and quirky, welded metal art objects. She paused to admire the different beds of local flowers. She hadn't exactly planned this trip—at all—but she couldn't have timed it better if she'd tried. Full blooms stood in a riot of color.

Above them, the sky was a brilliant blue, interrupted by only the puffiest of white clouds.

It was perfect, honestly.

Impulsively, she spread out her arms and did a little twirl.

"You seem happy," Han said.

"Who wouldn't be?" It was easy to shrug his comment off, but even she could recognize the buoyancy inside her was unusual. "Why have I never been here before?"

"Probably because you never come home."

The jab had no heat to it, so she reacted with a simple flick of her gaze toward the sky. "Touché." She glanced in his direction. His dark hair gleamed in the sun, and there was a sparkle to his eyes that she remembered. She bumped her elbow against his, making her whole arm tingle. "How did you find this place anyway? Not a lot of competitive research in a botanical garden."

"No, but you have to admit, it's a good place to walk off seven lunches."

"That it is."

They passed from the native plants section to one filled with European varieties. The more cultivated look of the garden reminded her of some she'd seen in Paris. It was a nice touch.

Beside her, Han tucked his hands into his pockets. "Dad brought me here, actually."

She almost tripped over a branch. "Oh?"

"It's a good place to walk off just one lunch, too." He smiled, but it was strained.

As they strolled on, she kept glancing at him out of the corner of her eye.

Han had always been a tough nut to crack. He spoke freely in general. He was even inclined to overshare at times, and he asked incisive questions. Most people would probably imagine he was frank to a fault; she was pretty sure that he imagined that about himself.

But she knew better. None of his openness was an act, but it was an effective distraction. He overshared about *this* to distract you from looking too closely at *that*. He asked you something cutting so you wouldn't see the blade sticking out of his own surprisingly tender heart.

This pause, his quiet statement about his father followed by silence... That was different.

He'd already said more about his father today than she'd expected him to ever say. But maybe there was a part of him that wasn't quite done.

Tentatively, she turned her head to look at him. He still had his hands tucked into the pockets of his jeans. The rest of his posture was open, though, his gaze entirely too intent on a row of budding roses.

"May I make an observation?" she asked.

One corner of his mouth curled up. "Can I stop you?"

She ignored the deflection and braced herself. "Earlier, when we were talking about your dad..."

Sure enough, he stiffened, but he didn't shut down. That was about as much invitation as she figured she would get.

"It struck me..." She chose her words carefully. "You had plenty to say about how losing him affected everybody else in your family. But not how it affected you."

He shrugged and kicked at a rock on the path. "You

mean besides it throwing my whole life out the window and bringing an abrupt end to the best relationship I ever had?"

And there was the oversharing. She was tempted to take the bait, too, her heart doing a little flip-flop inside her chest at him referring to what they'd had together as the best relationship he'd ever had. But it couldn't have been a more obvious misdirect if he'd tried.

"Yeah," she said calmly.

"What do you want me to say?" Shielding his eyes, he directed his gaze off into the distance. He let a beat pass before confessing, "I miss him." He dropped his hand. "All the time."

She pressed her lips together to keep from pushing.

They proceeded a few more steps forward before the dam inside him seemed to break. "He was my best friend, you know?" He shook his head. "It's so cheesy to say, but he was my hero. The guy who was always in my corner. Losing him meant..." He pulled in a deep breath before letting it go. "It meant I was on my own. But tied down. I was suddenly responsible for everything."

"Were you, though?"

He'd been eighteen.

"It felt like it. Still does."

Her hand had kept inching toward him as he spoke, but she'd forced herself to keep it by her side. They may have shared a few reassuring touches over lunch, but there wasn't any table keeping them separated, no server to interrupt them or food to distract them. They were utterly alone out here on a winding path beneath the big, blue sky, the scent of flowers in the air, and the weight of more than a decade's worth of pain pushing down on him.

She put her hand on his arm, and he shuddered, but instead of pulling away, he closed his own palm over hers. The heat of his touch took her breath away.

But she could stay focused. She had to, if she ever wanted him to talk about anything that mattered with her again. The fact that they'd gone thirteen years without talking about anything, weighty or otherwise, wasn't the point. She didn't want to lose this, and the consequences of that desire were another thing she'd have to face at some point, but not now.

His breathing was uneven for a second, but then he squeezed her hand. He let go, and she did, too, but some invisible barrier that had been separating them all afternoon had disappeared. Their arms brushed as they continued walking, out the back of the Parisian-style garden, through a trellised archway, and into a Japanese one.

He exhaled slowly, and when he spoke again, he was more composed. "It also doesn't help that he was the guy who kept my mom emotionally stable."

"You changing the subject again?"

"No." He glanced down at her, his eyes shadowed but his expression open. "But it's impossible to talk about losing him without also talking about losing parts of her."

"Oh, Han..."

"That was too heavy." He shook his head. "I just mean—the parts of her that could be spontaneous. The ones that knew how to have fun."

"She had any of those?" If she had, she'd kept them a secret from May.

Han blew out a laugh. "Of course she did. At home, when it was just us, anyway. But after my father died..." His throat bobbed as he swallowed. "She's better now. She has friends—your mom, for one."

"Well, that's nothing new."

"I'm grateful for it," he replied. "I think she's even happy, more or less. But she's brittle in a way she never was before. She leans on me. A lot."

"That must be really hard," she said carefully.

"Sometimes." He sucked in a breath and blew it out slowly. "I don't think I realized how much I let her expectations—the expectations I placed on myself... How much I let them dictate everything up until now."

"What changed?"

"We stopped having to pay Zoe's tuition bill, for one. And..." He glanced over at her before looking away. "I don't know. This old friend popped back into town." His throat bobbed. "I don't think I realized I needed an extra day or night off here and there until I had someone I wanted to spend them with."

It was all May could do not to swoon.

The backs of his knuckles brushed hers, and on impulse she took a chance, curling her fingers around his again. He threaded their hands together, holding on, and any remainders of the line between them fluttered off into oblivion.

Who on earth would have imagined this? Her strolling through a beautiful garden in this part of the world she'd sworn she hated and would never come back to? Arm in arm, and talking pasts and pains with the guy who broke her heart so many years ago?

The pain they'd caused each other was somehow easy to ignore right now, though. All she could think about were the good things. The way he'd always made her feel protected and special and safe, back when she struggled so hard to stand on her own.

They walked in silence for a few steps, the air between

them humming. She wished they could just keep walking like this together forever.

Finally, he said, "But it's all okay now, I guess. To answer your question. I mean, it's terrible, him not being here. There are so many things I want to talk to him about, or ask him. But it's okay, too. You know?"

No. Not even in the slightest.

Her own dad had been a temperamental jerk, who she mostly remembered as loud. When her mother had left him, it had been nothing short of a relief. May had only been a kid at the time, and she'd had her mother and her sisters. Before long, they'd moved down here, and her mom had fallen for Ned, and then May had had a pretty great stepdad, too. She'd never felt unsupported, or like she was missing much of anything.

But somehow, still, she was pretty sure she understood exactly what Han meant.

Terrible things could happen. People could be mean to you. You could get bullied, and you could feel like your own hometown was filled with painful ghosts. You could have the only guy you'd ever loved tell you that you should see other people.

You could have him force you to choose between everything you'd ever wanted and a friendship with him.

But you grew from it. You got stronger, and you forged your path.

And eventually, somehow, you could end up okay after all.

You could end up wandering through a beautiful garden, hand in hand with him, sharing feelings and secrets as if nothing had happened. Comfortable in a way that you'd forgotten you could be.

"Yeah," she said, leaning in. She let her head rest

against his shoulder for just a moment, until his warm amber and spice scent had fully permeated her senses. "Yeah, I guess I do."

———

Han's stomach was still feeling a little off by the time they made their way to the place May had selected for their dinner that night. Whether that was from the seven lunches—he hadn't eaten all of them, of course; just more than he should have, okay?—or how close he and his ex-girlfriend had gotten over the course of the afternoon, he couldn't say.

Sympathetic touches had turned into holding hands, and holding hands had turned into him putting his arm around her as they went under an archway with a particularly aggressive bunch of flowering vines draped across it. Somehow, he'd kept his head on straight enough to keep it from turning into more than that, but it'd been a close thing.

Temptation had eaten away at him the whole rest of the time they toured the garden, and it hadn't let up after that. They'd hit a couple of antique stores, a pottery studio, and a goat farm. He hadn't figured that any of those would be particularly romantic, but color him wrong.

How many times had he caught himself staring at her full, red lips? The memories of stolen moments back when they were teens had practically assaulted him, only the tension he felt as an adult, standing next to this gorgeous woman, was even worse. She smelled better than the bright spring blooms all around them. Her skin was soft, and his body was screaming at him to lean in. To find out how her mouth might taste after all this time.

His body was a fool, of course. He and May had spent half their first lunch recounting why things could never work between them. Nothing had changed.

So why was his heart threatening to lose its mind right along with the rest of him?

He still hadn't figured it out as she read off the directions to the place she'd chosen for their dinner. She'd promised they'd just be hitting the one restaurant, which was probably a good thing, both for his digestion and his heart.

"Okay, should be coming up on the left," she said.

A brightly lit red sign loomed, and he narrowed his eyes, tightening his grip on the wheel. "You've got to be kidding me."

"What?" The fake innocence in her voice had him shaking his head.

"You know what." He pulled into the parking lot of the Happy China Magic Noodle House with a scowl. As he put the car into park, he shot a glare at her. "And you think Buddha's Delight is an offensive name for a vegetarian dish?"

"I think it's trite and culturally insensitive."

He waved a hand at the sign on the restaurant. "And this isn't?"

"Of course it is. All the names for Chinese takeout places are."

Okay, she had a point there.

"Some stoop lower than others," he pointed out.

"And the Jade Garden is highbrow?"

He threw up his hands. "The Jade Garden is a name my uncle Arthur picked off a list, literally before we were born."

He'd never quite understand why this stuff bothered

her so much, but she always had been more introspective about the whole being-one-of-the-only-Asian-kids-in-town thing.

She wrinkled her nose. "It's still kind of gross."

Han pretended that didn't sting. Okay, yeah, the "Jade" part was sort of tacky, but it was like he'd said with the Buddha's Delight. Customers liked to know what they were getting, and tacky Asian references came with the territory of running a Chinese takeout place. As things went, the Jade Garden name was pretty enough. His family could have done worse.

Case in point, Happy China Magic Noodle House.

He jerked a thumb in its direction. "You seriously expect me to eat here?"

She patted his arm. "Remember? Competitive research."

Competitive research was a lot more fun when they were researching restaurants that weren't *direct* competition with his. Especially one that—ridiculous name or not—was actually pretty good.

Grumbling, he let himself out of the car. They headed inside together.

Unlike the Jade Garden, the Happy China Magic Noodle House had fully embraced the takeout dive aesthetic. A half dozen tables invited patrons to sit and eat, but the focus was clearly on the counter, where big pictures of popular dishes hung from a lit sign.

"Han!" Dave Chen, chef and owner of the place, greeted them from behind the register. He was only a few years older than Han, if maybe a little heavier and grayer around the temples. He rose and extended an arm.

Han slapped his palm against Dave's, then the backs of their hands and the knuckles of their fists. "Hey, man."

"What's up? Finally decided you wanted some real Chinese food instead of that crap they serve in Blue Cedar Falls?"

"Ha-ha." Han rolled his eyes. "Just in the neighborhood. This is my friend May."

Dave's smile shifted into more of a smirk. "Well, hello, May."

May stepped forward and held out her own hand, which Dave shook conventionally. If his touch lingered, Han shrugged it off the same way he did the dig at his family's restaurant. Dave was married with three kids. His flirting wasn't serious. And it wouldn't matter if it were, because it was none of Han's business.

Or at least that's what he was still trying so flipping hard to tell himself.

"You mind if we sit?" May asked.

"Not at all. Just lemme know what you want, and I'll bring it right out."

May surveyed the menu, which was about as standard as they came. After a moment's consideration, she picked the same things she'd chosen at the Jade Garden, but without any lip about the culturally insensitive names. Han did his usual and told Dave to just cook him up whatever he liked best, and Dave rubbed his hands together. Han sighed and mentally prepared himself for a box of the spiciest faux-Szechuan nonsense the guy knew how to make.

They grabbed a couple of drinks from the cooler and had a seat. May took a moment to pull out her notebook and jot down a few things.

Han craned his neck to see. "Are you writing down that this place is a dingy hole in the wall, run by a letch?"

"I'm mostly writing down the things I didn't have a chance to make note of from the goat farm," she informed him, unfazed.

"Well, let me know when you get to this place."

"I'm sure you'll have lots of helpful additions."

While she finished taking her notes, he got out his phone to check in and make sure things were going okay back home. His mom immediately replied, assuring him in her usual clipped texting style that she was fine. Returning to his inbox, he saw an article Devin had sent him about the newest roster changes for the Panthers, which led him down a rabbit hole.

As lost as he got in the wonderful world of electronic distraction, though, he never forgot that he was sitting across from May Wu. Their feet and calves brushed from time to time under the table. Some things had changed, but in other ways, it was just like it might have been a decade ago, her scribbling away on her homework while he perused the sports page of the paper.

Dave showed up in due course, their first couple of dishes on a tray. He set out paper plates and packets of chopsticks and stayed to shoot the breeze for a minute before he got the hint and wandered away.

Bracing himself, Han tried his chicken. He let out a fierce breath. Yup—spicy enough to peel paint.

"You feeling okay there?" May asked.

"Fine," Han choked. He shot a glance at Dave, who was watching in amusement. When Han flipped him off, Dave just grinned bigger, and Han shook his head.

He took a big bite of rice. He actually liked some heat—in moderation. This was way too much, of course, but he'd survive it.

May was delicately picking her way through her tofu

and vegetables, alternating them with noodles from her chow fun.

Han tipped his head toward them. "So what's the verdict?"

"They're good."

"But not as good as the Jade Garden."

"They're more traditional than the Jade Garden."

"Pfft." Han took another bite of Scoville-unit-defying chicken. "Tradition is overrated. Especially in American bastardizations."

"You're not wrong." Her mouth pulled to the side.

Oh, boy. Here they went again.

"But...?"

"But"—She gestured at their surroundings with her chopsticks—"This place knows what it is, and it isn't afraid to *be* it. Loud and proud."

"'It' being clichéd and mediocre."

"I can hear you," Dave called.

"Shh," May and Han both told him as one.

"Clichéd, yes," she admitted. "Mediocre?" She shrugged.

"Wait." He put his chopsticks down. "Are you trying to say this place is *better* than the Jade Garden?"

No way.

But she just lifted her shoulders higher. "It is what it is."

"Forgettable."

"Can still hear you," Dave chimed in.

They both ignored him this time.

"The problem with the Jade Garden," May said, her voice rising slightly, like she'd been holding this in for an entire day now, "is that it doesn't know *what* it is."

"It's a Chinese restaurant, offering both classic standards and bold, inventive new takes."

"Great website copy," she told him, and yeah, okay,

that was exactly what it was. June had helped him rewrite it herself last fall. "But my biggest issue is that it's trying to have it both ways. Your mom is still nailing the standards, granted."

"You brought me here to compliment my mother's cooking?"

She barreled on. "And the 'bold, inventive new takes' are good, too, but they don't fit."

"Well, maybe someday they won't have to," he blurted out.

"Wait." She held up a hand. "What?"

He glanced over at the counter, but Dave had apparently gotten tired of eavesdropping and had finally disappeared into the kitchen, leaving Han more free to speak.

So why was there a lump in his throat?

He'd been working on his secret menu for years now. Maybe too hard, fine. But he'd been getting his ducks in a row.

He'd never told anyone, concretely, anyway, what he was up to, though. Devin was the closest to having a clue, but Han had been vague with him, too.

But as May gazed at him with expectation in her eyes, he found the words rising to his lips. "I want to open my own place."

She blinked. "Seriously?"

"Is that such a surprise?"

"No. I mean, yes—I mean..." She shook her head. "I thought running the Jade Garden was, like, your life or something."

"It is." He swallowed, his mouth suddenly dry. "But it's not my dream. It never has been."

"Right." Her gaze softened.

They'd talked about this before, was the thing. Years

and years and years ago. The only person who knew more about his ambitions than May did was his father, God rest his soul.

"Zoe's out of college now, so our finances are looking better. Plus all the stuff your sister did with Pumpkin Festival, and your mom's famous cat brought a bunch more tourists back to town. This might finally be my moment."

"That's amazing, Han." Her smile lifted, and a warmth filled his chest.

So of course he had to go and undercut himself. "I mean, clearly I need to work on my menu. Since it's so overthought." He raised a brow.

"I didn't mean—"

"I know what you meant," he assured her. "And it was good feedback. I'm going to take it to heart."

"Does your mom know your plans are back on the table?"

"Of course not." His mom would be the absolute last person to know. This kind of venture would scare her out of her bitter gourd. "She doesn't even know about Taste."

As soon as he'd said it, he realized he'd opened a whole other, wrigglier can of worms.

"Taste?" May asked.

Well, he was in it now. "It's this foodie festival your sister is spearheading." He corrected himself. "Nominally, it's being thrown by the Main Street Business Association—"

"Yeah, yeah, but June is running it. Nothing new there."

"Right." He grinned, but his nerves were buzzing. Devin knew about this because he'd been there when the acceptance letter had arrived, but he was the only one.

"So it's hyped to be all super local, innovative, blah, blah, blah. I didn't think there was much chance they would take me, but I let them try some new stuff off this super-ultra-secret menu I've been working on."

"Seriously?" Her question dripped skepticism, but her smile radiated excitement.

"Shh, it's going to be great." That, or it was going to be a disaster, because he was an impostor, trying to be a culinary genius despite having half a semester of culinary training and a lifetime of takeout counter experience. "Anyway, it'll be my first foray as a solo operation."

She giggled, and her whole face lit up. "*Han Solo* operation, you mean?"

"Shut *up*." For heaven's sake, it was bad enough when Devin trotted that out. "It's a way to test the waters, you know? See if maybe it's worth trying to strike out on my own without rocking the boat too much."

A test to see if he could chase his own dreams without turning his back on the commitments he had made.

May smiled. "Well, I think it sounds like a great first step."

"You do?"

"Of course." She picked up her chopsticks again and started poking at her food. "When is it?"

"Um." He winced. "Two weeks?"

"Two weeks?" Her eyes went wide. "Are you ready for that?"

"Not even close, but I'm going to figure it out."

"You know..." A thoughtful expression crossed her face.

He furrowed his brow. "What?"

"Nothing. Just...That's not that long from now. I wonder if I should stay for it."

"Could you?"

When she'd first arrived, she'd been adamant she'd be here for as brief a stay as she could manage. Half a dozen times today, she'd had to pause what they were doing to answer questions from her editor, who'd seemed invested in this being a quick trip, too. Extending her visit for another couple of weeks seemed to run counter to all those plans.

"I don't know…" She picked up a chunk of red pepper and stared at it like it might hold the answers. "My mom and Ned would be delighted, and maybe it would appease June. She's always guilt-tripping me about not being around to help her more. And I do have a ton of unspent vacation days. Plus, it'd be nice to be able to relax. Spend some more time catching up with…old friends."

She popped the piece of pepper in her mouth and shifted her gaze to him. He suddenly felt warm under his collar. His stupid heart was in danger of getting ideas again. When her foot touched his beneath the table, she didn't pull it away. He didn't move back, either, and wow. This was playing with fire.

Since the moment she'd walked in the door of the Junebug, he'd known he was as attracted to her as ever. They'd nearly crossed a line that very first night, and all day today, they'd been dancing right along the edge of it.

But the overtness of her ankle pressed against his took things to another level. The line, wherever it had been, suddenly receded into his rearview mirror. An unmistakable invitation smoldered in her gaze, and his self-preservation instinct flew off into the distance, probably chasing that line they'd lost.

This was an invitation to do something unbelievably stupid. Something that was going to hurt.

Eventually.

In this moment, though, with her looking at him as if she were just any woman and he was just any guy...

Nothing hurt. For the first time in a decade, everything in his vision seemed to snap into place, and it all felt *right*.

Holding her gaze, he swallowed hard. And then carefully, deliberately, he placed his hand on her knee. "That'd be...great."

"Great," she agreed. She covered his hand with her own and stroked her thumb across his knuckles, sending warmth rushing all up his arm. "I'll talk to my editor tomorrow. Make sure it's okay."

"Great," he repeated.

"Great."

But he was pretty freaking sure, their verbal tics aside, that this was anything but "great."

He was pretty sure it was terrible.

And he Could. Not. Wait.

# CHAPTER TEN

The entire way home, May thanked the car for having seat belts. Otherwise, she wasn't sure how she would have stayed in one place. Heat raced just beneath her skin, twining with a kind of eager, nervous anticipation she wasn't sure she'd ever felt in her life. Over and over, she fought to calm herself down, doing the breathing exercises she'd learned at that yoga class Ruby had convinced her to try the last time she was getting too caught up in the stress of her job.

But every time she so much as glanced at Han, sitting there in the driver's seat, his profile illuminated by the dashboard lights, or caught a whiff of his cologne, she had to start the process all over again.

Of course, he seemed cool as a cucumber. But there was an energy coming off him, too. As if he could sense her restlessness—how could he not?—he reached over and put his hand on her knee, and fireworks went off inside her.

This was ridiculous.

Yes, they'd been flirting all afternoon, and yes, when she'd suggested she might try to stick around for an extra week or two so as to include Taste of Blue Cedar Falls in her article, she'd maybe grazed her foot against his. Okay, fine, she'd practically batted her lashes at him, and he'd answered her with fire in his eyes.

The intensity of her attraction to him blew her away. After all this time, shouldn't it have faded? But if anything, it had only grown. He'd changed. She couldn't have imagined anything—except his stubborn streak—getting better, but somehow everything about him had. His voice, his physique, his hair. His quiet confidence and his charm. His soulful way of looking at her as if she were the missing piece he'd always been searching for.

Wow, this was going to be a mess.

Finally, Han passed the sign welcoming them to Blue Cedar Falls. He turned onto Main Street, and her scatter-shot mental breakdown where she cycled wildly between arousal, anticipation, worry, dread, and back again picked up in speed until she was just a raging jumble of emotions. He rubbed his thumb against her leg, the weight of his hand growing firmer. How was it possible for that touch to both ground her and wind her up tighter?

As they reached the heart of Main Street, Han slowed the car. It was just after dusk, and the restaurants and cafés along the strip were lit with flickering lights and the hum of people enjoying good food and good conversation. The Junebug appeared to be hopping, as she was starting to understand was more or less the norm.

Han put on his blinker and pulled over in front of the Sweetbriar Inn. Fairy lights and softly colored lanterns cast the front porch in a warm glow. Inside the lobby, she was pretty sure she could make out her sister June in silhouette, working away as usual.

The sheer normalcy of it all rocked her conviction. A

flicker of doubt lit inside her. Getting any closer to Han was probably a mistake. She should just go inside and forget this ever happened. Staying for some festival and getting more invested in whatever was brewing between the two of them was foolishness. She should wrap up her research and get out of town as quickly as possible. That would be the prudent choice.

But then she turned to Han, and irresistible, unfathomable heat burned in his eyes. "May..."

He leaned forward, reaching out to graze his fingertips against her cheek. All her doubts melted into a big, imprudent pile. Their gazes caught. He flicked his toward her mouth, and she stopped breathing altogether. Almost imperceptibly, she nodded.

Closing the gap between them, he brushed his lips ever so gently against the corner of her mouth. Something in her chest gave way. When he started to pull back, she threaded a hand through his hair and hauled him in again.

This kiss was warmer, tentative and familiar, new and exciting and yet exactly, everything she remembered and had longed for. She parted her lips for him, and his tongue slipped past them, and she *couldn't breathe*.

"Han..."

She was ready to lose herself in him completely, every nerve in her body screaming at her to deepen the kiss, but he pulled away for real this time. Pure, black desire filled his eyes, and seriously, prudence was stupid; who had even suggested it in the first place?

Before she could second-guess herself any further, she breathed, "Your place?"

Without a moment's hesitation, he dropped back into his seat. In one smooth movement, he put the car into drive.

The three minutes it took to arrive at his family home on Cherry Blossom Way passed in a flash. As he pulled the key from the ignition, she glanced up at the darkened windows. Her doubts were gone, caution thrown thoroughly to the wind, but her nerves about some logistics remained.

"Your mom—" she started.

"Won't be closing up the restaurant for another hour yet. And even then—she'll come back, watch *Jeopardy!* on the DVR in her room, and go to bed."

She laughed nervously, but deep down she was a mix of giddiness and soft, wanting anticipation. "You sure know her schedule, huh?"

"Hasn't changed since Dad died." He opened the door on his side. "But don't worry. A few other things definitely have."

She let herself out and followed him to the front door.

The instant she stepped inside, it was like she was transported back in time. The darkened living room was set up a little bit differently, and there was less kid junk lying around. The couch and the TV were both new. But she recognized the family photos and the ink paintings hanging on the wall. The whole place still had the same light scent of incense and laundry and fresh lemon Pledge. She filled her lungs with it, scarcely able to believe she'd forgotten, its familiarity was so strong.

He excused himself to go check on the dog, leaving her to look around. He didn't dally long. When he returned, he grinned. "Wanna come check out my room?"

She swatted at him fondly, fluttering all the while. "Is it still covered in Legos?"

"Ha-ha." He led the way toward the stairs, shooting over his shoulder, "I'll have you know they're in the closet now."

"You are such a dork."

"Guilty as charged." Instead of stepping off at the second-floor landing, though, he kept climbing to the third floor.

"Moving up in the world?" she asked.

"Just a little."

At the top of the stairs was a door that he opened with an actual key. Now that was an improvement she could get behind. He flipped on the lights and welcomed her inside.

As she entered, she whistled long and low.

Back in the day, his sisters had shared the big, converted attic. Their parents had never gone for decorating it too wildly, but there had been posters of boy bands and pink curtains and a big flowery area rug separating their twin beds and desks and shelves.

All of that was gone now.

In its place stood a studio apartment that rivaled her own. Small by Blue Cedar Falls standards, but as Manhattan real estate went, it was a steal. The only thing it lacked was a kitchen, honestly.

"You got your mom to put in a bathroom up here?" she asked, peering through the door in the corner.

Han's eye roll was clear in his voice. "*I* put in a bathroom up here."

During their game of Never Have I Ever that first night she came back to town, he'd explained that he still lived here both to save money and to look after his mom. He'd been clear they'd reached an arrangement where it was *their* house—not his mom's—that he happened to live in. Considering how controlling his mother could be, May hadn't entirely believed him, but she regretted being so skeptical now.

"Nice," she commented, turning her attention from the new bathroom to the rest of the space. As she took a few more steps inside, its *Han*-ness radiated through her.

His taste was everywhere. The LEGO stuff might be in the closet, but his books filled the shelves. The walls had been painted a pale gray, and black curtains framed the windows. A flat-screen TV hung on the other side of the room, with a couple of video game consoles tucked into a cabinet underneath it. Two recliners faced the television, separating the space into two halves.

But they weren't unoccupied.

"Oh no." She strode across the room to the side table positioned between the chairs. She picked up the stolen garden gnome that had been creepily standing on top of it. Watching them.

"You told me to take care of him," Han protested.

"Yeah, but, like, in a drawer or something."

Han grabbed the gnome and set it down on one of the recliners. He shoved a throw pillow over top of it.

"I still know it's there," she pouted.

"Try not to think about it too much."

She turned. As she did, she lost track of what she'd been saying as she was confronted with the big, dark wood-framed bed that dominated the other half of the room.

As she took it in, a shiver hummed under her skin. Everything went quiet. They weren't here to talk about gnomes.

Han's scent surrounded her as he came to stand behind her, his breath near her ear. His hand grazed her side.

"May…"

She turned her head to find him right there, mere inches separating them. His voice still held a question, though.

She flicked her gaze up to meet his. His dark eyes

smoldered. The first, tentative kiss they'd shared in the car flashed back to her—followed immediately by the need she'd felt to take it further.

And there was nothing stopping either of them now.

She leaned up onto her toes, and he shifted down.

Their second kiss in a decade was gasoline poured over the spark that had been growing between them these past few days. She wanted to take her time and relearn every single thing about him, but she couldn't focus. All the heat and longing she'd been trying to push aside since they'd reunited came to a boil too fast.

She opened her mouth to him, and he pressed forward with his tongue. Again, there was the impossible instinct to cry at the taste of him, still the same after all these years.

Other things were different, though. He was more confident than he'd been when they were teenagers, taking command of the kiss with a gentle dominance that made her go weak in the knees. He made no effort to overpower her—they'd always been good at the push-pull, the call and answer and the ask and accept. She breathed softly into his kiss and threaded the fingers of one hand through his thick, soft hair.

He pulled her into his arms. Her other hand went to his chest, and she quaked inside. Now, that was different, and in the best of possible ways. Han had always been physically attractive, but back in high school he'd been one of those guys who could eat and eat and never put on a pound. He'd filled out since then, his chest firm with lean muscle.

He made a low sound of approval in the back of his throat as she walked her fingertips down his torso. When she reached the hem of his shirt, she slipped her hand beneath it to touch the hot skin of his waist. More fire-works went off inside her when he drifted his palms lower on her body, too. Breathless, she pulled away.

She glanced at his face to find his eyes dark with desire, his mouth kiss-bitten and wet. She sank her teeth into her own lip and flicked her gaze over her shoulder.

Taking her meaning, he swallowed. Then he pulled her into his arms again.

Together, they crossed the room toward his bed, kiss-ing and touching the entire time. She undid the buttons on his shirt, and he shrugged it off and away. The dips and ridges of muscle on his chest were a feast, and she would have dined on it all day, but then his hands were on her waist, pushing at her top, too.

They left a trail of clothes across his floor. By the time they made it to the bed, she was in nothing but her bra and underwear. She ran her hand over the hard bulge of him through his black boxer briefs, and he sucked in a breath that felt like half pleasure and half pain.

Breaking their kiss, he pushed the covers down. She sat on the edge of his mattress and stared up at him. Hot need prickled along every inch of her exposed skin, and she was ready to reach up and pull him down to join her.

Something in his expression made her pause, though. He gently brushed a lock of hair back from her face.

"I never thought we'd do this again," he said, voice gruff.

Her heart panged. Curling a hand around his wrist, she nodded. "Me, neither."

Another breath passed. It felt like they were both acknowledging the miracle of this moment.

But also the tragedy.

They were opening up a whole new well of pain

between them now, heading back down this path. Unlike the last time around, they were both doing it with eyes wide open.

That had to count for something, right?

Pushing aside her fears about the heartache she was setting herself up for, she leaned back onto the bed. His throat bobbed.

He set one knee between her splayed legs, and a resolve that seemed to match her own finally filled his eyes.

When he climbed over top of her, relief sang through her body. She wrapped her arms and legs around him. Their lips crashed together once more, and she moaned. His weight settled over top of her, his hips rocking into the cradle of her thighs and sending crackles of pleasure racing up her spine.

He slipped a hand beneath her to unhook her bra. She pulled her arms free of the offending fabric, and his hot palms cupped her. He groaned, dragging his mouth down the column of her neck before sucking the tip of her breast between his lips. Arching into his touch, she held him there until the sensitivity got to be too much. Then she pulled him back up and kissed him hot and hard. He tugged her underwear down, and she shoved at his. When she took him in her hand, he let out a sound that went straight to the aching space between her thighs, and she couldn't wait a second more.

"Condom," she panted.

He fumbled in a side table. Once he was sheathed, he fit himself to her opening.

She gazed up into his eyes, one hand on his cheek, the other gripping his hip.

He pressed inside.

Lightning shot through her as he slowly filled her. It was like a part of herself she'd forgotten about shifted back into place. Like a piece of her heart that she'd locked away for all this time was finally let free.

Worried she'd betray the depth of emotion welling up within her, she tugged him down. They kissed and kissed as he moved inside her. It was exactly as good as she remembered, but also better somehow.

As they hurtled toward their peaks, a sudden certainty fell over her.

It didn't matter that this was a terrible idea. It didn't even matter that she was almost certain to regret it later.

Right now, being here with him—having him with her like this again...

It was worth it.

———

It was after midnight when Han flopped onto his back on the bed, struggling to catch his breath.

"*Wow.*" May stared up at the ceiling. Sweat glistened on her skin, and he grinned in smug satisfaction. Shooting a glance at him out of the corner of her eye, she fluttered a hand at him before dropping it back limply to her side. "Don't be so impressed with yourself."

He only smiled wider, pride welling up inside him as he leaned over to kiss her lax mouth. "I don't know. I think I'm just the right amount of impressed, considering..."

He ran a hand down her naked side. On his way back up, he brushed her where she was still sensitive, and her entire body twitched.

Letting out a shuddering breath, she nudged his hand away. "Okay, fine, fine," she allowed. Closing her legs, she turned her head toward him. "Somebody's picked up a few new tricks over the past ten years."

"I'm definitely not the only one." He cocked a brow.

Running her fingers through his hair, she admitted, with maybe about the same amount of ruefulness that he felt, "Fair."

Sex with May had always been incredible. From their fumbling first time in the back of his car to the slow, bittersweet love they'd made the night before May left for New York, physical connection had never been a problem for them.

If it had been up to him, he would have been perfectly happy never having sex with anybody else.

Their time apart and his handful of other partners had certainly been...educational, though. May had never hidden what she wanted from him, back in the day. But she'd been shy about correcting him when he wasn't doing something right, and there'd been a lot of trial and error involved.

He knew his way around a woman's body better now, as could be seen from the way her chest was still heaving, her voice ragged from so many muffled pants and groans.

But increased technical proficiency on his part was only a small part of the story.

She'd clearly learned a few things, too. Gone was the innocent, shy girl who was too embarrassed to draw him a map when he tried to touch her. There was a new confidence to her, and it turned him on like he couldn't explain. They were in sync in a way he hadn't known that he could be with a woman.

There was also the small matter of thirteen years' worth of pent-up longing and regret.

He leaned in to kiss her again, but before they could get too carried away, his stomach growled.

"Are you seriously hungry?" she asked, pushing at his chest.

*"Starving."*

She laughed, relaxed and free. "You had seven lunches."

"That was hours ago." He stole one more quick taste of her lips before pulling away. He rolled off the bed and stretched his arms over his head. "Plus there was just the one dinner, and I couldn't concentrate on it with you impugning the quality of my food." He grabbed a fresh pair of boxer briefs out of his drawer and pulled them on. Then he scowled. "Plus there was the matter of Dave making eyes at you the entire time."

Snorting, she flicked her gaze upward. "'Making eyes'?"

"I saw what I saw." He dressed in a T-shirt and sleep pants before tipping his head toward the door. "C'mon, I'll make some real food for you."

She sat up, bottom lip between her teeth. "I don't know. Your mom..."

"Sleeps like the dead. Remember all the times we snuck around back in the day? And that was when my room was right next door to hers."

"The stairs creak."

He grabbed a pair of boxers and another T-shirt from his drawer and tossed them her way. "Not if you know where to step. Just follow me."

Still, she hesitated, worrying the bundle of clothes he'd lobbed in her direction. "I don't know..."

He let out a rough breath and moved to sit beside her on his bed again. Taking her hands in his, he leaned in to look her in the eye. "May. I'm a thirty-year-old man. I'm allowed to have girls in my room."

She laughed, shaking her head, but it wasn't a happy laugh this time.

He opened his mouth but shut it before any words could come out. This next argument was a risky one, but it wasn't like they were hiding anything from each other now. Lowering his voice, he told her, "I've had girls in my room before."

"Scandalous." She put her hand over her mouth in feigned shock.

"It's fine. My mom and I even talked about it."

"You talked about *this*?" She gestured at her still-naked body in his bed, and he should really stop being so gobsmacked about the whole thing. Good luck on that happening anytime soon, though.

"Not this, specifically." He rolled his eyes. "Not about much of anything specifically. You know how conversations in this family go."

They never talked about anything of consequence. His mother occasionally made incisive comments that made him feel incompetent at life, but otherwise she left him alone. His living at home made sense, financially and logistically. They both saved a ton of money and they didn't have to sell the house. She was getting up there, too. After Uncle Arthur had his heart attack the previous fall, she got all worked up about her own health and what she would do if she needed someone to take care of her. She'd even made some noises about moving into an old folks' home, but he wasn't hearing any of that. He'd promised he would always be there for her.

Good, old, dependable Han. She knew she could rely on him.

She also knew, in her own blunt and yet evasive way, that he was a guy who needed privacy. When he'd moved upstairs after Zoe left for school, his mom had told him specifically that she couldn't hear anything upstairs, and any lady callers were welcome to leave out the back at any time, if they didn't want to run into her.

He hadn't taken her up on that assurance many times, but he was pretty sure she meant it.

Even if he weren't, he was in the mood to throw caution to the wind. Taking May downstairs and feeding her felt more important than any judgy looks he might be setting himself up to receive in the morning.

"C'mon." He separated out the shirt from the pile. Finding the neck opening, he put it over her head.

"I can't believe you're trying to get clothes *on* me." She moved to help him, a softer, happier laugh escaping her.

"I know, it's a tragedy."

For some reason, though, it wasn't. Sure, he liked her naked, but he liked her dressed and beside him, talking to him with a familiarity and a frankness and a fresh perspective he didn't get from anyone else.

And this was a dangerous train of thought to be boarding, considering the tracks were bound to slam him right into a mountain wall. But he couldn't help himself. He wanted to make love to her in every way humanly possible. But he also wanted to go out to restaurants with her and cook with her. He wanted long nights, and he wanted scallion pancakes and bacon in the morning. He wanted to see her bleary-eyed and undercaffeinated. He wanted strolls through the farmers' market and hikes with his dog and movie nights on the couch, curled up together.

For a blinding fraction of a second, he imagined that maybe he could. That maybe she might decide to move back here—or heck, maybe he could follow her to New York. It was all part of an impossible fantasy. He had responsibilities here, and Blue Cedar Falls was his home.

But it was nice to imagine, even if only for a moment.

Shaking her head at him, she consented to finish getting dressed. She looked ridiculous in his clothes. They were so big they were ready to fall off her. She was also so sexy he had to fight his own inner caveman to remember he was the one trying to get her dressed and down to the kitchen with him.

He gave in and hauled her into his arms for one last fiery kiss before releasing her.

They tiptoed their way down the stairs together. She stuck close to him, following his feet with such exaggerated precision she was practically on top of him. He couldn't help but be distracted by the warmth of her, her soft scent, and the brushes of her body against his, and it tripped him up.

The last step right before the first landing creaked.

And downstairs, Ling-Ling lost her flipping mind.

"Crap," he cursed as the dog started barking her head off. Forgetting stealth, he dashed downstairs.

"What—"

His dog basically launched herself at him the second he reached the first floor. She was still worked up, but as he rubbed a hand over her head, she at least stopped barking so loud.

He shook his head as she licked at his face with the kind of vigor that meant he'd been gone too long and she'd assumed he was dead. He'd checked on her when he and May had gotten home, and she'd seemed fine hanging out in the yard. His mom must have let her in when she got back from closing up the restaurant.

He might not get any lip from his mother about having a girl over, but leaving her to deal with his dog might do the trick.

"Okay, okay, I get it," he mumbled into her fur.

"Well, hello there." May crouched down behind him and held out a hand.

Ling-Ling looked comically between the two of them. Han nodded at her, and she inched closer to May. After a delicate sniff of her palm, she leaned in closer and licked her face. Laughing softly, May took the cue to pet her flank, and Han's heart gave a little squeeze.

He prided himself on having a dog who was an excellent judge of character. The fact that all it took was a nod from him and a quick sniff and she was cool with May spoke volumes.

"May, meet Ling-Ling," he said, fighting the hitch in his voice. "The other love of my life."

May glanced up at him, and yeah, he was wearing his heart on his sleeve a little too blatantly with that one, but May was kind enough not to call him on it.

The three of them made their way to the kitchen. Han tossed Ling a couple of biscuits and gave her an extra scritch behind the ear. He palmed another biscuit to May before turning to the fridge.

His stomach was still grumbling, and he couldn't lie—his ego was, too. Dave's decent but unremarkable Chinese takeout had only egged him on.

His gaze caught on what was left of the pineapple he'd cored and chopped for his breakfast that morning. Inspiration struck him—he was pretty sure he had some pork in here somewhere. Spring onions and wonton wrappers and half the sauces crammed into the little shelf set into the door joined the rest of the ingredients on the counter.

"You really are still hungry, huh?" May asked.

"Shh, I'm working."

He'd really meant to come down here and fire up some nachos or something simple, but when an idea snagged him, he couldn't help but run with it.

May appeared at his elbow as he started getting out a couple of pans. "Want any help?"

"You can chop those onions if you want."

She took her place as his sous chef without complaint, asking questions about the specifics of what he was looking for. Before he knew it, they'd settled into an easy rhythm, cooking together like an old married couple, and wow, yeah, there went the train, careening along the tracks toward the wall of rocks again, but whatever.

As they cooked, they chatted, mostly about the food, but about other things as well. He was just getting the oil going in a frying pan when she paused.

When she spoke again, her tone was more serious. "So, earlier. You were talking about having other girls up in your room."

He tensed, which was stupid. There was no reason for him to be embarrassed about that. "Yeah?"

"Just. Curious." She glanced up at him through her lashes, and was that jealousy he heard? "You said you hadn't had any long-term relationships, but was there anybody you came close with?" Her mouth pulled to the side. "Anybody special?"

His stomach took a little dip. He turned his attention to the stove. He dropped a few of his improvised dumplings into the hot oil, letting the sizzle cover for his silence.

But he could only hide behind it for so long.

"No," he confessed. It wasn't a lie, either. "Far from it, honestly."

"What's that mean?"

Crap. How much to tell?

He shrugged, gaze focused on the pan. "After Dad died and you left for good, I wasn't in a great place. I made some crappy decisions."

"Like, STD levels of bad decisions?"

He laughed and flipped one of the dumplings to reveal a perfectly browned bottom. He turned the other ones over, too. "Fortunately, no." He glanced at her over his shoulder. "But that was mostly good luck on my part."

"Oh."

Guilt pressed against the inside of his chest. He was tempted to confess the worst decision he'd made of them all—the one she'd find the least forgivable. But it was ancient history. Even if she was staying an extra couple of weeks, was there any point telling her things that would hurt her?

Deflecting, he cleared his throat. "How about you? Anybody special?" He raised a brow. "Or any STDs?"

"No to the latter."

Oh. "But the former?"

He scooped the first batch of dumplings out and added the second. As they cooked, he stirred the sauce he'd been simmering on the other burner.

"No one I was with for more than a year."

Yeah, she'd said as much that first night at the bar. "So, what? Eleven months, twenty-nine days?"

"Pretty close," she confessed.

At this rate, he was going to burn the dumplings, but he was glad to have the food to concentrate on. The idea of her with someone else for that amount of time made him want to punch the wall.

"What happened?" He managed to keep his voice more or less even.

"Nothing, really. We just wanted different things."

"You really have to start screening your boyfriends earlier in the dating process," he told her tightly.

"I'll have to work on a questionnaire."

"What did he want?"

"Me to quit my career and stay home with our kids."

He flipped a dumpling with a little too much force. "Wow. And y'all made it an entire eleven months?"

"You aren't the only one who made mistakes, I guess." Real sadness colored her tone.

"I'm sorry," he said. Not sorry she'd ended up single and in his bed tonight, but sorry for how things had ended up with her and her dud of an ex. Deep down, even if he wished she'd stayed here with him, he still mostly just wanted her to be happy.

"It's fine. Josh and me—we were never a house on fire anyway. Not like..."

He snuck a glance at her, and their gazes caught. He wasn't sure if it made it better or worse that they both knew what she meant. The two of them had been the house on fire. For both of them, it seemed, no one else could ever hold a candle.

"Anyway," she continued. "It wasn't a huge loss. Just a disappointment."

She went quiet after that. He held his tongue, trying to give her space in case she wanted to share anything more. It killed him to hear her talk about other guys, but anything she wanted to tell him, he wanted to know.

She seemed to be done, though, and the food was, too.

Turning off the burners, he relocated the rest of the dumplings to the plate where he'd been keeping the cooked ones tented with foil. He poured the sauce into a shallow bowl he was pretty sure his mom had picked up at a secondhand store.

It was a far sight from the nice bone china he served his secret menu items on at the restaurant, but for some reason, that felt right.

"Here," he said, bringing both over to the island where she stood. "This'll make you feel better."

"Pretty confident, there." Her tone brightened, and she bumped her shoulder against his arm, leaning into him for a second. "Considering I'm pretty sure you just made this one up on the fly."

"Darn right I did."

Improvising in the kitchen used to be one of his biggest joys. While her comments about his food being too fussy still stung, they had reminded him about how bogged down he'd gotten, refining and tweaking things he'd already done instead of playing and creating anything new.

There was something about having her here with him that inspired him, though. This was the most fun he'd had cooking in he didn't even know how long.

He picked up a dumpling and dipped it in the sauce. "Bottoms up."

She grabbed one of her own, copying him. They touched them together as if they were pint glasses, then each took a bite.

Her eyes went wide, and he was pretty sure his did the same.

"Wow." She blinked, dipped again, and ate a bit off the other corner. "I mean, like—*wow*."

He looked at his own creation with similar fascination. He didn't want to toot his own horn, but yeah. That was awesome. Sweet from the pineapple but savory with the pork and soy and garlic. The green onions added a fresh pop, and the dipping sauce just brought it all together.

He frowned.

"Hold on." He grabbed a garlic chili paste he'd been tempted to add earlier and scooped a dab into another little bowl. He poured in a splash of the sauce and mixed them together with a pair of chopsticks. When he was done, he dunked his dumpling in the spicier iteration, and..."Oh, yeah." He pointed at the new sauce. "That's what it needed."

"It didn't need *anything*," May argued, though she tried it all the same. Her eyes flew open even wider. "Crap, you were right. How is that even better now?"

Pride swelled in his chest. "Told you I knew what I was doing."

"Like I could ever doubt that." She finished the rest of her dumpling before reaching for the collar of his shirt. She dragged him in for a kiss that tasted like her and sex and overly complicated midnight snacks.

Put a fork in him. He was done. It was all of his favorite things combined into one. He hadn't even known that that was possible.

For a second, his eyes stung.

Oblivious to the moment he was having, May released him. He fought to contain his excessive reaction—the unexpected, overwhelming rush of feeling that washed over him. He probably did a crap job of it. He never had been great at keeping his emotions to himself.

Fortunately, she was distracted, plucking another dumpling off the plate. She licked her fingers as she ate, and for the first time in his life, he got the whole saving-time-in-a-bottle thing. If he could snap a picture of this and keep it in his heart forever, he would.

"What?" she asked.

He jerked his gaze from her mouth to her eyes. "Huh?"

One brow rising, she reached for a paper towel from the roll in the center of the island. "Do I have something on my face? You're looking at me like..."

He was looking at her like a lovesick fool. Crap.

"Uh, yeah." He gestured at the corner of his own mouth, grateful she didn't see through him, but also somehow amazed by it. Did she seriously have no idea?

She dabbed at her lip before looking to him for approval.

"You got it," he assured her.

"Thanks."

She kept eating, and he kept berating himself in his head. Getting invested again was pure recklessness. She might have extended her trip, but she'd still only be here another couple of weeks. While it might be fun to fantasize about throwing his entire life out the window and finding a way for them to be together long term, they'd been down this road before. It just wasn't possible.

When she left, it was going to annihilate him.

He should wrap this up. He should tell her she should go. He should put up some walls around his heart now, while he still had a chance of keeping himself intact.

But like a stupid masochist, instead, he snagged another dumpling.

Might as well enjoy it now. He'd never make anything like this again and not think of her.

Swallowing down her last bite, May licked her lips. "Seriously, though, Han. These are so good. Forget the secret menu. This is what you should be serving at that food festival you've been prepping for."

He finally pulled himself out of his stupor. Tearing off a paper towel of his own to wipe the sauce from his hands, he shook his head. "Dude, it's in like two weeks."

"So? Clearly you know how to come up with stuff on the fly."

"I can't create a whole new menu in that amount of time." He started to laugh, but then he stopped himself.

The idea of starting from scratch with a fresh concept, two weeks out from D-Day, was ridiculous. He'd already put in his orders to suppliers.

But the stuff coming in was versatile. Lots of staples. He could work with all of it. Hit the market—even drive out to Asheville or Charlotte if he had to get any specialty items to supplement.

An entire new set of courses started to form themselves in his mind. He couldn't serve exclusively dumplings, of course, but it could be sort of elevated street food. Fusion, small plates, with classic Chinese takeout fundamentals underpinning everything.

Foodies would eat it up, and he would, too.

"Crap." His unfocused gaze zeroed back in on her expectant face. "I have to create a new menu."

"Well." Grinning, she reached for another dumpling. "What are you waiting for? Let's get cracking."

# CHAPTER ELEVEN

❊ ❊ ❊ ❊ ❊ ❊ ❊ ❊ ❊ ❊ ❊ ❊ ❊

Hold on," Ruby said, squinting at May over the video chat. "You're waiting around in Backwater Falls for what now?"

Sighing, May explained again, "It's this food festival thing that Han is doing."

"Han your ex who you cried yourself to sleep over for years?"

There was no point beating around the bush with this. "Yes, that Han."

Ruby narrowed her eyes in suspicion. "Who you hadn't spoken to in more than a decade."

"Yes."

"And who you're now just chummily hanging out with like nothing happened between you two."

Crap. May's cheeks warmed. She bit her lip and glanced around, but she was alone in the apartment at the moment. She still lowered her voice. "I mean, I'm not sure I'd say we're acting like *nothing* happened between us."

Ruby gasped. "May Wu, you walking, talking cliché. Did you go home and bang your ex?"

"Like a screen door in hurricane." She couldn't stop the giggle from rising to her throat.

Maybe she should be embarrassed. She was as much of a cliché as Ruby was making her out to be, and yes, she was fully aware of just how terrible an idea last night had been.

It had also been incredible. Sleeping with Han had been fun and athletic and emotional on a level she wasn't prepared to examine right now. While she would probably regret falling back into bed with him at some point, for now she was giddy, and she felt no reason to try to hide it.

Ruby broke out into a huge smile. "Well, all right then. Good for you." She paused. "It was good for you, right?"

"So good," May confessed.

"Then I'm happy for you."

"Really?" May raised her brows. "You're not going to give me some sort of talking to about how I'm setting myself up for disaster?"

"Oh, please. I know you, and you've already given yourself that talk about a dozen times today."

"True..."

"Honestly, I'm much less worried about you two banging than I am about the part where you said he's the reason you're staying an extra couple of weeks."

And okay, there it was—the concern May knew she'd get when she brought her best friend up to speed.

"I'm not staying for *him*." She fought her own instinct to cringe. That sounded weak even to her own ears. "I'm staying for Taste of Blue Cedar Falls, which is an event where he happens to be showcasing his new menu."

"Uh-huh."

"For the article." May mimed giving her friend a swat upside the head. "This area is undergoing a revival, and I think it would be good to see one of the new events that's helping turn things around." Another thought occurred to her. "Besides. My sister is one of the people organizing it. I'm staying here to support her, too."

At the mere mention of June, May heard movement in the office that connected the Wu family's apartment to the Sweetbriar Inn. Internally, she rolled her eyes. She'd known her sister was working behind the desk this morning, and she'd been prepared for eavesdropping, but could June be a little bit more subtle?

"All right, all right." Ruby held up her free hand. "If that's what you want to tell yourself."

"It's true."

"Well, you and Han"—Ruby's brow arched pointedly when May started to interrupt—"and your article and your sister have a great time." She panned the camera so May could see her tortoise, Todd, chilling in his little terrarium on one end of Ruby's kitchen table. "We'll be fine for an extra couple of weeks."

May waved at Todd through the screen, which was stupid—he was a tortoise, not a toddler or a golden retriever. He was pretty indifferent to her even when she was there in person.

Returning her attention to Ruby, she smiled. "Thank you. I really appreciate it."

"It's no bother."

They spent a few more minutes catching up, and then it was time for Ruby to get on a work call, so they said their goodbyes.

Setting her phone down, May ticked off the box next to "call Ruby" on her to-do list for the day. That had been the most pleasant task she had to handle, regarding prolonging her trip. Messaging her editor Zahra to tell her she wanted to stay an extra couple of weeks had been a lot less fun. For better or worse, Zahra was at a conference this week herself, so all she'd gotten in reply had been an out-of-office message. May had proposed taking one of the two weeks as long overdue PTO and using the other week to round out her research for the article. She was still expecting an exasperated call at some point in the next few days.

Getting away from the office had been good for May's mental health, but it wasn't as if she had forgotten the restructuring going on at *Passage* since the title had been acquired. The pressure to perform and keep up with tight deadlines remained. For now, all she could do was trust she'd gotten as many of her ducks in a row as possible.

Which meant she had a minute to deal with the fact that her sister was still noisily puttering around in the office next door.

With a shake of her head, she closed her notebook and laptop and tucked her phone into her back pocket. As a pretext—and because it wasn't as if she couldn't use another cup of coffee—she grabbed her mug.

She didn't stomp across the room, but she did make sure her footsteps were loud enough so as not to startle June. When she opened the door to the office, she found her sister rifling through a filing cabinet.

June looked up. "Oh, hey."

"Hey."

May continued past her sister and through the open door to the lobby to refill her cup. The two of them had already exchanged some basic pleasantries earlier in the morning when May had wandered out for her first cup of caffeinated goodness and also answered the phone and booked a couple of rooms for a wedding party coming in toward the end of the summer.

June hadn't noticed—or at least hadn't remarked on—May sneaking in during the wee hours, though May had few illusions she'd gotten away with it. June or her mom or who knew, maybe even Ned, would undoubtedly bring it up out of nowhere at some point in the day. Her family loved conversational time bombs. May was a grown woman, though, and she had nothing to be ashamed about. She could sleep with her ex like the worst kind of cliché, and anybody else's opinion about it didn't matter.

Besides, she was pretty sure June had something even more complicated she wanted to discuss.

Surprise, surprise, June followed her out as far as the front desk. "So I couldn't help but overhear you when you were talking on the phone."

Uh-huh. "Oh?"

"You're planning on extending your trip?"

May splashed even more fancy creamer into her mug. "Yeah, an extra couple of weeks. Han said there was a food festival coming up that might be a good addition to the article."

"Taste of Blue Cedar Falls?"

"That's the one." As if she could have been talking about some *other* food festival happening in two weeks.

"You're helping run that, aren't you?"

"Yeah. We've been doing lots of stuff, trying to build on the momentum from Pumpkin Festival last fall. Not to mention Mom's whole...cat...thing."

"Right." May snickered. The whole cat thing being the reason Zahra had sent her here in the first place. "Who would have guessed that Sunny would save the day."

"Yeah..." June's voice trailed off, but May could practically hear the thoughts she was choosing not to say.

Oh boy, here they went. Pouring her coffee, her back still to her sister, May took the bait. "What?"

"It's just funny. The whole time I had it in my head that you were going to come save us. But then our mom's cat did."

Ouch.

"Look—" May started.

June continued, "Apparently I shouldn't have spent so much time trying to nail you down. Seems like all I had to do was get Han to ask you."

May took a deep breath and counted to ten. "You know that's not true."

"Really?"

Finally turning, May leaned against the table and crossed her arms over her chest. She found June standing behind the front desk in more or less the same position. The two of them always had been a pair.

"Last fall was a completely different situation. Do you know how many air miles I logged in October alone?"

"I'm sure you'll enlighten me."

May had looked it up. She might not have anticipated this precise conversation, but she'd been under no illusions she could escape some sort of a confrontation about her last-minute cancellation the previous fall. "Twenty thousand."

June sighed in exasperation. "Okay, fine, you were traveling a lot."

"I took on double my normal number of assignments. Those first few months after the acquisition were a nightmare." May's pulse skyrocketed just thinking about how anxious she'd felt. "They laid off half the staff. Rumor had it, they were thinking about letting literally everybody go and switching to a one-hundred-percent freelancer model."

In a particularly paranoid bout of insomnia, May had looked into her own options for transitioning to freelance writing, and they hadn't been great. While she had a lot of connections and probably could have done all right for herself, there was no way she could have afforded to keep her home base in New York.

"I get it," June said.

But that was just the thing—and since they were laying it all out there... "Do you, though?"

June flinched.

The words were out there on the air, though, now. May couldn't pull them back. She wasn't even sure she wanted to. "I have my dream job in New York. I know it's not what anybody here wanted for me."

Her mom, her sister, Han. All of them wanted her here. But she had a life. A dream she'd worked so hard to pursue. It'd be amazing if she could just snap her fingers and have her family and her job and her travel schedule all magically align, but that wasn't reality.

She braced herself, ready for June to jump down her throat. Instead, her sister exhaled, long and slow. "I want you to be happy. I know you love your job and your life."

The frankness in her tone took May by surprise. "You do?"

"Of course I do." She gestured around expansively. For the first time, May noticed an issue of *Passage* magazine on every coffee table. The framed copy of her first article to be reprinted in the *Times*, hung up behind the desk. "We're so proud of you. It's just..." When she spoke again, a new vulnerability cracked her voice. "Last fall. This whole past year. I needed you."

Guilt echoed in the hollow space behind May's ribs. For once, it wasn't colored by resentment. June wasn't trying to guilt-trip her—at least not at this particular moment.

If June could be vulnerable, then crap. Maybe May could, too.

Swallowing any defensiveness that might have wanted to seep out, she nodded. "I know. I'm sorry."

A chuckle escaped June's lips. "How much did it kill you to say that?"

"So much."

June finally dropped her arms to her side, and the tension in the air dissipated.

"I'm sorry, too," June said. "I didn't need to jump down your throat. You staying for Taste is great." She rolled her eyes. "Even if it was Han who convinced you."

"I thought you two were friends."

"We are." June waved a hand back and forth. "Or anyway, he and Clay are tight, and me and Clay are..." A light flush appeared on her cheeks.

May grinned and did her best impression of an old-school adult film soundtrack as she shimmied her hips. "Bow-chicka-bow-wow."

June raised a brow, as if to say *You really want to go down that road?*, and no, May really, really didn't.

Grabbing her mug, May came back over to the desk. No reason to keep talking at each other across the entire width of the lobby. She plopped into the spare chair behind the desk, and June likewise sat down at the one by the computer.

"So that's really going well, huh?"

June's flush deepened. "Yeah, it is. Though it's hard."

"I bet it is." May pursed her lips in insinuation, and June kicked her ankle.

"What are you, thirteen?"

Hardly, but she was just so relieved to have some of the air cleared between them that apparently she was regressing.

"I just mean," June continued, "that it's difficult, me managing the inn and Clay running the Junebug. Not to mention all the other stuff I'm doing with the Main Street Business Association, trying to keep things hopping around here. Neither of us has a lot of time."

"Yeah. That sounds tough." May chewed her lip. "My work schedule always messed my dating life up, too." Taking a risk, she nudged her sister's foot. "Not just my family life."

June laughed, accepting the joke for once.

May regarded her sister for a second. On the surface, she was the same old June, clearly working herself to the bone and trying to run not just the inn but the entire town. But there was a new softness to her, too.

A thought occurred to May. She'd mentioned it to Ruby this morning, as well as to Han the previous night, but she'd never actually brought it up to June. "You know, since I'm going to be sticking around a little longer, maybe I could pitch in more here at the inn. Give you some time to spend with Clay. Or doing whatever else it is you haven't had time for since Mom got sick."

June's brows scrunched together. "Are you sure? You mentioned how much work you have to do."

There would never, ever be an end to the work. That was just a factor of life.

"I'm taking some of this as vacation. I still have an article to write and research to do. But I can make some room to help my sister out, too."

A soft, hopeful smile spread across June's face. "I mean, that would be amazing. If you're sure..."

The light in June's eyes made May's chest squeeze.

Like that, her decision was made. "I'm sure. You deserve some downtime."

"And you do, too. Don't spend all your vacation helping me."

"Don't worry." May laughed. "I won't."

Oh, no. She definitely had some other plans for her looser schedule these next couple of weeks.

Plans that involved a certain ex-boyfriend of hers and cementing her position as the biggest cliché ever.

June reached over and squeezed May's knee before standing up. "Great. And maybe we can find some time to relax together, too. Wu girl mani-pedi date?"

May put her hand to her chest in mock disbelief. "You're going to leave Ned here with the computer system?"

After that time he accidentally erased an entire month from the calendar, May half thought he'd never be allowed to touch the mouse again.

June rolled her eyes. "For brief stretches."

"Wow, you really have changed."

Pausing, June looked back at her. "Yeah, I guess I have." She gently arched one brow. "But I don't think I'm the only one."

———

"Look," Clay said the next day, coming to a halt in front of the big prep table Han had cleared off in the kitchen of the Jade Garden. "When you said to come on over for lunch, I didn't realize you meant 'come on over for lunch and bring literally everybody you know.'"

Okay, fine, by "cleared off," Han actually meant "cleared of prep stuff and replaced with fourteen different kinds of experimental dishes."

Han shook his head, spooning a new chili-mango relish he'd been working on into a sauce dish. "Friends and family only."

Zoe, who'd arrived a few minutes earlier and was already munching her way through the first few samples, shook her head. "You've known Han long enough that you should have been prepared."

"No one could have been prepared for this," their mother said dryly.

Han stifled an annoyed sigh. She was only being snippy because she was handling the takeout orders that had come in while he'd been cooking up all of... well, this.

"Pull up a stool," Han told Clay.

"Where's Devin?" Clay asked.

"Ugh." Zoe shot her gaze skyward. "Working. So boring."

"Which leaves me with you two to tell me which of these are any good." Han set down a plate, a pair of chopsticks and a fork in front of his friend. "Now shut up and get eating." For good measure, he gave Clay a pen and some paper, too. "And take notes."

"He's in a *mood* today," his mom said, sotto voce.

The thing was, she wasn't wrong. But while she seemed to be trying to imply he was in some sort of crummy, testy mood, her assessment couldn't be much further from the truth.

For years now, he hadn't realized how he'd been slogging through life. He'd been doing okay, more or less, but there hadn't been any passion. He'd worked and cooked and nursed some vague ambitions about taking his career as a chef to another level, but deep down, he'd been stuck. Unwilling to change anything else in his life or take any real risks.

Not anymore.

May's reserved commentary on his secret menu, followed by her enthusiastic approval of the new dish he'd whipped up for their midnight snack, had launched him out of his rut with a vengeance. As soon as she'd proposed re-envisioning his menu for Taste of Blue Cedar Falls, the gears had started turning.

Ever since, he'd been cooking like a fiend, inspired for the first time in he didn't even know how long.

The best and worst part of it was that he knew exactly who to thank.

May waltzing back into his life had shaken him up in every possible way. She'd given him a new lease on life in the kitchen, not to mention a reason to want to spend some time outside of it. He liked hanging out with his buddies, of course, but when was the last time he'd had so much fun?

She'd also ended an embarrassingly long dry spell in the bedroom. Their first night together had been explosive. Her touch had felt both nostalgic and new. She'd snuck over again last night, and they'd proved that their chemistry was the exact opposite of a one-night thing. He didn't think he'd ever get tired of kissing her.

Who was he kidding? He didn't think he'd ever get tired of doing *anything* with her. Kissing, making love, talking. After they'd put their clothes back on yesterday, they'd just sat around, discussing everything and nothing. Considering he'd gone more than a decade without a single word from her, he'd soaked in the tiniest, most mundane details of her life.

No matter what happened next—or how badly it hurt when she inevitably left—he refused to spend another thirteen years not speaking. He didn't know how on earth they'd manage it, but there had to be some way to stay in each other's lives after this.

He'd find a way. Somehow.

"Holy crap," Clay sputtered, his mouth full.

Zoe swatted at him with a napkin. "Ew."

Rolling his eyes, Clay swallowed. He pointed at the hoisin shrimp taco he'd just tried. "That's amazing."

"Yeah?"

"It's even better with more of the bok choy," Zoe added.

Game as ever, Clay gave that a shot, piling the shredded greens Han had turned into a sort of a ginger slaw on top of his taco. He took a bite and groaned. "I want to marry this taco."

Zoe giggled. "Don't let June hear you say that."

"Whatever, I can have multiple wives—especially if I plan on just eating this one."

"Y'all have got the weirdest relationship," Zoe said.

Han held his hands up. "I'm not judging."

"Because he has no room to," their mother said in a sing-song voice from over near the register.

Clay and Zoe both swung their gazes comically to him.

"Oh no," Zoe said.

Han shook his head. "Shut up."

"So you and May . . . ," Clay started.

"I said shut up." He shot a meaningful glance in the direction of his mother.

"They're not telling me anything I don't already know," she called out.

Han wanted to thunk his head on the counter. "It's not a big deal."

"What's not a big deal?" another voice asked from the other side of the restaurant's front counter.

Han looked up to find Caitlin there. She passed a credit

card to his mom and peered into the giant box of takeout she was apparently there to pick up.

"Nothing," Han said, at the same time that Clay said, "Han hooked up with May, we think."

"We know," his mom corrected.

"Seriously?" Han asked.

"Seriously?" Caitlin echoed. She'd moved here a few years ago, so, like Clay, she didn't know the whole dramatic saga of it all, but Bobbi had presumably filled her in.

"I hate everybody," Han muttered, staring upward.

"Are those tacos?" Caitlin asked.

Clay nodded, reaching for another one. "The best tacos I've had in my life."

Han just about swatted his hand away. "I appreciate the praise, but save your appetite, man."

"You want one?" Zoe offered.

"I mean..." Caitlin looked to their mom, who shrugged indulgently. Taking that as the tacit permission it was, Caitlin came back to the kitchen, where her eyes went wide. "Wow." She looked to Han. "Slow day?"

"No," his mom said.

Han ignored her. "Just trying out some new stuff."

"Instead of working," his mom chimed in again.

Normally, he'd let that roll off his back, but today, it got to him. "R & D is just as important as what happens on the production line."

He'd always done his test kitchen stuff on his own time before, but he wasn't blowing smoke or making excuses. Working on the menu was real work.

Caitlin accepted the taco Zoe had arranged for her and took a bite, then made the same noise of approval Clay had. "Dang, why wasn't this on the menu for our wedding?"

"Because we don't do catering," Han's mom reminded them.

"We do for friends of the family," Han shot back. She might try to argue with him about that later, but again, he stuck to his guns. He half expected the ceiling to open up and lightning to strike him where he stood, but when it didn't, his confidence only grew. To Caitlin, he said, "It can be if you want it to be."

She finished wolfing down the rest of her taco. "I do." Her mouth pulled to the side as she chewed. "Though Bobbi should really try it all, too. She's the mastermind."

"Tell her to come on over," Clay suggested. "Goodness knows there's plenty."

Caitlin shook her head. "Bakery doesn't close until three." She jerked a thumb behind her at the box of take-out she'd left on the counter. "Besides, I have a half dozen folk waiting on their lunch. I don't get back there soon and they're going to get cranky."

"I can whip up another tasting menu. Restaurant's closed on Tuesday. We could do it after you both get off work?"

"Sounds good," Clay said, grabbing an egg roll. "I'll get Zoe to cover the bar."

Zoe gave him a dirty look. "Hey!"

"I don't remember inviting either of you," Han said.

"Please," Zoe said dismissively. "You're going to cook up just as much food as you did today. No reason not to turn it into a party."

Caitlin had been tapping away at her phone while they'd been inviting themselves over. She looked up. "Bobbi's cool with a tasting party on Tuesday."

"I said it's not a party."

"Devin's in, too," Zoe said, setting her own phone aside. "I'll get Kenny to cover the bar."

"I'll get more fire insurance," Clay grumbled.

"See?" Zoe grinned. "We're all set."

"I'm sure June'll want to come, too. She can have May handle the inn." Clay raised his brows meaningfully. "Unless you think May will want to come to your party, too?"

Han opened his mouth to protest that he hadn't even agreed to have a party, but then he stopped and looked around. Caitlin and Bobbi, Devin and Zoe, Clay and June. These were some of his favorite people in the world, all planning to come to his house and test-drive his new food.

Yeah, he was definitely having a party.

That said, he was used to being a third wheel—sometimes even a fifth. But a seventh?

When May was here and helping him create this new menu?

Yeah, no.

With a little grumble of mock resignation, he shook his head at them all. "See if June can get Elizabeth to cover."

Clay broke out into a grin. Zoe did, too, but there was a bit of reservation behind it. Considering Han hadn't mentioned the whole sleeping with May thing to Devin yet, he mentally braced himself for another come-to-Jesus talk with his best friend after Zoe filled him in. But it would be worth it.

"Seven o'clock?" he asked.

They all agreed that worked for them.

His mom clucked and heaved out a sigh. "Guess I'd better find someplace else to be."

# CHAPTER TWELVE

* * * * * * * * * * * * * * *

The following Tuesday, May strolled down Cherry
Blossom Way to the Leung house, repeating affirmations
to herself to try to keep her nerves in check.

The past few days had been a whirlwind. Stepping back
into working at the inn had been surprisingly easy. The
computer system and some of the procedures might have
changed, but not much else had. As a teen, she'd always
been so focused on school and her desperate need to get
out of this town that she hadn't appreciated the simple
rhythms of her family's business. Changing out linens and
dusting and chatting with guests were all...surprisingly
satisfying. She was pitching in to give June and the rest
of her family a break, but she still found herself working
side by side with them as often as not. Little conversations
with her sisters and her mom and stepdad had her regretting staying away for so long all over again. Blue Cedar
Falls and the Sweetbriar Inn weren't her home anymore,
but somehow she felt more at home here than she had in
she didn't even know how long.

When she wasn't covering shifts at the family business, she was off researching more neighboring towns for

her article. At every turn, she found herself pleasantly surprised by how much the area had to offer. This wasn't a plum assignment, compared with the more luxurious destinations *Passage* had sent her to, but she liked it all the more because of that. The Carolina mountains had more character and quirk than pretty much anyplace she'd been in the past year. It was refreshing, honestly.

But not nearly as refreshing as doing half of her research trips with Han.

It probably wasn't fair to the other half, where she had to go alone. Han's presence gave all the places they visited together a glow that couldn't be matched. They joked over appetizers and held hands through museums. He gave her an insider perspective on the food they ate, and she regaled him with stories of other places she'd been. She had *fun*. Nothing seemed boring or stale or like just more of the same when he was around.

And after…

Her grip tightened on the neck of the bottle of pinot grigio she'd brought as she flashed back to what they did together after their research trips.

Tonight wasn't going to be another night of giggling, panting, moaning fun between the sheets, though.

Oh, no. Tonight was going to be their first time hanging out with all his friends.

And to make matters worse, there in the driveway, she spied Han's mother's car.

She took a deep gulp. Instinct told her to go hide in the bushes and wait until Mrs. Leung left. Han had said she'd made plans with May's mom and a couple of their other brunch crowd friends. She'd probably be leaving soon.

But May was a grown-up. This wouldn't be the first time she'd interacted with Mrs. Leung since she'd started sleeping with her son again. To be fair, all their previous interactions had been both fleeting and public; by some miracle, she had yet to run into her on the stairwell or on the way out the door any particular morning. Saying hi to her in her own house before a bunch of Han's friends joined them would be no big deal.

Having—barely—convinced herself of this, she took a deep breath, and strode to the front door.

As soon as she rang the bell, barking sounded from inside. Han pulled open the door, Ling-Ling trying to push her way past his legs. Laughing, May dropped to a crouch. She probably should have braced herself better as the dog leapt at her.

"Okay, okay, I'm happy to see you, too," she told the sweet thing.

"And I'm just chopped liver?" Han asked.

May rose to her feet and nudged Ling-Ling back inside. "I mean, most dogs really like liver."

"And you?"

May swallowed as Han turned the full power of those dark eyes on her. He pulled her in, and the warm, spicy amber scent of him threatened to overwhelm her.

"Not a huge fan of liver," she said breathlessly. Then, like a dope, she added, "But I do like you."

A flash of emotion dashed across Han's face, but before she could examine it too closely, he reeled her in closer. When their lips met, it was with the same mix of desire, longing, comfort, and this inexplicable thrill that she should probably be used to by now, but somehow she wasn't. She hummed and opened for him, letting the kiss grow deeper.

"At least close the screen door," an irritable voice called from inside.

Han winced, and May grinned. No matter how much had changed in the past ten years, at least it was nice to know that some things were exactly the same.

"Come on." Han tipped his head down the hall. "You're the first one here."

That had been by design. He'd told her she could swing by early and help him prep ingredients for the dinner party he was throwing, both as a test run for the new menu and a chance for his friends Bobbi and Caitlin to taste some options for their wedding. She'd hoped "prep ingredients" was a euphemism for "make out," but oh well.

"No bugs got in," Han assured his mom.

Mrs. Leung sat at the dining table, the newspaper spread in front of her, a pair of sparkly pink reading glasses perched on her nose. May had to hold in her giggle. The older woman usually dressed pretty severely in black, and the decorative frames made quite the pop.

Mrs. Leung made a little sound of disapproval, but at least it was directed at Han and not at May. "Bugs always get in." Her gaze shifted to May. She raised a brow, but instead of sounding judgmental, her voice came across as a bittersweet greeting. "Hello, May."

"Good evening, Mrs. Leung."

That one brow arched higher. "Nice to see you coming in the front door this time."

Ah, there was the judgment. May wanted to shrink into the floor, but she did her best to stand tall.

"Be nice," Han warned.

"I'm always nice." Moving on, apparently, Mrs. Leung tapped at something in the paper. "You see all this non-sense? Big food festival next weekend at the park?"

Han blinked. "Uh..."

Forget not being able to make out. Getting here early

was seeming like worse and worse of an idea every minute.

"Of course you've seen it." Mrs. Leung rolled her eyes. "Perfect for you. Fussy food here, fussy food there."

"I wouldn't say—" Han started.

"When June got it approved at the Main Street Business Association, I told them. Waste of money, waste of time." She glanced at May. "No offense."

"None taken," May said.

Han swallowed, his jaw flexing. He lifted his chin. "Actually, Mom…"

A nervous pang fired off inside May's chest as she glanced between the two of them. Were they really having this conversation now? May knew Han had been working up to telling his mother about his plans for Taste, and it was about time he broke the news. He'd gotten so stuck in his head about the whole thing, though, convinced she'd disapprove or kill his enthusiasm for all the new creations he'd been cooking up.

May chewed the inside of her lip. He had good reason to be worried. His mother had always been a pessimistic killjoy, and Han had always let her have an unreasonable amount of sway over his life.

But there was something different about the way he was looking at his mother now. Resolve seemed to fill his gaze, and her heart squeezed. Some things never changed, but some things did. Could the relationship between the two of them possibly be one of the things that was ready to change?

Before he could put his announcement out there, though, his mother took her reading glasses off and set them aside. In a put-upon voice, she said, "Why anyone would possibly want to enter such a thing…"

All the air seemed to get sucked out of Han's sails. He scowled. "How long have you known?"

May let out the breath she'd been holding. Watching these two talk was always an experience. So much got said without any words being spoken at all, but she could hear the silent parts loud and clear right now.

His mother shone a sly smile. "They released the list of vendors days ago. I've been wondering when you would come clean."

"Look, I didn't mean to keep it from you."

"Oh?"

Han let out a breath. "I just thought—"

"I thought we made business decisions together."

"We do," Han told her, and pride and concern mixed in May's chest. He was standing his ground, and she was glad for that, but he was also acting defensive in a way that rarely won arguments. He let out a rough breath. "But this isn't a decision about our business. This is my decision about *my* business."

And May should keep out of this. She had no right to say anything in a family matter—especially after how long she'd been gone. But Han's mother had started this discussion now, while May was standing right here. Whether that was because Han was clearly getting ready to test his recipes for the event or because she wanted a witness to keep things from getting too heated, May didn't know, but it didn't matter. She was here, and she'd been encouraging Han all week. Staying silent now felt wrong.

"I think it's a great idea," she blurted out. "And Han's new menu he's been working on is incredible."

"I never said it wasn't," Mrs. Leung said carefully. She kept her gaze on her son. "But he's been working on it at our family business, using our supplies. Our resources."

"Are we keeping track of that now?"

"We've always kept track of that. Your father handed us down a budget."

"A budget that's changed in the years since he's died, Mom." Han's color was up, his hands clenched tightly at his sides. "We changed it when Lian went off to college, and again when Zoe did, and now they're both out, and it can change again."

His mother stood. "Do you know how many restaurants fail in their first year?"

"A lot." Han's answer made it clear they'd had this discussion before. "But I'm not launching a new restaurant. Just a pop-up at a festival. Testing the waters, if you will."

"Because you want to open a new restaurant."

"I've always wanted to open a new restaurant!" He threw his hands up. "Me and Dad used to talk about it all the time."

"Your father isn't here now."

For the first time, Han seemed close to losing his cool. "Believe me. I know."

May shivered. She'd only ever heard that edge to his voice once before, and that was the day after they'd put his father in the ground.

He and his mother stared at each other wordlessly for a moment that dragged on and on. Neither of them appeared to be ready to cede an inch.

But neither of them seemed to want to turn this into an actual fight, either.

Finally, his mother shook her head. "I hope you know what you're doing."

"Believe me," he breathed quietly, "so do I."

That was the end of the discussion, apparently. As if

nothing at all had happened, Mrs. Leung headed for the entryway to gather her jacket and purse. "I'll be at Ms. Smith's, if you need me."

"Okay, Mom."

Han kept his posture straight as his mom let herself out. Only after she was gone did he let out a rough breath and scrub his hand over his face. He muttered a couple of curse words. "Sorry. You didn't need to hear any of that."

"It's fine."

"Maybe she's right. Maybe I shouldn't have..."

May shook her head furiously. With his mother gone, there was no reason not to curl herself around him. She took his face between her hands, staring up at him with a fierce burning in her heart. "Of course you should have entered Taste. This is a great opportunity for you."

"It's a risk."

"And you have to take those sometimes." If there was anything she wished she could have drilled into his head, it was that.

"I know."

Did he, though? "You deserve the chance to chase your dreams, Han. No matter what she says."

He let out a dry chuckle. Dipping his head, he brushed his lips against hers. "Seems so easy when you put it that way." He pulled away by a fraction. "It helps. Having you here. Reminding me that it's all right to want more from life."

The low fervor in his tone made her swallow hard.

"You know me," she said. "Always here to tell you to keep reaching for the stars."

Even as she said it, she regretted her phrasing, though. Because wasn't that the problem?

She wasn't always here.

She wouldn't be.

And she had a really bad feeling she was just giving him more things to regret after she was gone.

———

"Spring rolls are up!" Han called, setting the last one of this batch on the platter before drizzling them all with a new mole teriyaki sauce that shouldn't work but totally did.

Devin swooped in to grab the lot of them. Han shook his head, lifting it out of his reach and passing it to Bobbi.

"Remember?" Caitlin told Devin. "Happy couple gets first shot at everything."

It was a rule they'd had to institute an hour into this shindig, when Devin and Clay had managed to wolf down an entire tray of bacon-wrapped shrimp with spicy basil sauce before either of the people whose tasting this was actually supposed to be got so much as a bite.

"Oh, *man*." Bobbi's eyes rolled back in her head a little as she tried a spring roll.

Caitlin nodded. "I didn't know your cooking could get any better, Han, but you've outdone yourself."

"Glad you like them." Han's throat tightened, but he swallowed past the lump that was threatening to form there.

Without his permission, his gaze darted to the far side of the room, where May was chatting with Zoe and June.

These spring rolls were yet another dish he'd invented with May after a round of bedroom shenanigans. They were flipping fantastic, so it'd be boneheaded not to serve them, both at Bobbi and Caitlin's wedding and at Taste

of Blue Cedar Falls. But deep down he was pretty sure
he was screwing himself over, big time. No way he was
ever going to be able to make these, much less eat them,
without thinking of May standing barefoot in his kitchen,
her lips kiss-bitten, her hair mussed from how he'd run
his fingers through it as they'd made love.

"Is it our turn now?" Devin needled.

Bobbi grabbed a second roll, her mouth still full from
the first one, before nudging the platter his way.

"Grab me one, babe?" Zoe called.

Clay snagged one of his own as Devin walked the
whole tray over toward the girls. He ate it in three bites
and hummed his approval. Swallowing, he reached for
the dirty pots and pans on the stove and tossed them in the
sink. He'd been a real buddy this evening, helping with
cleanup and prepping ingredients. "What's next, boss?"

"Deep-fried dumplings?" Han raised a brow at Bobbi
and Caitlin.

"Good by me," Caitlin agreed.

Clay turned up the heat on the fryer. "On it."

Han got to work. This wasn't how he usually organized
his dinner parties. In the past, he'd always cooked and
cooked, shooting the breeze with his friends and maybe
showing off a bit. He was still doing that, to be fair, but
instead of presenting some big four-course meal at the
end of it, he was making one batch of stuff at a time and
just letting everybody have at it as it came off the stove.
It was a lot less stuffy of a presentation—a lot more informal. But Caitlin wasn't the only one to comment that
his performance tonight was blowing them all away.

He'd cracked something open, creatively, with this
new menu. He was having fun, playing with flavors and
textures, and the results spoke for themselves.

He had a lot of work to do, streamlining his process and getting this whole operation to the point where he could fill orders in a festival setting, but the challenge excited him.

So what if his mother didn't think he could pull this off? Her skepticism from earlier in the evening haunted him, but he did his best to shake it off. She hadn't even tried any of his new food. How could she tell him that he wasn't going to be able to hack it?

His friends had faith in him.

May did, too, and yes, she was biased. But she was also a professional, and she'd never lied to him, which was more than he could say about himself.

Unbidden, his gaze was drawn to hers again. As if she could feel his stare, she looked up. It wasn't the first time their eyes had met across the space tonight. If they weren't careful, they were going to turn into two of those repressed weirdos from those period dramas she loved so much, staring longingly at each other from opposite ends of the room.

He just couldn't seem to stop himself was the problem. He was under no illusions about the source of his sudden trove of inspiration.

May had always been the yin to his yang—dark and contemplative where he was fun-loving and light. But somehow, in their new incarnation, she'd become the yang to his yin. Her confidence and insight had jolted him out of his rut and helped him remember the joy of discovery in his work. Talking with her about his own cooking and about the places she'd visited around the world had put his ambitions in perspective. He didn't just want to open a new restaurant because he'd set it as his goal when he was sixteen. He wanted to do it because food was meant to be shared. His new takes on the classic recipes that were a part of his heritage deserved a chance to be enjoyed.

Once he'd recognized that, everything else clicked into place. His new menu. His newfound will to push back against his mom's crushing expectations; turned out, it was easier to stand up *to* someone when you were standing up *for* something you believed in.

His chest tightened.

Thanks to this woman, he'd found his purpose and his passion again.

But it raised the question: What kind of purpose-filled, passionate life could he have had if she had stayed?

What kind of life would *she* have had? She purported to hate Blue Cedar Falls so much, but she seemed relaxed and reenergized, the exhaustion she had shown up with slowly fading from her eyes. If she had tried, maybe she could have found a way to be happy here.

And then there was the flip-side of the coin.

Maybe he could have found a way to be happy in New York.

What might he have discovered if he had followed her? If he'd put aside his duty and his discomfort about leaving home—and put his relationship with her first?

Would there have really been room for him in her solitary, globe-trotting life?

He swallowed hard, forcing himself to look away.

It was all idle, self-torturing speculation, of course. She was never going to choose Blue Cedar Falls or him. And he could never abandon his family. Nothing had changed.

So why did it feel like everything had?

And what on earth was he going to do once she was gone?

# CHAPTER THIRTEEN

❖ ❖ ❖ ❖ ❖ ❖ ❖ ❖ ❖ ❖ ❖ ❖ ❖ ❖

A couple of days later, Han was having brunch with May for another "research trip" in a town an hour or so west of Blue Cedar Falls when she suddenly flashed pale.

"Crap, hide."

"What?" Han jerked his gaze up at the same time that May ducked behind her menu. He glanced around. The Tranquil Toad Café in Newborough didn't seem to hold any threats—unless you counted an unfortunate number of pictures of toads.

"Shh." She peeked out from behind the side of the menu. Then she let out an exaggerated sigh of relief and set the thing down. "Never mind—false alarm."

Chuckling, he shook his head. "What did you think you saw?"

"Nothing," she said, trying at breezy and failing miserably. "Just somebody I didn't want to run into."

"Who, Hitler?" He shot his gaze toward the door.

And then he didn't have to ask anymore. Because right there, currently being led to a table on the other side of the café, was a dead ringer for Jenny Sullivan.

"Oh." His stomach dropped.

"Looks just like her, right?"

It was uncanny, honestly. The woman had the same gym-rat build and the same pale coloring, the same shoulder-length blond hair. One good look at her face, and she was clearly someone else, but he could understand the mistake.

"Yeah."

"So what're you thinking?" May gestured at the menu, less than subtly trying to shift the conversation.

Han wasn't quite so easily redirected.

He could understand the mistake, all right. What he couldn't understand was her reaction.

"I'm thinking that was super weird." He pointed toward the door.

She scoffed and pulled out her notebook. "I'm thinking a turkey club and the salmon special."

For a moment, he wavered. It'd be easier to let it go.

But this was something they'd circled around enough times. From the bitterness in her tone when she'd insisted that Jenny must have been the one to tattle on them about breaking into the mini golf course after hours to the way she'd frozen up in front of the real Jenny at the Junebug that once.

Now she'd all but dived behind a potted plant at the first glimpse of someone who looked a little bit like her.

"What gives?" he asked.

"I don't know what you're talking about."

"Yeah, I'm gonna call BS."

He closed his menu and reached across the table to shut her notebook, too, but she wasn't having any of that. She batted his hand away and folded the notebook in half, making it so there was nothing to close.

"Look—" she started.

"What does Jenny Sullivan have over you?"

She flinched, but it wasn't just nerves. Her gaze darted to his, and the wideness to her eyes made his breath catch. He hadn't expected the mix of both hurt and anger she turned on him, and oh man. He'd really stepped in it, hadn't he?

But he'd stepped in it on purpose, and her reaction only made him want to tread deeper.

"What?" he asked in response to the betrayed expression on her face. "You clearly have a problem with her, considering your first response to seeing someone with the same haircut was to hide."

He wasn't sure what he was expecting, but it wasn't for her to laugh.

The sound was raw, and her eyes flashed again in a way that made it clear she found this anything but funny. "How can you ask me that?"

Whatever he'd stepped in was starting to feel suspiciously like quicksand. "Look, okay, I know you hated her in high school—"

"More like she made my life a living hell in high school."

And Han knew that. More than once, May had shown up red-faced and fighting back tears after some stupid stunt Jenny had pulled, but she'd never wanted to talk about the details back then. He'd tried to get her to explain, but she always shut him down. Eventually, he wrote it off as a girl thing.

Internally, he winced. That probably wasn't making him out to be a real hero in the whole scenario, huh?

"What happened?" he asked, trying to be as neutral as possible.

Her mouth opened and closed about a dozen times,

and she made a few complicated, aborted hand gestures that almost had him wondering if she was trying to communicate with him in sign language. Finally, he reached out and took her hand in his. He rubbed the center of her palm with his thumb.

"May, it was ages ago." He softened his tone. "What could be so bad that it's still bothering you so much?"

"I don't know how to explain it." She shook her head. "When you boil it down, it seems so stupid." She pitched her voice higher, as if mocking herself. "She called me mean names." She rolled her eyes. "Pathetic."

"It's not pathetic." He wasn't trying to say he understood, because he was completely freaking lost. But the anguish in her tone was genuine. "What kind of names?"

"You really want to know?" When he nodded she blew out a breath, like she was so annoyed to even have to admit it. "Like, racist awful stuff. Chink, gook. Told me to go back where I came from—which is New York, by the way, not China."

Han fought the urge to recoil. Guilt churned inside him. "Wait—"

When she laughed this time, it was even more ugly and raw. "I assumed you knew. Figured she was giving you the same crap."

Some guys on the football team had tossed insults at him here and there. He'd just written it off. Neanderthals were gonna Neanderthal. None of it meant much to him. Yeah, he was the weirdo with the different-toned skin and the funny eyes and the gross lunch—according to them; he knew full well his lunches were freaking delicious. But so what?

"I mean," he started. "I kind of knew, but I didn't realize."

"She and her mean girls made me feel like a social pariah for my entire life, Han. Like—it was so *insidious*. It wasn't until I was in college that I realized how racist it was." A new fire lit in her eyes, regretful and angry. "At the time, I thought it was just the price of being anything other than white. Like I deserved it."

His whole conception of all those times she'd been upset about some crap someone had said or done to her at school was being rocked. Yeah, he knew their race had something to do with it. But he'd had no idea it was like that.

If he had...

What would he have done? He couldn't exactly go beat up a girl. He and Devin could have tried to take on the football players, half of whom were dating girls who ran with Jenny's crowd. They would have gotten their rear ends handed to them, but they could have tried.

More bile rose in his throat. His regrets from after May had left...The things he'd done in anger that he never should have done...

They took on a whole new light, and he had to slam the door on that entire train of thought before it flattened him into the tracks.

May swabbed at her eyes, which looked suspiciously glassy. "It wasn't just that, of course. I was also a giant nerd, and I sucked at dodgeball."

"Definitely reason to be tormented," he said sarcastically.

"But seriously. They were *awful*."

"I wish..." What did he wish? He'd known some of what was going on. He just hadn't understood the depths of it.

He wished he could have helped her more, or beaten someone up, or gotten them to stop it.

He wished he could have been there for her.

She seemed to hear all the things he couldn't figure out how to say. "I know." She squeezed his palm before pulling her hand away. "But when you say 'What do you have against her?' I feel like—I mean, what do I not have against her? She and her friends..." She chewed the inside of her lip, slightly shaking her head again, and the glassiness to her eyes was back. "There wasn't a day in school when I didn't wish I could sink into the floor, or hate myself, or pray I could just disappear or something."

"May." His chest threatened to crater.

Some of the intensity to her expression faded. She swallowed. "But I'm fine now." She was fighting so hard to keep her voice even. "I'm wildly successful and living my best life far away from this hellhole town, remember?"

Right. This hellhole town that he loved almost as much as he loved...

Well.

He reached for her hand again, and she gave it to him. He considered her knuckles for a minute, tracing them with a fingertip. Gathering himself.

When he was finally ready to speak, he did so softly, trying to put as much meaning as he could into his words. "I wish everything had been better for you, back then. I wish *I* could have made it better."

She shook her head. "You were one of the only people who made it bearable at all."

"I wish Jenny hadn't been such a witch, and I wish you'd had more friends who could have seen you for the amazing person you were, who absolutely did not deserve any of that. But I also wish—" Oh, man. He was hip deep in the quicksand now. Slowly, carefully, he raised his gaze to hers. "I wish it hadn't made you hate Blue Cedar Falls so much."

The bitter darkness in his tone surprised even him, but he couldn't help it. She disparaged his hometown, a place that had been good to him and his family. The weather was great, the people were nice—at least for the most part.

He liked it here. It was home. Hearing her trashing it invoked this strange sort of sadness in him that was defensive and disappointed and misunderstood all at once.

She let out a breath and looked away. When she turned to him again, her gaze was calmer. "I don't *hate* Blue Cedar Falls."

He raised a brow in skepticism.

"I don't," she swore. "I just—I was really unhappy here, growing up."

"Clearly." There was that bitterness again. Good grief, he had to get ahold of his tone. They were talking about how a bunch of mean girls had basically tortured her. His own crummy feelings about her dumping on his hometown and leaving him as a speck in her rearview mirror didn't matter.

She gave his fingers a squeeze again. "Like I said. You were the bright spot." She sucked in a deep breath. "And being home these past couple of weeks...it's given me a lot to think about."

Yeah, him, too. Mostly, his chances of ever being happy again after she left, but that was just him being melodramatic.

"Oh?"

Begrudgingly, she admitted, "Blue Cedar Falls has more going for it than I remember." Her gaze shifted toward the distance, and a hint of a smile curled her lips. "It really is beautiful."

"Right?"

"And people I care about are here. My family." Her smile shifted into a grin, and she looked to him again, rubbing her thumb across his knuckles. "Among other people."

"Bobbi and Caitlin and Clay are pretty great."

"And Devin, when he's not giving me death-glares."

He rolled his eyes. "He barely gave you a single death-glare the other night."

"It's been a good trip," she said firmly. "I'm glad I was forced to come."

His heart constricted painfully. The silent "but" hung deafeningly in the air.

Like a masochist, he had to put it out there. "So someday maybe you'd want to stay?"

The way her face fell was the worst thing about the entire afternoon, which was saying something. It had some stiff competition. "Han..."

He waved her off. "I know, I know. Believe me, I know." Why was it suddenly so hard to breathe in here? "Don't worry. I won't ask." A vision of her from thirteen years ago flashed across his vision. Telling him no. Outraged that he would be so much of a dick as to put it out there. His voice broke. "No ultimatums this time."

He pulled his hand away to reach for his water, but before he could get far, she clasped his palm in hers again.

She waited until he met her gaze before saying, "Maybe I'll visit more." She raised a brow. "Or maybe you could bear to be parted from this place for a weekend now and then? Let me take you to some fancy restaurants in New York? Or the Maldives?" Her foot nudged his, and the flirtatious note to her voice should have made him feel better. But it didn't.

"Maybe," he allowed. He'd had the same thought himself, and it had made this bubble of lightness grow in his chest.

But where would that leave them? She'd breeze into town once or twice a year, he'd go visit her about the same, and all for what? So they could each get their hearts broken more often?

Quietly but firmly, like she could read his mind, she said, "My life is in New York, Han."

"Your life could be anywhere you wanted it to be," he told her. "But I understand. I respect your choice."

That didn't have to stop him from hating it.

Her throat bobbing, she released his hand. "Just like I respect yours."

Too bad staying here had never felt like a choice to him.

Then again—had hers ever felt like one to her?

They sat there in silence for a minute before a waitress tentatively sidled over. It was a good thing they were in Newborough. If they were home in Blue Cedar Falls that Lady Gossipmonger character from her bodice-ripper show would be in a tizzy.

The waitress glanced between the two of them, her notebook at the ready. "Y'all made any decisions?"

"Yeah." When Han pulled back this time, May let him. He took a big gulp of his water. He looked up at their waitress with a smile that he hoped wasn't too obviously pained. "Pretty sure we're decided on everything."

———

That night, after the second-most awkward ride home she'd ever taken in Han's car, May sat at one of the tables in the back of the Junebug, nursing a margarita with

Elizabeth, Graham, and their friends. They were debating some new artist who'd gotten famous for slapping literal gallons of paint onto canvases on the internet. May was more or less letting it all pass over her head.

She hadn't really wanted to come out tonight. Her argument with Han was still rattling around in her head.

How could he be so oblivious? He'd known she was miserable in high school. Surely he'd had at least some idea of what kind of bs Jenny was pulling. They'd parted on decent terms, with vague plans to meet up later in the evening after he closed the restaurant, but the low, simmering betrayal in her gut hadn't gone anywhere.

When she'd gotten back to the inn, Elizabeth had taken one look at her and told her she was coming out with them, no ifs, ands, or buts. As much of a party pooper as she'd felt, she hadn't had the energy to protest. So here she was. Out. But definitely not having fun.

Especially considering that none other than the wicked witch of the west herself, Jenny Sullivan, had wandered in ten minutes ago.

May's only consolation was that Graham had been sensible and ordered an entire pitcher of margaritas, so at least she wouldn't have to slink up to the bar for more anytime soon. The last thing she needed was to go all knock-kneed and sweaty, having to wander by the mean girl squad again.

Instead, she'd content herself trying to set Jenny's head on fire with her mind.

"You ever think about actually, literally, murdering somebody?" May asked during a lull in the conversation.

Elizabeth followed May's glare and shrugged. "I'd help you bury the body."

Graham face-palmed. "I did not hear this conversation."

"Aw." Elizabeth patted his arm fondly as he turned away. "You may be a narc, but no one can say you're not a loyal narc."

"I work in the mayor's office," he cast over his shoulder. "Trying not to become an accessory to murder is just part of the job."

"And you do great at it," she assured him. To May, she asked, "Any particular reason you're considering homicide today?"

So many. May flailed a hand in Jenny's general direction. "She ruined my life. And this town." She huffed out a breath. "Probably my...non-relationship."

She expected her sister to press her on that last part. Instead, she just put on this way-too-sympathetic, knowing look and nodded. "No jury would convict."

"I just—" May dug the heels of her hands into her eyes. When she dropped them, it took a second for her vision to refocus. What was she even saying here? Then her gaze caught on her sister.

While she and Elizabeth hadn't had so much in common back when they were kids, they'd ended up becoming closer over the years. Conversations with June were often fraught, what with June constantly implying she had heartlessly abandoned the family and all. But Elizabeth was easy to talk to. Plus they had the same taste in trash TV.

Han may not have gotten the same kind of xenophobic bullying as May had when they were in school; if June had, she'd let it roll right off her back. Which left the question...

"Did you get crap about being Chinese when you were a kid?"

Elizabeth pursed her lips, the little space between her

brows scrunching up. "I mean...a little?" She waved a hand flippantly, as if trying to encapsulate her entire self. "I wasn't exactly your model minority stereotype, though."

That was true. Elizabeth had been a rebel from the outset, not caring about anyone's opinions and never coloring inside the lines. She'd hung out with a whole crew of misfits and weirdos—and Graham—and maybe that had helped.

But it still sat wrong with May as any kind of answer. "What? And I deserved to get treated like some kind of alien species because I played the part as the awkward Asian nerd?"

She'd worn glasses, studied, been good at math, for all that she'd never really liked it very much. Heck, she'd played the violin.

Didn't mean she'd been asking for a target painted on her back. That was as messed up as her old internalized notions of "deserving" to get bullied for the crime of being Asian American in the first place.

"No! Jeez." Elizabeth pulled a face. "Just...the fact that I *wasn't* probably made it easier for me—at least on that front." Taking on a more self-deprecating tone, she said, "I already stood out because I was covered in paint and had blue hair. What was a little ethnic diversity on top of that?"

She was overgeneralizing, but she probably had a point. Setting yourself up as an iconoclast kind of took the wind out of the sails of anyone trying to label you as "different."

"So you're happy here?" May asked. Because that was really the heart of the matter.

Elizabeth chuckled and picked up her glass to take a

sip. "I mean, I did tell you about the applications I was putting in for artist residencies pretty much everywhere else in the country, right?"

He acted like he wasn't listening, but Graham put his glass down a little too hard. His jaw flexed.

Uh-oh. Looked like the platonic best friend slash roommate wasn't on board with the whole leaving town thing. At least he seemed to be taking Elizabeth's aspirations better than Han had ever taken May's.

Ignoring that entire minefield, because it was absolutely none of her business, she pressed, "But you've stayed here this long. You can't have been completely miserable."

"What can I say?" Elizabeth gestured around at their surroundings. "Blue Cedar Falls is fine. I like it here well enough, I guess, but I'm not going to evangelize about it like June always does."

May chuckled and raised a glass. June was a walking, talking promotional poster for this place. Why shouldn't she be, though? To her mind, Blue Cedar Falls had taken them in and sheltered them after their useless dad walked away. It'd been the happiest place she'd ever known.

While May had always been dying to go back to New York. Back home.

Only there was a weird pit in her stomach as she thought about that now. New York was her home, but it didn't feel as clear-cut as it did a couple of weeks ago.

Stupid Han. Stupid loving, supportive family. Stupid, beautiful, imperfect Main Street in all its glory.

Clinking her glass against May's in solidarity, Elizabeth continued, "It's comfortable, you know? Easy."

May nodded, not exactly sure she'd describe it that way, especially when her high school tormentor was still on the other side of the room, her head still regrettably flame-resistant. But she could see how, absent that kind of living, breathing reminder of the worst time of your life, a person could see this place that way.

"If that were all I wanted," Elizabeth said, "I could hang out teaching art classes at the community center and working at the inn forever." She shrugged. "I'm just not sure easy and comfortable are my main goals in life anymore, is all."

There was that bulging vein in Graham's temple again, but May stood firmly on her sister's side on this one.

"I'll drink to that, too." May lifted her glass again.

Elizabeth returned the gesture before taking a sip. "I just feel like if I'm going to make my move, then now's the time to do it, you know?"

"Hear, hear."

But there was that unexpected twisting in her gut again.

May had made a lot of moves in her life. Once upon a time, she'd had that same starry look in her eyes that her sister had now.

Good grief—Han really had gotten in her head, hadn't he?

How many of those moves had made her happy? Her career satisfied her. She loved writing and traveling, and she'd never lose her ambition to keep climbing. But her expectations for just how much joy her next move would bring her had become more and more tempered over the years. The past year or two they'd practically flatlined. All the deadlines and the extra assignments and the mergers and looming layoffs had left her feeling like she was on more of a treadmill than a mountain.

She just hadn't had a chance to realize it until now. Funny how it took slowing down for once to notice exactly how sore and exhausted you had gotten.

Pulling her out of her thoughts, Elizabeth shifted and asked, "Why all the questions, anyway? You thinking about moving back here or something?"

"No." It was out of the question, no matter the weird doubts swirling around inside her. She waved a hand dismissively. "Han just got in my head earlier."

"Is that the only thing he got in?" Elizabeth waggled her eyebrows.

"Oh my God, shut up." May tossed her napkin at her. She considered for a second, trying to think of how to put this. "He really loves it here. I always used to think he hung around because his mom was controlling him, or he had this weird, overwhelming sense of duty or something."

She was still pretty sure both of those things were true. But they didn't paint the entire picture. His whole face had changed when she'd started dragging on Blue Cedar Falls again. The acid in his voice had spoken to real hurt. Was it possible her complaints about the town had always bothered him so much? Had she just not noticed it bugged him—same as he hadn't noticed some of the crap she was facing?

"Between him and June," May said, "I just wonder what I'm missing."

Elizabeth regarded her levelly over the rim of her glass. "You want an honest answer to that?"

"Sure. Why not?"

"What you're missing, sister mine"—Elizabeth took a decent sip, swallowed, and set the glass down—"is any kind of ability to sit still for five freaking minutes."

Oh, please. "I've been sitting here listening to you hipsters talk about Instagram artists for, like, an hour."

"In life, May. You're always off to the next thing."

Elizabeth fluttered a hand toward the ceiling. "And that's not how life works here."

"Because it's a backwater town that time forgot." Why was she still beating this drum so hard? Even she didn't completely believe it anymore.

Elizabeth gently kicked her under the table. "It's really not *that* backwater these days, you realize."

"I know, I know." Her gaze darted unconsciously to the other side of the room, where Jenny and her friends were settling their tab. Finally. Maybe after they left, May could get her head on straight.

"I mean, it looked like it was heading into the toilet this time last year, with the new highway cutting us off. But then there was Pumpkin Festival and Mom's cat thing took off."

"Right."

"And June's running with it." Elizabeth looked around, as if their older sister might be behind her instead of home, taking care of the inn tonight. Assured the coast was clear, she said, "Don't tell her, but she's doing a really great job. Bringing in new people. Folks are moving here, too. Construction on the edge of town is booming, and not everybody who's coming is a stupid bigot." She tipped her head back to where Jenny and the rest were heading out.

Sure enough, May breathed a little easier the moment the door swung closed behind them.

"I can appreciate that things have changed," May said. She'd been touring around both Blue Cedar Falls and its surroundings, and the evidence of the area's evolution had been everywhere. The place had held on to its cute, homegrown, vacation-town vibe. But it had kept up with the times, too. She swirled the last bit of lime-green goodness in the bottom of her glass. "The problem is that I don't think it's changed enough." She swigged it down. "Or even if it has, I'm pretty sure I have not."

Elizabeth's foot against her ankle this time was less kicking and more reassuring. "I don't know about that." She smiled. "You'll figure it out."

"You say that with so much confidence."

"Of course I do. You're you. Eventually, you always do." Genuine emotion filled Elizabeth's voice.

Only to disappear a second later when Graham, perhaps sensing the moment had passed, turned back to them with the remains of the pitcher. "Anybody ready for a refill?"

"Always," Elizabeth said, pushing her glass toward him and shoving May's along with it.

And who was she to refuse an offer like that?

She sipped her fresh drink slowly for a while, letting herself slip back into the conversation. Her sister shot her a couple of glances, as if checking in to make sure she was cool moving on, and she definitely was. That had been more than enough heaviness for her.

Which was too bad, because not another half an hour had passed before the door swung open.

And in walked Han.

# CHAPTER FOURTEEN

* * * * * * * * * * * * * * * * * * * * * *

H an met May's gaze across the length of the bar. It was so stupid, how it was like he could sense her even across that much space. She'd mentioned she might be heading to the Junebug with her sister tonight, so it wasn't a surprise to find her there, but he hadn't exactly gone looking for her or anything. Their plans to meet up again had been tentative at best.

Deep down, he'd kind of imagined they were bs plans. The kind of thing people said when they wanted to make it clear they weren't mad, or about to walk out of your life for a decade or two. But not anything real or concrete.

He'd mostly come in to have a drink, shoot the breeze with Clay for a minute if he was free, and try to decide whether or not to text her.

She looked like she was having a good time. He fought his brain's impulse to point out that, see, she could have fun in Blue Cedar Falls if she wanted to. That kind of thinking was only going to make him crankier.

Leaving the ball in her court, he gave a little wave and a smile that he was pretty sure came across sadder than he wanted it to be. He tipped his head toward a set of empty seats by the bar. She nodded, hopefully realizing this was an open invitation. No pressure.

He put his back to her as pulled out a stool and sat down.

Clay caught his eye and moseyed over. "Tough day at the office?"

Han let out a sound that wasn't quite a laugh. "You could say that."

The look Clay shot him didn't even bother to hide his concern. He glanced meaningfully at the back corner where May was still hanging out with Elizabeth and her friends. "This about . . . ?"

"Isn't it always?" He was so tired of pretending he didn't care, or that his relationship with May was no big deal.

Wordlessly, Clay reached under the bar for a glass. He filled it from the tap and passed it to Han.

Han accepted it and took a sip. He glanced at Clay, who showed no signs of moving. He glowered, but there wasn't any heat in it. "Is this one of those things where you just shut your trap and wait for me to spill my guts?"

"I learned it from the best." He raised a brow, and okay, yeah, Han had done that to Clay a bunch last year when Clay was aggressively sabotaging himself through falling in love with June.

"I regret everything," Han said.

"Doubt it."

Han glanced at him over his beer. "I regret giving you such a hard time when June didn't like the bar and you acted like she'd killed your puppy."

"I don't. I needed someone to help me get my head out of my rear." Clay's raised his brows. "You ready for me to return the favor?"

"Not yet."

Clay nodded. "For what little it's worth." His gaze went to a spot behind Han. "If you're a numbskull like me who thinks your lady friend doesn't give a crap about you, I can tell you for sure that that's not true."

Han let out another not-quite laugh. May giving a crap about him had never been the problem.

It had been her giving enough of a crap about him to get over everything else. The hopes and dreams and apparently racist bullies that had propelled her farther and farther away from him until he tried to yank her back. And the line broke.

Clay gave him a small salute and stepped away.

Han felt May before he heard her.

"Hey."

"Hey," he replied.

He didn't look up as she took the seat beside his. His skin prickled where she wasn't quite touching him, but the tension crackling between them was about more than attraction, unfortunately.

They were both silent for a minute, Han contemplating his glass and her fiddling with her own. Finally, she sighed. "I'm sorry. About this afternoon. I never meant for things to get so heavy."

Of course she didn't.

"That's what we get for breaking the 'no emotions' rule." He couldn't quite manage to keep the wryness from his tone.

"Pretty sure we broke that one a long, long time ago."

He liked the "we" part of that sentence, but that was about all. He chanced a glance her way.

"I just—" she started again. "I don't want this festering. I don't know how to fix any of this, but the fact of the matter is that you love it here, and I might not hate it any-more, but I have a ton of bad memories." She swallowed deeply, her throat bobbing. "And I have to go back to New York in a week." She cast her gaze toward the ceiling. "Or wherever it is they end up sending me."

Like he'd said to the waitress this afternoon. It was all decided.

And like usual, it wasn't like he really had much choice.

Except in how he handled this last bit of time they had.

Turning to face her more fully, he sat up straighter. Heaven help him, she was beautiful. He'd always loved how she looked at the end of a day, when she let down her hair a bit, metaphorically. She'd done it literally, too. It fell in long sheets to just past her shoulders. Her eyes were soft and deep, her mouth full.

In so many ways, she was the same girl he had fallen in love with fifteen years ago, and in others, she was an entirely different woman. Confident and strong, insightful and worldly. A woman he'd only just barely begun to get to know, but who he couldn't stand to let go of a single second before he had to.

"I don't want it to fester, either," he told her.

She licked her lips. She shifted her weight, and her leg fell against his. Open in a way she hadn't been until now, she tossed the ball to him. "So what are we going to do?"

———

They crashed through the door to Han's bedroom fifteen minutes later. He locked it behind him, even as he was tugging her in. Their mouths met in a fiery kiss, the same way they had against the brick wall out back, behind Clay's bar. He tried to pour everything he felt into the press of his lips to hers, but how was that even possible? He'd never felt more connected and more alone, more exhilarated and so crushingly, terrifyingly sad.

"May," he tried, but she shook her head, threading her fingers through his hair and only hauling him closer. Her own desperation and conflict seared into him.

Flipping their positions, he pushed her into the door. She tipped her head back, and he attacked her jaw, kissed his way down to the pulse point of her throat. She was still here for another week, and he had no doubt they'd do this again. Neither of them could seem to get enough. Every touch felt like the last, though. He tried to savor each one, but he couldn't seem to control himself.

He scrambled at her top. Her skin was so hot against his eager palms. She helped him pull the shirt up and off, and he shoved at the cups of her bra. He sucked on each soft tip and then sank to his knees.

As he undid her pants, he gazed up into her eyes. She had her lip between her teeth. Her eyes were glazed with desire, her cheeks pink, and he wished that he could take a picture. That he could carry this image in his pocket forever, but it was like everything else with this woman. His to hold in his heart, but never to keep.

Pressing his face to the softness of her belly, he drank in the scent of her. He parted her legs.

When he put his mouth on her, she let out a moan that was familiar and heart-breaking and perfect. He coaxed every bit of pleasure he could from her, working her up until she was shuddering and tense. She called out his name as she slipped over the edge, and it was as if he'd come himself, it felt so good.

But before she could even recover, she was pushing him away. He sat back on his heels. Fire sparked in her gaze, and she dropped to straddle him, crushing her mouth to his. She tore off his clothes, and they should go to the bed—it was right there.

Neither of them could wait.

He grunted aloud the second she took him in her hand. She gave him a few rough strokes before rolling on a condom, and then she was lifting up.

She sank down onto him, and he practically lost his mind right then and there. She was so wet and soft and hot. No other woman had ever felt like this. No other woman had ever made him feel anything at all, and he thrust up into her, clutching her too tightly, only she held onto him with the same frantic need.

She gazed down at him, moving over him fast and hard, and for a minute, he swore that he could see into her soul. That maybe she wanted the same things he did, or that maybe he could take the leap and turn his back on his family and his job and his home, following her wherever the wind might take her. That maybe this could go on and on, and that it never had to end.

But that wasn't how anything ever worked for him.

Relentlessly, he climbed.

"May," he gasped, "I can't."

"I know. I know—"

She snuck a hand into the space between them, touching herself, and when her breath skipped, there was no more holding back.

They came together, flying off into a pleasure too deep to fathom.

When it was over, she collapsed onto him, and he buried his face in her hair, so in love he couldn't breathe.

He clenched his eyes shut tight.

He might have survived her leaving him the first time.

But this time was going to destroy him.

# CHAPTER FIFTEEN

$S$ee, now there's your problem." Rising with a grunt from behind May's parents' TV, Clay held up a frayed wire.

May's mom was practically standing on top of him. "Ai," she tutted. "What would we do without you?"

"I'm sitting right here, you know," Ned grumbled from his spot in the recliner. He turned another page in the paper without looking up.

"Exactly—sitting. Clay, here, though—*working*. Helping." May's mom petted Clay's biceps, and May had to look away before she made a comment she'd regret. She couldn't stop the way her brows rose, though.

June, who was sitting across from her at the kitchen table, caught her gaze and made a show of rolling her eyes. Okay, so at least her sister was in on the fact that their mom had a crush on her boyfriend. Even Sunny had wandered off, since their mom wasn't paying any attention to her.

Ned kept his gaze on the paper. "Apparently, you missed the part where I handled the entire breakfast crowd this morning."

"I refilled coffees," May chimed in.

"That you did," Ned agreed, "but I cooked about a hundred eggs, so don't mind me if I take a load off my feet for a minute."

"It's no bother, Mrs. Wu." Clay smiled, slipping by her to get to his toolbox. "Little electrical tape and this'll be good as new."

"My hero," their mother simpered again.

Even June couldn't hold back her giggle-snort at that one.

Their mom didn't miss it. She pointed an accusing finger at June. "You mess this one up, and I'm taking him."

"Still sitting right here," Ned commented.

As Clay patched the wire, they all fell into the usual hum of bickering and teasing that had been the backdrop of May's home life since she was in middle school. It was nice, being surrounded by her ridiculous family.

It was also making it completely impossible to concentrate on work.

Over the couple of weeks she'd been here, she'd set up her little makeshift office at the family's kitchen table, and for the most part it had worked out all right. June was always off doing something or other. Ned was usually busy with the breakfast crowd or general maintenance around the property. Her mother could get chatty, and had the strange need to show May every single cat meme she found on the internet—including the ones she'd made of her own cat—but for the most part that was fine. Great, even. Spending some time with her mom had been one of the perks of being home.

Today, though, none of them seemed to have anything better to do than sit around, watching Clay wrap tape around a wire. May tried and failed yet again to concentrate on a piece she was pulling together from her last trip. The fact that it was due this afternoon didn't help matters. Tight deadlines always made her anxious. She *could* take her laptop and head to her "room," but there was no place to work with the old treadmill and boxes of junk scattered around.

Finally, after futzing around with the same sentence for the eighteenth time—and with her mom now steering a victorious Clay from the patched TV wire to a dripping faucet Ned hadn't had a chance to look at yet—May had to call it.

She closed her laptop and reached for her bag. June shot her a questioning look.

"Think I'm going to head out for a bit," May told her. She glanced at her mother, who was still fluttering around Clay.

June chuckled, and it didn't feel like a guilt trip when she said, "Pretty tough, trying to get any work done with this circus."

"Exactly." Relieved that June seemed to understand, she tucked her laptop and notes in her bag and stood. "I'll be back before dinner."

"Tell Han hi for me," Clay called, his head in the cabinet under the sink.

May suppressed a groan. A couple of days had passed since they'd had their sort-of-fight—and their explosive post-sort-of-fight sex. Nothing had been resolved since then. They'd still been seeing each other, but a dark cloud had taken up residence over their heads.

In reality, it had probably always been there. The miracle was that they'd managed to spend a happy week together before they'd remembered its existence. But there was no forgetting it now.

"I'm not going to see Han. I'm going to a coffee

shop to work. Like most grown-ups do in the middle of the day."

"Have a nice time, dear," Ned told her.

"Take a coupon." Her mother waved at the book of them by the fridge.

Of course. May raised a brow at June. Coupon books full of discounts for Main Street businesses had been her sister's idea, but her mom had latched on to it with gusto. She'd bought a dozen of them, and at the rate she was going through them, she was going to turn a tidy profit.

June shrugged, and May obligingly riffled through the book for a ten-percent-off discount at Gracie's Café. She tore it out, said another quick goodbye, and headed off.

Outside, the sky was a bright blue, but some gray clouds in the distance had an ominous cast. She hurried along the sidewalk, smiling and waving in response to greetings from a few longtime Main Street denizens. She shook her head. Amazing, how normal that felt after such a short time back. In New York, she hardly even knew her neighbors, much less felt close enough to them to say hi on the street.

"Afternoon, May," Gracie said, standing behind the register at the café. She was an older Black woman with long, gray braids, and she brewed one of the best cups of coffee May had had outside of Kona.

"Afternoon." She ordered her cold brew, presented her coupon, then proceeded to toss the ten percent discount in with the tip, and Gracie smiled.

The café was pretty busy today. May recognized a few girls she'd gone to high school with at a big table in the corner, and her heart pounded, but to her relief, Jenny was nowhere in sight. The rest of her gang could be casually mean back in the day, but they never had the same edge of cruelty without their leader. Ignoring them, she parked herself at a high-top by the window and got to work.

Only to be interrupted about two paragraphs in by her phone. She was all set to be irritated, but Zahra's name flashed across the screen, and that took the wind out of her sails.

She and her editor had exchanged a few messages since May had decided to extend her trip, but they had been brief. Zahra had been traveling, and May had supposedly been on vacation, so she'd been trying—with mixed degrees of success—not to sweat the limited communication. May was back on the clock now, though, finishing up her research and banging out some articles based on previous trips. Apparently, Zahra was back in the office, too, and the much-awaited earful May had been waiting for seemed to have finally arrived.

"Hello?" May hated it when businesspeople in coffee shops shouted on the phone, so she did her best to keep her voice down.

Zahra launched right in. "Do you or do you not remember that I promised you a choice assignment the minute you were done profiling your mom's weird cat?"

May pinched the bridge of her nose and exhaled. "I do."

"Just checking, because for a minute there I had to assume you'd gotten amnesia, because how else do you explain *extending* your trip?"

"A trip you sent me on despite my protests."

"All the more reason I am mystified by your time line."

"Look, you know how it is." Dropping her hand, she gestured helplessly—not that Zahra could see it. "My sister roped me into pitching in with the family business, and I reconnected with some"—she winced—"old friends."

That wasn't technically a lie, but it still felt like one.

She was putting in a bunch of hours at the inn, and June had expressed her gratitude more than once. She'd also reconnected with old friends. Graham and the rest of Elizabeth's crew. Devin and Bobbi and Caitlin—to name a few.

But none of that explained her decision to stick around.

"Plus it just made sense," she tried. "Taste of Blue Cedar Falls is shaping up to be a really cool event."

May could almost hear Zahra's eyebrows hit her hairline. "A 'really cool event.' Wu, you've been to Burning Man, Carnival, and Holi. Are you kidding me?"

"I just think it'd be a good addition to the article." May tried to put some conviction in her voice, but even she could tell it was forced.

Yes, Taste of Blue Cedar Falls was going to be a really cool event. It would be a great inclusion in the article—a centerpiece for it, really. Her coverage of it would help tie together her entire evolving thesis about how this quiet, frozen-in-time little pocket of the world had grown, and in a good way. Instead of becoming big and commercial, it had built itself up from its own foundation of unique, local businesses. Blue Cedar Falls and its surroundings were a worthwhile destination for anybody looking to escape the monotony of cookie-cutter resorts and the encroachment of the same twenty chains that had taken over the leisure industry all over the world.

She wanted to stay for the festival for every one of these completely valid reasons.

She wanted to stay here for her family.

And heaven help her—she wanted to stay here for Han.

Their not-quite-fight the other day had driven home the fact that she was only here temporarily. That she would always leave, and he would always stay.

And yet neither of them wanted to call curtains on this *thing* they'd been doing.

After the intensity with which they'd ripped each other's clothes off at the end of the evening, there was no denying that they were both in too deep. She'd been trying to hold back her heart, but she had no doubt that it was going to get cracked wide open all over again when it came time for her to leave.

But like the masochist she'd once accused Han of being, she was in this now. She didn't want to miss out on a second of this limited time with him.

And she was going to be here to support him on the biggest night of her career, for Pete's sake.

Zahra muttered something under her breath. "Fine, fine, it's your funeral. Just so you know, I am totally sending Xan to that new underwater resort that bonkers billionaire is building in Iceland, though."

May's heart leaped in her chest, and the straight-A student inside her strained something, it tried to raise its hand so high. The career-obsessed travel writer inside her flopped onto its bed in utter despair.

She'd been angling for that assignment since the moment construction had been announced. The resort was going to be one of a kind. It was one of the only new destinations she'd been looking forward to in ages.

But she swallowed hard and sent both her inner over-achiever and the jet-setter to their rooms. Through gritted teeth, she managed to say, "Good for them. I'm sure they'll love it."

Zahra whistled, as if impressed that even losing her prize assignment wasn't going to get May to change her plans. "Well, all right then, off they go." She paused a second, but when May continued to hold her tongue, she sighed and moved on. "That said, I hope you're spending your little vacation in the middle of nowhere writing. You may be taking some time off, but nobody else here is."

"I am—the article I owe you is almost done." Ha. She tapped on the trackpad of her laptop just for the fun of staring at the blank space where the other thousand words of it were supposed to go.

"Next round of layoffs is rumored for end of the quarter."

"Right."

"But I've got your back. In fact...I've managed to fast-track your cat tourism article."

Now she had May's attention. "Oh?"

"Yup. You know how these viral stories are. Boom and bust. We don't get that cat on our pages soon and everybody will have forgotten about Backwater Falls."

"Blue Cedar Falls," May said automatically, but the intensity of her annoyance with the slip took her by surprise.

Since when did she care about people misquoting the name of her hometown?

Since when did it rankle her to hear someone calling it forgettable?

"Whatever."

May mentally shook her head at herself. "I mean, I'm grateful to have it fast-tracked." That meant Zahra was really rooting for her. The more high-profile positioning her articles received, the better off she would be. Still..."But being back here...There's a lot here for our readers. I think this is going to have some staying power."

"Yeah, right." Zahra laughed, and forget rankled. May was getting pissed about the dismissiveness now.

"Look—"

"Prove me wrong," Zahra offered. "I'd love it if you did, but the day a place like that really ends up on the map for anything other than a weird viral gimmick is the day I start playing the lottery. Just get your article in on time, Wu."

"I will."

Still irritated in ways she couldn't quite explain, she ended the call. An email from Zahra hit her inbox almost simultaneously with her hanging up. The new due date for the article stared back at her, and she swallowed. It was only a week and a half after Taste of Blue Cedar Falls. That would be tight, considering everything else she had waiting for her upon her return.

The shortness of her time here made her throat constrict, and it had—almost—nothing to do with how fast she'd have to type.

It had to do with something else entirely.

Something she wasn't sure she was ready to face.

"Excuse me."

May somehow managed not to fall off her stool as she jerked her gaze from the computer screen to find a woman standing right next to her. She put a hand to her chest, but her surprise quickly morphed into fight-or-flight as she recognized the person as Tori Gonzalez. Her once poofy brown hair was sleek and shiny now, and she'd traded her gold hoop earrings for some cool beaded ones, but she was unmistakable.

Tori had always been one of Jenny's crew. She'd never been mean to May directly, but she'd been beautiful and she'd fit in at school without any trouble, so May had always lumped her in with the rest.

"Sorry," Tori said, smiling genuinely. "Didn't mean to startle you."

"Uh-huh." May's own smile was more forced. She glanced past Tori, half expecting an ambush of thirty-year-old girls assembling behind her to revisit their sixteen-year-old antics. But the rest of the mean girl minions had left. Not that that made May any more interested in a chat. She gestured at her laptop. "I'm actually in the middle of something..."

"I won't keep you long." Tori sat down in the seat across from May.

She had to be kidding. May should be firm and tell her to leave, but the connection between her brain and her mouth seemed to be broken.

"I've actually been hoping to run into you. You know, with fewer people around." Tori rolled her eyes, but the gesture was warm—like she was making fun of herself and not of May. "You probably get this all the time, but I am a huge admirer of your work."

May blinked owlishly and resisted the impulse to pinch herself. "You what now?"

There was that eye roll again. "Oh come on. *Passage* magazine? That's the big time."

Yes, it was, and May was proud of it. "It's a great publication. I'm lucky to be on staff."

"And we're lucky to have you visiting." She raised a brow. "Assuming you're here for work, that is, and not just to visit your folks."

"It's a little bit of both," May allowed. She probably shouldn't let down her guard, but there was something about Tori's inviting posture that set May at ease.

"Good. Otherwise I'd have to give you my sales pitch for why you absolutely should be here to write a feature about Blue Cedar Falls." She lifted a hand in front of herself. "Sorry—I should have disclosed—I work for the tourism bureau now. It is literally my job to give sales pitches about this place."

Oh. That made May feel both better and worse somehow. "I didn't realize."

"It's new. I was at the *Chronicle* until this past winter. Tourism really picked up after this big Pumpkin Festival thing." She laughed and tapped her head. "Which of course you already know all about, since you're June's sister. And Li Mei's daughter."

"That I am." May's nerves were still all wonky, but she was actually starting to relax now.

"Anyway, they expanded the department, and I was a lucky hire."

As much as she was aware she was being chatted up on account of her position, the flow of conversation was easy to fall into. May had always liked talking shop; it was easier than talking about personal things. No matter how different of circles she and Tori had run in a decade ago, they were both professional women in the media now, and they had a surprising amount in common.

So much, in fact, that she was shocked when her phone pinged and she glanced at the time on it to find an hour had passed. "Oh, yikes. I completely lost track of the time."

"And here I promised I wouldn't keep you." Tori winced. "Sorry about that."

"No, don't be. It was...nice." Which was the last thing on earth she'd been expecting, especially when she still had a thousand words to bang out, but it was true.

"I'm glad you agree." Tori slung the strap of her purse over her shoulder. She hesitated before she stood, though. "Maybe we could get together again sometime before you leave. I'd love to pick your brain for a new print product we're trying to get off the ground. Little local spotlights, that kind of thing."

"Sounds great." If her research weren't already dog-eared for *Passage*, she'd even volunteer to help.

"Awesome." Tori paused again. "I—"

May had already opened her laptop again, and for real, she going to finish this article. "Yeah?"

"I feel like I owe you an apology. For, you know."

"Huh?"

Tori grimaced. "Back in high school."

Oh no. May had gotten so comfortable, but sweat broke out on the back of her neck. Her voice rose. "I don't know that—"

"Don't pretend Jenny wasn't awful to you. I always wanted to stop her, but I never knew how." Real remorse colored her gaze. "I wish I'd been braver, back then. I feel really guilty for being a part of it."

May waved her off. "Water under the bridge," she lied.

But for once, it was less of a lie than it used to be.

"It wasn't okay. I—" She sucked in a deep breath. "I hated the things they said. I was always afraid they were going to turn on me next, though, you know? Being Mexican had its own whole *thing*."

"I know," May said quietly, and this time, it was one hundred percent the truth.

Tori gave her a hopeful look. "No hard feelings?"

May had so many hard feelings. But she didn't doubt what Tori was saying. Would it have been cooler for her to be a bigger person and call out racist bullying for what it was back a decade and a half ago? Uh, yeah. But late was better than never.

"We're cool," May promised.

"Phew. For what it's worth, Jenny's a lot less awful now than she was back then."

"Well, that I'm going to have to take your word on."

Tori held up both hands as she stood. "Fair enough."

They said their goodbyes, and Tori headed out. May set a timer on her phone and put everything on do not disturb—the way things had been going this afternoon, that was her only chance of actually accomplishing anything.

But even as she got back to writing, her thoughts kept wandering. To Han, of course. To her family.

To the version of Tori that had stood idly by while May was going through the most miserable years of her life.

To the version of herself that had never stood up to any of it either. Who had never gone to anyone for help. Not even Han; apparently, she'd hidden it so well he'd hardly even known it was going on.

She didn't blame herself for any of it. She hadn't deserved to be treated that way.

But the blame she did hold in her heart—for every one of Jenny's friends, for the entire school. For Han.

For this town.

Was any of that real?

Did any of them deserve that?

Did they deserve a second chance?

# CHAPTER SIXTEEN

One minute, Han was prepping his rear end off for Taste of Blue Cedar Falls, savoring his last days with May, and trying to act like he wasn't a freaking masochist for both.

The next minute, time was up.

The day of Taste, he arrived at Pine Meadows Park the earliest he was allowed to start setting up. He still wasn't the first one there. Making his way toward his stall, he passed the culinary giants of Main Street, not to mention some of the best restaurateurs from the next five towns over. A few hailed from as far away as Charleston. His stomach churned. Taste of Blue Cedar Falls had been advertised as the best of the best from both the region and the town, and he'd known that would be true. But as he stopped in front of his designated stall, the reality of the moment settled on his shoulders like a ten-ton weight.

"All right, boss." His official helper for the day was Naomi, one of the part-timers from the Jade Garden. "Point me in the right direction."

"Us, too," a familiar voice said. He looked up to find Devin, Caitlin, Bobbi, Clay, Tyrell, and a handful of his other friends standing there. Devin, who had spoken, lifted a brow. "What, did you think we were going to just leave you to it?"

Han laughed, some of his anxiety melting away.

Then he realized what these jerks were wearing.

He swabbed at his eye, even as he scolded them. "I told you to knock that stuff off—not get custom T-shirts printed."

The shirts were an emerald green, just like the banner he'd gotten made up for what he was currently calling the Jade Garden Annex. Except instead of saying the name for the actual pop-up restaurant he was running tonight, they all said, in giant letters, HAN SOLO.

"There's no reasoning with them," a quieter voice said.

He turned to find May standing there wearing the same stupid shirt, though she'd tied it in a knot at her waist, because even when she was ganging up on him with the rest of his friends, she had to do it in the sexiest way possible. She took his hand in hers, and it was just like the moment when she'd declared that his late-night fusion food should be the foundation of his new menu. Her confidence in him reached right into his soul.

He gazed down at her, and his heart was too big for his chest.

Back thirteen years ago, he'd known she was his perfect match. Yet somehow, in the intervening time, she'd become an even better partner than he could have imagined back then. Her support radiated through the air toward him, making him feel about ten feet tall. Giving him the space inside his chest to feel the support of all his other friends who had shown up for him today.

And this was what he'd been missing for all this time. Not just her love—though God knew he'd been missing that. But also this conviction. This openness to believing in himself and in his ability to work toward his goals. She'd given it back to him.

Even later, after she left. He would still be able to be grateful for that.

His throat scraped. "I thought you were here to cover the festival."

"I am." She squeezed his hand. "And to support my favorite chef in Blue Cedar Falls."

"Just like the rest of us," Devin said. "So now, seriously, dude. Tell us how to help you get set up."

He laughed and leaned in to plant a hard kiss on May's lips. She smiled, kissing him back before pulling away. "Knock 'em dead."

He rubbed his hands together and surveyed his make-shift army of volunteers. "All right, then, y'all. Let's do this."

Thus began a few of the most frenetic hours of his life.

The Jade Garden had done enough street fairs along Main Street to have a decent mobile kitchen ready to go, but the beast was cantankerous at best. He was grateful for the many hands that pitched in as he and Naomi led the way. The burners got assembled and hooked up to power and gas, the banner got hung and the table decorated, the ingredients and cooking implements organized. There was a brief issue with their water hookup, but May just shook her head and called June, who got a tech over within minutes to straighten everything out.

Before he knew it, June herself stood at the center of the festival, microphone in hand. Beside her stood Main Street Business Association president and local gallery owner Patty Boyd. After June tried and failed to get everyone's attention a couple of times, Patty fired off a blast from a bullhorn before putting the thing to her mouth. "Welcome, everybody, to the first annual Taste of Blue Cedar Falls!"

People at stalls all around them applauded. Really taking in the scene for the first time in hours, Han realized exactly how many folks were here. In addition to the staff and helpers surrounding each of the stalls, random people were milling around, checking out what was on offer.

He gazed off into the distance, where more people were arriving. The festival wasn't even open yet, but already the turnout was incredible. To think—this time last year, they'd all been worried the town was going to sink into oblivion.

Its vitality shone tonight, though. Locals and tourists alike had shown up in droves. He didn't miss the fact that not a small percentage of the visitors wore shirts with pictures of May's mom's cat on them, but that was beside the point. Pride welled up in his chest. This was his hometown, and it was thriving.

Now, he was going to show it a whole new side of himself. One that was creative and ambitious. He had the support of the best friends a guy could ask for.

He had the most beautiful woman in the world by his side.

As June gently elbowed Patty out of the way and launched into her welcome speech, Han looked over to find May standing right beside him. He curled his arm around her waist, so grateful for her presence here. For the kick in the pants she had given him that helped shake him out of his rut. For her inspiration and her support and—

And for her love. Whatever form it came in, and for however long she could offer it.

As if she could feel the intensity of his stare, she tilted her head up. Their gazes met.

"Did I tell you how glad I am that you came back," he told her, his chest and throat tight.

"Me, too," she admitted, but in her eyes, he could see the regret. The impending goodbye.

Her time was almost up.

"I'm really proud of what you've done here," she told him.

"What *we've* done," he insisted, even though it hurt.

He squeezed her close, and she squeezed back.

"Without further ado," June said into the microphone, rounding out her speech, "let's dig in!"

Hollers went up throughout the crowd. Lines instantaneously began forming in front of every stall—including his own.

May let go of him. With a little gleam in her eye, she shooed him forward. He cast exactly one last glance back her way as he stepped in front of the cooktop.

Naomi handed him the first order.

And that was the last quiet moment Han had to himself all night.

———

A couple of hours into Taste, the enthusiasm of the crowd had only grown. May wandered the park, nibbling on a pretty great garlicky shrimp skewer she'd gotten at a stall her sister June's friend Ella was running. She was trying to sample fare from as many different booths as she could, which was helped by the fact that pretty much everyone was offering special, smaller "tasting" portions. She caught herself smiling, remembering how Han had groaned after eating too much at each of seven different lunches on their first research trip together.

She glanced down the row to where the Jade Garden Annex was doing a brisk business. She'd heard people talking about it all night. It was a surprise hit of the evening. Her heart squeezed at the number of locals who'd been thrilled to see their favorite Chinese takeout joint proving itself. Not one person made a disparaging, othering remark about it being foreign food.

Maybe Jenny really had been the outlier back in high school. The cracks she'd made the couple of times May had been forced to bring leftovers of her mother's cooking for lunch still stung.

But had anybody else really cared? People had always gone to the Jade Garden for a cheap, filling, delicious meal.

Had May been cursing herself for a decade now for inviting that kind of abuse—when it hadn't been her fault at all? She'd missed out on her mother's cooking because of what some stupid girl had said about it. She'd steeped herself in shame, and for what?

She looked around, and everything Han had said about Blue Cedar Falls rang true. It had changed. People of every race and creed and gender and orientation had assembled to eat amazing food, and it was incredible. It was something she was so proud to be a part of.

At least for this stolen little pocket of time.

As if she needed the reminder, her phone pinged in her pocket. She finished the last bite of shrimp, wiped her hands, and tossed the stick and napkin in the trash before checking the notification. Ruby had sent her a picture of her pet tortoise, Todd, wearing what looked like a tiny party hat that her friend must have made for the little guy.

The caption read, *Can't wait to (finally) see Mom!* It was followed immediately by a selfie of Ruby making a stink face, captioned: *(And Ruby can't wait to stop dealing with tortoise poop.)*

The pride in May's chest flipped on a dime. She tapped out a flippant response about how she couldn't wait to see her precious baby and rescue him from the clutches of the mean lady who body-shamed him for normal biological functions.

Deep down, though, dread filled her all the way up from her toes.

Her flight to New York was booked for tomorrow night. She had so much to get back to. Work, friends. Todd. Normally, she'd be champing at the bit, searching to see if she could catch an earlier flight.

Nothing about leaving felt normal this time, though.

"Hey—watch where you're going!"

May blinked a stray bit of mistiness from her eyes and looked back to find eighty-something-year-old Dottie Gallagher driving a motorized scooter down the path. She was selling bouquets from her flower shop out of the back of it and grumbling something about "youths and their phones" as she passed.

At least it was good to see some things hadn't changed.

Making sure she was out of the flow of traffic, she returned her attention to said phone, switching to Facebook, where she had posted a live video of Taste of Blue Cedar Falls to her professional account. A bunch of comments and reactions had come in, mostly supportive, expressing excitement to see her covering more off-the-beaten-path destinations. A few, less kind ones questioned what on earth she was doing in some Podunk town nobody had ever heard of before, and she had to hold a tight leash on herself to keep from firing back anything equally rude. Everybody had a right to their opinion, but the comments grated the same way Zahra's had when she'd dismissed this town, too.

Mentally rolling her eyes at herself, she exited the replies section and scrolled down. She bit her lip. She'd also maybe possibly posted a selfie of herself next to the Jade Garden Annex, expressing her support for a "friend" and his amazing food. The comments there were a mixed bag, too, with everything from people dragging her for making a personal endorsement when she was supposed to be a journalist to someone who was apparently here and had replied with a picture of one of Han's dumplings, captioned with about thirty-seven heart emojis. She liked that one and then forced herself to blank the screen.

Figuring it was time for some dessert, she set off again. She'd just picked up a Nutella and berry crepe when her younger sister Elizabeth sidled up to her out of absolutely nowhere.

"There she is." Elizabeth draped her arm across May's shoulder. "The one who got away."

"What?" May tried to slip out of her grasp, but she held on tight.

"How did you do it?" Elizabeth asked, her face way too close to hers.

It was then that May smelled the liquor on her breath. She wrinkled her nose. Her sister's eyes were glazed, her cheeks pink with the Asian flush that plagued everybody in their family.

"Elizabeth," she hissed. "Are you—"

"Drunk as a skunk," Graham confirmed, helping to tug Elizabeth off May. His jaw was tightly set, but the rest of him was just a little bit more rumpled than his usual prim appearance.

"Seriously," Elizabeth persisted. "How did you get away?"

"I don't know what you're—"

"Away from here." Elizabeth listed closer again, swaying against Graham's hold. "This town."

May blinked rapidly, gripping the little box that held her crepe. Good grades and grim determination didn't seem like answers that would help right now. "I mean..."

"I'm never getting out," Elizabeth moaned. She reached into her crocheted bag and pulled out a crumpled piece of paper. "Form rejections. Can you believe it? The residency I thought I was a shoo-in for didn't even bother to write something nice." She put on an affected voice. "Dear Ms. Wu: We regret to inform you that you are utter trash—"

"That is not what they said," May and Graham said all but in unison.

"They might as well have." Elizabeth scowled and shoved Graham off.

The poor guy let her go, misery writ large on his face.

Elizabeth stumbled forward and poked a finger into May's chest. "You got out. You made this great life for yourself, because you're great. And I'm stuck here forever, teaching toddlers and getting paint thrown at me, because nobody wants *my* paintings."

"That's not true," May swore.

"What? That nobody wants me or that I'm stuck here?" Elizabeth made a sweeping gesture with her arm, but she lost her balance.

May and Graham both moved to catch her. May "won," but with how her sister sagged into her, she wasn't sure it was that much of a victory.

"Your paintings are great," Graham reassured her.

She shook her head. "You have to say that because you're my friend, and you're stuck here, too."

"I'm not—"

"Nobody's *stuck* anywhere," May interrupted. Shoring her sister up, she gave her a little shake. "You're not stuck anywhere you don't want to be."

"Easy for you to say." Elizabeth slumped her head on May's shoulder again, and her voice was slurred. "You can go anywhere, and you're here. Like a freaking chump."

"Like a person who loves her sister," May countered, but she felt like she'd been socked in the gut.

Elizabeth snorted. "That's not all you love."

*Ow.*

"Okay, drunkie." Graham reached for Elizabeth, and May let her go. "Let's get you home."

"I'm going to die in that apartment, Graham."

"Not for another sixty years, God willing."

"Sixty years," Elizabeth moaned, but when Graham started walking her toward the parking lot, she didn't resist.

"Sorry about that," Graham mouthed at May.

May shot him a sympathetic glance. "Make sure she drinks lots of water."

He saluted, but almost lost his grip on her sister and had to lurch to keep her upright.

May kept an eye on them until she was pretty sure Graham had things under control. She dusted herself off. When she went to open up the box that held her dessert, she hesitated, though, her appetite suddenly gone.

She felt bad for Elizabeth. Her sister had been so excited about the prospect of focusing on her artwork in a more formal setting. The rejection must have been crushing, but her over-the-top reaction made May cringe.

Then she cringed even harder at her own hypocrisy.

May had spent the entirety of her teenage years convinced she was stuck here, too. She'd worked endlessly to get out, sure, but she'd also made sure nobody could be left with any doubts about her opinion of Blue Cedar Falls.

Elizabeth had been drunk and disappointed, but May had been insufferable. How had people who really loved this town put up with her? How had June, her mom, Ned—Han?

Embarrassment burned in her cheeks.

The worst part of it all was that she'd been so unfair in her assessment. Yes, Jenny had been mean, and being one of the only Asian kids in town had been difficult, but the entire place wasn't to blame for that.

Rattled, she turned back toward the festival. She still had a bunch of stalls she wanted to visit, but her sister's breakdown had derailed her pretty thoroughly. She checked her watch. There was another hour left before things shut down. Maybe she should swing past the Jade Garden Annex and see how things were going...Maybe offer Han a taste of her now-cold crepe.

She bit the inside of her lip. When had it become her first instinct to go check in with Han when she was feeling unnerved?

Did it matter?

She headed toward Han's stall, moving through the crowd with a forced smile.

Of course, who did she spot standing directly in her way?

Jenny Sullivan had her back to May, and for a second, May considered turning right around. The queen of mean was surrounded by a bunch of her friends, though, and

Tori caught her eye. May fought her deer-in-the-headlights response and waved.

Digging her nails into her palm, she waded on over. The gaggle was parked right in front of the Jade Garden Annex, so there was really no avoiding them. She glanced past Jenny, Tori, and her friends to see Han grinning like a fool as he dished out orders and chatted up the front of the impressively long line of customers waiting patiently for their food. Her heart sank. She was delighted for him, but no way he'd have any time to spare until things closed.

She planned to just keep walking, but Tori held out a hand, signaling her to come over. May shot Jenny a glance, but Tori rolled her eyes and encouraged her to join them anyway.

This was a terrible idea.

She and Tori had gotten along so well the other day, though, and she had just finished telling herself that she'd let Jenny poison her opinions of Blue Cedar Falls for too long.

She still didn't make eye contact with the queen bee as she came over.

"Hey," Tori greeted her, reaching out for a quick hug. "How's it going?"

"Great." The back of May's neck was hot, but she maintained her composure as she gestured around. "This whole setup is incredible."

"I know, right?" Grinning, Tori tipped her head toward the Jade Garden Annex. "And who knew Han had this in him, right?"

May had known. All along—even when they were kids.

Jenny muttered something, but May couldn't hear it, and she clenched her hand into a fist.

One of the other women munched on a pineapple pork

dumpling, just like the ones Han had invented the night he and May had fallen back into bed together. The woman beside her—Kelsey, May thought—sighed. "A bunch of reporters keep circling around him. He's going to be famous by the time this is all over."

Tori agreed. "Think he'll remember all the little people he knew back when?"

"I know he'll remember me," Jenny said.

Kelsey shoved her teasingly. "Well, of course he'll remember *you*."

Another of their friends, Madison, rolled her eyes. "Or at least that thing you do with your tongue…"

The box with May's crepe slipped out of her hand. She couldn't help the way her gaze swung automatically toward Jenny, and oh, the witch. Her blue eyes gleamed like a predator's, her mouth curled into a smug smile with just a hint of teeth, and May had been fighting so hard for so long to stop making herself look like prey.

Her brain spun. Madison's comment—the look on Jenny's face—

None of it could be true, could it?

Her ears rung.

In her head, she flashed back to all the times she'd told Han that Jenny had tortured her. He'd looked at her like she was out of her mind. He hadn't quite leaped to Jenny's defense, but his mouth had pursed in this specific way.

Like there was something he wasn't telling her.

Her eyes stung.

Han had known how evil Jenny had been to May. He might not have grasped the full extent of it, no, but he'd known enough.

And—according to Madison—he'd let Jenny do "that thing" with her tongue to him, anyway.

Her face on fire, she stooped to pick up the box she'd dropped. She had a brief flashback of these same girls looking down at her, of a pointy-toed shoe coming down on her fingers as she scurried for her fallen textbooks.

She stood up.

She looked Jenny freaking Sullivan right in the eye. Levelly, she said, "I don't know about that. He's certainly never mentioned it to me."

Then she turned around. She walked away, head held high.

Trying to pretend her world hadn't just shattered into pieces.

# CHAPTER SEVENTEEN

❁ ❁ ❁ ❁ ❁ ❁ ❁ ❁ ❁ ❁ ❁ ❁ ❁

Taste of Blue Cedar Falls didn't so much end as taper off. All the vendors had instructions to stop serving and start cleaning up at ten p.m., but who was Han to turn away hungry people who'd heard the spicy basil bacon-wrapped shrimp were amazing? He'd run out of just about everything else a while ago, but he filled as many of the last stragglers' orders as he could.

In the meantime, Naomi got to work packing up. His mom had arrived around the time the Jade Garden proper had closed—"Nobody there anyway," she'd scoffed, looking around at the crowded festival like it was personally to blame. Which it probably was. She took over the register, tallying receipts, which he was more than grateful for. That had always been his least favorite part of the job. Devin pitched in for a bit, too, but when things seemed like they were in hand, he said good night and headed out to meet Zoe at the Junebug. Han said he'd try to catch up with them there, but he wasn't sure.

He'd been riding high on adrenaline all night. He hadn't had a second to rest, and it had been incredible. His food festival pop-up had been such a hit. Maybe that solo restaurant he'd been dreaming about since he was ten could actually be a reality. New possibilities for his future kept dawning on him.

But the only one he wanted to share them with was May.

May, who against all his better judgment he'd fallen back in love with. May, who was leaving tomorrow.

May, who had been his biggest supporter. May, who'd helped him climb to where he was right now.

As busy as he'd been all night, he had found time to occasionally scan the crowd for her. He'd spotted her wandering around, talking and sampling, taking pictures and making notes. Their gazes had connected more than once, and each time, he'd felt it in his soul. She'd disappeared at some point in the evening, though. As soon as he was done here, he'd text her and see if she wanted to go to the Junebug to celebrate...or if they should have their own, more private celebration.

His blood heated at the thought. He was restless and buzzing on the high of an incredible night. Working off some of the excess energy with her between the sheets sounded like the best solution.

As much as he wanted victory sex, he also just wanted to...*talk* to her. He wanted to tell her all about the best night of his career, about his ambitions and the fuel he'd been feeding to the new fire of his dreams. About how much of his new energy he owed to her.

He wanted to hear about her night. He hadn't gotten to see a single bit of Taste outside his own patch of the lawn. What had she enjoyed? What had other people been doing?

Had she had a good time?

He chuffed out a laugh under his breath.

Even he wasn't delusional enough to think that she

could have had so much fun as to change her mind about leaving Blue Cedar Falls—*again*—but he still had this stupid, irrational hope buried somewhere deep inside him that she might at least soften her position. A little.

Finally, things were more or less settled. He and Naomi split the tip jar, then took a cart full of stuff back to the truck. There wasn't much left at the stand, so he sent her home and walked back through the maze of other half-deconstructed stalls alone.

His mom spotted his approach and pressed a few buttons on her old-school giant calculator, making a big show of it as she did.

"So how'd we do?" he asked.

"Depends." She took off her reading glasses and set them aside. "Did you want to make a profit or not?"

Was this a trick question? "Uh, yes?"

For the first time all night, a sliver of doubt threatened his happy bubble.

His mother shook her head. "Then it did not go well."

"Wait—" That didn't make any sense.

She held up a notebook full of her usual chicken scratch. If he hadn't been watching her do the books at the restaurant for literally his entire life, he wouldn't be able to make heads or tails of it. As it was, he still needed a primer.

"These"—she pointed at the number at the bottom of the first column—"your receipts for tonight."

His eyes bugged out. The number was better than even he had expected.

"Plus tips." She held up what was left in the jar.

"All right," he said, pumping his fist.

"This." Her tone was sharp as she pointed at the second column of numbers. "Your expenses. Ingredients, paying

Naomi—both tonight and the nights you've been away from the Jade Garden wasting your time on this."

She might as well have slapped him. But for some reason, the judgment failed to sink in this time. She might be making him doubt himself, but she wasn't taking the wind out of his sails. "That's not fair."

Raising her brows, she tapped a fingernail against another number. "Plus wear and tear on the equipment."

"It was one night, Ma." Irritation rose in him. Was she really going to rain on his parade like this? On tonight of all nights?

She barreled right along. "Booth fee for venue."

"Okay, I get it, I get it—"

"No, you don't."

"Maybe you don't," he finally exploded, and oh man. He never raised his voice to his mom, but this was important. The conviction he'd gained over the past few weeks fueled him. "We had a great night! Everybody loved the food. It was all over social media. We sold out of almost everything. Our line was ten-people deep for almost the entire night."

He had something here. Something special, something that resonated.

Something that could pull him out of the rut he'd been in for these past thirteen years.

Only his mom seemed intent on anchoring him down to its bottom. "You barely broke even," she said sharply.

"On a test run! This was a word-of-mouth builder, not a retirement plan."

She started counting off his issues on her fingers. "Expensive ingredients, time-intensive prep."

"Screwball accounting."

She slammed her palm down on the counter. Her eyes

blazed. "I tell it like it is! You—you have always been dependable. Always did what the family needed. Your sister Zoe—she had her head in the clouds forever, but you I could rely on. But I can't rely on this."

"Mom…" His chest was so tight he could scarcely breathe.

"This is not good business, Han."

"But it could be."

She shook her head. "No one pays top dollar for Chinese food." She spat on the ground and muttered an unkind word for "cheapskates" in Mandarin under her breath. "There's a reason everybody runs the same Chinese takeout place."

"Because they don't have any better ideas."

"I had an idea to keep my family alive. Your uncle Arthur and your father and I—we all had that idea."

"And you did." His voice broke. "You built this incredible life for us, Mom."

One his dad had always told him to make the most of.

She reached a hand toward him across the makeshift counter. "It can disappear in a moment, Han."

Pain echoed in her words. Grief.

Ever since his dad had died, his mom had been obsessed with security and stability. She feared losing everything his dad had worked with her to build.

Han had indulged her for the most part. He'd seen through his duty, helped her run the family business, gotten his little sisters through college and off into their own lives, and a part of him had thought… He'd imagined…

Maybe, someday, it would be his turn.

"Mom."

She flexed her fingers insistently. Something in him cracked. He put his palm in hers, and she squeezed tightly.

"This dream of yours—your own restaurant—"

"I never said—" He'd thought it, sure. But he'd never said it. Not to her.

"You think your mother a fool?" She gazed up at him with eyes that were incisive but also sad. "I know what you really want. But this isn't it."

His rib cage felt like it crumpled.

"Maybe someday," she continued, "when business is better."

Business was the best it'd been in years.

He shook his head. "I know I can make this work."

"Not like this," she promised.

With that, she released him. She picked up her reading glasses, slipped them in their case, and dropped them in her purse.

The sucker punch to the ribs hadn't receded at all. He couldn't get enough air. "So, what? That's it? You just decree that this isn't working, conversation over?"

"Nothing else to say."

"Well, I have a lot more to say."

She raised her brows, as if inviting him to go ahead and spit it out, then.

But all he could do was sputter. "You didn't even taste the food." She hadn't given him a chance. "Tonight was a *win*, Mom."

She snorted. "For your ego."

"That's not fair."

"*Life* isn't. You show me the numbers for how you can make this a success, and fine. Great." She fluttered a hand at her own chest. "Happy to be proven wrong. But until then?" She gestured around. "This is a dream, Han. Welcome to reality."

He bit down on his tongue so hard he tasted blood.

This wasn't over.

But even as a part of him geared up to keep fighting, another part wanted to slump to the ground. Arguments with his mother always went like this. She loved him. She was proud of him. But she made him feel like a dunderhead, too, and his tongue tied itself in knots.

He'd been an Eagle Scout, once, but he couldn't seem to get this knot undone.

It occurred to him that he didn't *need* her approval. He could strike out on his own tomorrow. He had savings, the support of his friends—the support of the entire town, apparently. But the idea of telling his mother to get lost chafed against something so deeply ingrained in him he couldn't begin to get the words out.

Taking his silence for the momentary cease-fire it was, his mother slipped from behind the counter, car keys in hand. "We can talk about it more in the morning. You're on the schedule to open."

"I know the schedule," he said sharply.

She walked away. He stood there motionless for long moments.

Finally, he squared his shoulders. He wasn't giving up. His friends, May, the people who'd come out to eat his food tonight... they all believed in him.

He'd figure out a way to make this work.

Somehow.

He just had to talk this through with someone who would understand. Someone who'd support him, no matter what.

And exactly one person came to mind.

———

By the time Han had unloaded all the equipment at the Jade Garden and dragged his stinking carcass back home, he'd calmed down a little bit. Manual labor had been good for him; exercise always helped settle his brain. His mother's discouraging words kept circling in his mind, but his resistance to them hadn't lost any of its strength.

Neither had his instinct to talk this through with May. He knew full well she was leaving imminently, but what they'd built while she was here was so strong, he couldn't help but want to lean into it.

He'd texted her while he'd been unloading things. She'd agreed she wanted to talk, but she'd been unusually terse about it, and they hadn't settled any logistics. He fired off another message, asking where she wanted to meet up. He just needed a quick shower, and he'd be ready to go.

With that goal in mind, he headed toward the stairs. Ling-Ling was passed out in her bed in the living room, which was disappointing. He could use a quick snuggle and a doggy grin to lift his spirits. From the second-floor landing, he could see his mom's door was closed, so she was probably already asleep, too—thank goodness. If she tried to pick another fight, he didn't know what he might say.

He kept climbing. Three steps from the top, he stopped.

His door was open. Brow scrunched, more worried his mom had been going through his stuff than about a home invader, he continued up.

Only to find May perched on the foot of his bed.

Instant relief crashed over him, like cannonballing into a pool on a muggy day. This was so much better than having to go meet her somewhere.

"There you are." He closed and locked the door before reaching behind his neck to tug off his shirt, even more ready for that shower now that May might be joining him. "You would not believe this night."

May stood. "Did you or did you not sleep with Jenny Sullivan?"

He froze. He regretted taking off his shirt.

Slowly, trying to unscramble his brain, he asked, "Like, tonight?"

Her glare sharpened. "Like, ever."

Crap. "Look—"

"Answer the question."

He shook his head. How did he buy himself some time here? "Where did you even hear that from?"

"That's not a denial."

He squeezed the balled-up wad of cotton in his fist. Turning, he dropped it in the hamper. He wasn't going to put it back on—it was disgusting. He was disgusting, sweaty and covered in kitchen grease. All he wanted was a shower.

He wanted to go back in time thirteen years.

Since neither of those were options, he wordlessly opened the drawer of his dresser, plucked out a clean T-shirt, and pulled it on. He already felt stripped naked by her question—no way he was answering it without wearing some clothes.

Finally, he faced her again. The accusation in her stare cut through him. The soft, warm smile she'd shone at him earlier this evening was a distant memory.

"Did I sleep with Jenny Sullivan? No," he said truthfully. His gut burned. May opened her mouth to speak, but he cut her off. No sense dragging this out. "Did I have sex with her? Like a dozen years ago, when the dirt on my dad's grave was still fresh? Yeah. I did."

The betrayal on May's face was a whip slashing through the air. "How could you—"

Nope. No way. "A dozen *years* ago, May. You were gone, remember? Out of the picture."

God, he'd been such a mess back then. Culinary school was gone, his dad was gone. May had come back, and like a dolt, he'd leaned on her. He'd begged her to stay, and she'd said no, and he'd been so *angry*. It was like there'd been nothing left of him but rage and grief and guilt.

May sputtered. "But you knew how awful she was. You knew how much she hurt me."

"Do you have any idea how much *I* was hurting?" he hurled at her. Why couldn't he keep this in? Dragging up these ancient injuries was only going to make things worse.

But how much worse could they get? She was leaving again. Tomorrow. She'd always been planning to leave, and he'd never protected himself one bit. He hadn't imagined he could convince her to stay. Even his fleeting, manic dreams of following her had been just that—dreams.

He also hadn't imagined her learning the truth.

"So is that what it was?" Incredulous and disappointed, she jerked a hand toward the side. "You screwed Jenny to get back at me?"

He flinched.

But could he deny it? He'd been lost and angry and in pain, and he'd been flailing about for a way to make it better. He never thought May would find out what he'd done, but he had to admit that knowing it would hurt her was a plus.

It hadn't been the whole reason, though. "Unlike you, Jenny was there. She was nice to me."

Unexpectedly so, honestly.

The two of them hadn't had much to do with each

other back in high school. She'd sent him a flirtatious glance once or twice—especially after he'd filled out a bit and grown another half foot between junior and senior year. But it hadn't mattered. He'd been head over heels for May, and she'd always been dating some football star or another.

But then, after his dad died, the Sullivans were just…there.

"She knew what it was like," he said. "After her mom…"

Mrs. Sullivan had died more slowly. Cancer, back when Jenny was only ten. Han hadn't known Jenny well at the time, and she'd never let anyone outside her inner circle see how it'd affected her. It was before May had moved to town, but she had to have heard about it.

The anger in her gaze flickered, because yeah. She knew.

"She and her dad brought over about fifteen casseroles." Two or three of them were even good, but he didn't need to mention that. "They ordered from the restaurant twice as often as they used to. Volunteered at Harvest Home, even."

His uncle had almost had to shut down the food bank and soup kitchen that he ran. He and Han's mom were reeling in those first, awful weeks.

But Blue Cedar Falls had rallied around them. The Wus, the Gallaghers, the Boyds. And yeah—the Sullivans.

It was after a shift at Harvest Home that it had happened, actually. Jenny had been between boyfriends, and they'd been headed to the parking lot, and she'd given him this look.

He'd had a moment to make a decision. He'd been a mixed-up jumble of grief and hurt and loneliness, and she'd offered him a chance to get out of his own head—and yeah. A chance to get back at May, too, but that hadn't been the point.

They'd ended up in bed together a half dozen times. She was the first person he'd had sex with besides May and it had been . . . good. Awkward.

Neither of them had pretended it was anything serious. He felt like crap—like he was using her, but he was pretty sure that in some way or another, she was using him, too.

In the end, she caught the eye of some new guy who moved to town, and they parted ways. He felt a certain gratitude. She'd helped him when he was at his lowest. He didn't love her—heck, he barely more than liked her. And she still had some pretty close-minded views. She wasn't perfect, but then again, neither was he.

"Look, I don't expect you to understand," he said.

"Good. Because I don't. At all." May crossed her arms over her chest, her fingers digging into her biceps. "Not a day went by when she didn't tell me to go back to China—or worse. You think she didn't think the same stuff about you, too?"

He raked a hand through his hair. "Of course she did. There's no excusing any of it. Maybe she learned something from hanging out with me. Maybe . . ."

"Maybe what?"

Oh, he was treading into dangerous waters now. "Maybe you were so intimidating and smart and gorgeous that she latched on to anything she could to take you down a notch."

"By being super racist and making me feel like crap."

"Making people feel like crap is what popular kids do."

"You still sound like you're making excuses for her."

"I know, I know, and I swear I'm not." He huffed out a breath. "She bullied you. She said terrible things. You could never forgive her in your life, and nobody would blame you."

"But?"

"But..." He didn't want to humanize someone who had been bigoted and cruel. But the truth was the truth. "When I needed it, she showed me kindness. I'll never forget that."

May's eyes shone. Shaking her head, she swabbed at them, but her mouth was a grim line. "I can't believe you."

"What do you want me to say?" The unfairness of being confronted like this now clawed at him. "I'm not going to apologize for something I did over a decade ago when you weren't even here, because you *left* me."

"You told me to go."

His voice cracked. "Right after I begged you to stay."

Fires blazed in her black eyes. "To give up everything. Drop out of college. Come back to this place where I was never happy."

"Then why did you even come back at all? Why show up for the funeral and give me a taste of having you?" It had meant everything to him at the time, but it had been its own exquisite form of torture, too.

"How could I not?" She blinked and swiped at her eyes again. "I loved you."

"But you were never going to stay."

She shook her head. "Not since day one. You knew that. Before we got together, even."

Of course he did. She'd never stopped talking about it. They'd be hanging out while their moms were playing bridge, him goofing off, her studying, and she'd rambled on and on about all the places she was going to go someday. If she hadn't been so beautiful and passionate, it would have been annoying.

So yeah. He had always known. But… "I thought maybe, at some point in all those years, you'd change your mind. Remember that this is *home*." He sucked in a harsh breath. "Look, I know it wasn't always perfect. I wish I could have protected you from all the crap that people threw at you."

God, he wished that. People had been awful to her here. But it hadn't all been bullies and jerks, had it? Didn't any of the good stuff count for anything? "I hoped you'd remember that this is where your family is." His throat threatened to close. "That this is where we had been happy together."

Only she wasn't listening to any of it. Her knuckles were white, she was clenching them so hard. "Just like I thought maybe you'd change your mind, too—you know, because you literally lied and said you had."

"I never—"

"We made all those plans to go to New York *together*, Han."

"You made them." She'd found him applications to culinary schools up there. Even started filling them out.

But ever since his dad had taken him to visit, he knew he didn't belong there.

"What, so it was all me?"

"Of course it wasn't." How was this getting so twisted around? "But I should have been clearer. Earlier."

Her eyes widened in disbelief. "Uh, ya think?"

"You were a force of nature, May." Heaven help him, she still was. "You were so excited, and I couldn't figure out how to break it to you that it wasn't for me."

He had his family to think about. They had expectations of him.

So did she, and the choice had always torn him apart.

She laughed, an ugly sound that cut off with a croak. "Well, I can't imagine you could have come up with much worse of a solution. 'Oh, hey, it's the last day to change anything about our life plans, and by the way, I turned down the fancy school I got accepted to in the restaurant capital of the world for a freaking state school.'"

"Don't knock NC State."

"You could have done better."

"I couldn't even do what I did." His chest hurt. Letting May go, losing his dad, dropping out of school. It was all a jumble in his heart, and every part of it hurt. "Remember? I lasted three months."

"That's not true."

"It is." He did all right in school; he was never in any danger of failing out. But his love of food was the only thing keeping him there. Everything else inside him told him to go home, to the mountains where the fresh air and flowing falls and smiling faces made him feel like *himself*. Out there, he felt like an impostor. Here, he knew who he was.

But May still didn't get it. "Only because of your dad."

"Only?" He was losing it. Any shred of calm he'd walked into this ambush with, he'd lost.

"You know what I mean."

"Losing my dad and having to take his place here is the biggest, worst thing to happen to me." He sucked in a deep breath. "Followed only by how much it sucked to let you go."

A huff of a laugh escaped her lips again, and he'd had it.

"You think that was easy for me?" he asked. He was

talking too loud. He was going to wake his mom, but he didn't care. Let her hear this. Let her get some inkling of what he'd been going through. What he'd sacrificed.

May glared at him. "It sure seemed it." She put on her mocking impression of him again. "'While we're at school, I think we should see other people.'"

The acid in her voice threatened to burn him.

But not as deeply as the memory. "I told you how much it killed me to say that."

"Then why did you?" The tears that had brimmed at the edges of her eyes finally spilled over. "Why break my heart like that?"

Twist the knife. "I broke my own heart, too, you know?"

"Why?" She practically shouted it this time.

So he dropped his voice low. He ground out the admission he'd been holding on to for all these years. "Because I refused to be the selfish prick who dragged you down."

She flinched, taking a half step back. *"What?"*

"Wasn't it obvious?" He wanted to laugh, but if he opened up a single bit further, he'd cry. "I loved you. You were it for me."

"But—"

"But you had all these dreams that I was never going to be a part of."

She shook her head harshly. "You were a part of all of them."

"I was a chain around your neck." From the minute she came home with that dream school acceptance, he felt the weight. "I couldn't go. My family needed me." He'd had no idea how much. "Even before my dad. And I needed them."

That was the part he couldn't lose in this. It wasn't

just about the duty he felt toward his family. It was about what they gave him, too. He valued his roots, and those ran deeply here. After he moved home, he never once again considered leaving.

Not until she came back, and all these fantasies of making a home for himself wherever she happened to go started entering into his head. The past thirteen years had taught him a lot, and the past three weeks had somehow taught him even more. He was strong enough to hold a family together. Strong enough in his convictions to launch a new business, based on his own vision. Strong enough to stand up to his mom and all her expectations. Maybe strong enough to strike out on his own, too.

But did it matter? Those fantasies of trying to figure out how to assemble a life with May were built on a dream. He and May had seemed to slide right back into their old, comfortable patterns, but the fault lines underneath were still there.

She still wanted things that he could never give.

"I loved you too much to hold you back," he admitted. The fissures in his heart cracked wide.

Only she wasn't done. Would she ever be? "You wouldn't have. We could have made it long distance."

"For how long?" As if he hadn't gamed this all out in his head. "A few months, even a few years? Sure. But you were never coming back." No matter how much he'd deluded himself that she would. "A long-distance forever isn't the kind of life I wanted. And I sure as hell didn't want it for you."

"That wasn't your choice to make."

The vehemence in her tone took him aback. He opened his mouth to defend himself. Somebody had had to cut the cord, and she'd been so convinced they could have it all. He'd been the realist. He'd hurt them both to save them months—maybe years—of pain.

He shut his trap against the words that would have made him out to be some sort of self-sacrificing martyr.

She was right.

"I know. I'm sorry." He let out a slow breath. "But I don't regret it." The bitterness of bile seeped into his throat. "After all, we both saw how well it went when I did try to hold you back."

"Look—" she started.

He held up a hand, overwhelmed for a second by flashbacks of the stupid, self-sabotaging ultimatum he'd leveled at her. *I need you. Stay. Or never come back.*

Of course she'd left.

"We're going around in circles." They always would be. Neither of them would ever change. "We just keep ending up in the same place."

It was time he sucked it up and got used to it.

"I know," May said. At least she sounded as miserable as he was.

But that didn't make him feel any better.

He pushed his hair back from his eyes. "I don't know why I thought I could do this."

"Me, neither," she said quietly, and the devastation in her gaze struck him to the core.

He'd thought their parting thirteen years ago had been final, but there'd still been tendrils of hope.

This time, there was nothing left but the grim truth.

He couldn't believe he was saying this, but... "I think you should go."

She nodded, a sharp, quick jerk of her head. Another tear slipped down her cheek, but she brushed it away.

She had to go past him to get to his door. He moved to step back, but they both stopped.

Heaven help him.

They both reached for each other at once. He pulled her into his arms, crushing his lips to hers. His blood stirred, the same way it always did when she was close, but he was too sad for this to be about sex. The kiss was fire and need.

But it was also farewell.

She drew back. He released her. She lifted a hand and touched his face, smoothing away a tear he hadn't even realized he'd shed.

Voice shaking, she said, "Goodbye, Han."

He couldn't bring himself to say the same to her. He opened his mouth and he didn't know what was going to come out, but none of it could be good.

Like she understood, she nodded again. She headed to the door. She pulled it open and cast him exactly one backward glance, and he had to bite his tongue to stop himself from trying to talk her out of going.

The sound of the door closing behind her echoed. Long after her footsteps on the stairs had died away, he stared after her.

But she was gone.

And this time, she was never coming back.

# CHAPTER EIGHTEEN

This was *not* how May had expected to spend her last morning in Blue Cedar Falls.

She, her mother, and her sisters sat together at a booth in the dining room of the inn, working on a delicious breakfast that tasted like ashes in her mouth. June was trying her best to carry on a lively discussion of how great Taste had gone. Their mom was nodding and asking politely worded questions, but she wasn't getting much help. Elizabeth and May both looked like something the cat had dragged in—but that would be insulting the cat.

Setting down her fork, May rubbed at her eyes, but the lids were sore from crying herself to sleep. She mentally shook her head at herself in despair. How had she turned into even more of a cliché? Not only had she banged her ex, but she'd let him break her heart again.

And she'd walked into this with her eyes wide open, was the thing. She'd thought she could be a mature adult and take her lumps.

Hearing about his past with Jenny had somehow tossed all her rationality out the window, though. It hadn't been fair of her to be angry about something he did such a long time ago, but she'd suddenly realized exactly how little he understood about what she'd gone through in high school. Which meant he hadn't understood her reasons for leaving. He hadn't understood *her*.

And she could have let it go. Heck, she could have thrown all her stuff in her suitcase and driven away to catch an early morning flight. Thirteen years ago, that's exactly what she might have done.

She'd deserved answers, though.

And she'd gotten way more of them than she'd been prepared for.

All these years, she'd been nursing so much resentment over the way Han had treated her. His decision not to follow her to New York had rocked her world, and his declaration that they shouldn't be exclusive while she was away crumbled what was left of her foundations.

Finally, after his father died, his demand that she come back home had leveled her. None of it had made sense.

Until last night.

He'd loved her as much as she loved him. She hadn't imagined any of it. But he'd still chosen home and family over her dreams, and that was fine. It couldn't have been an easy decision.

The way he took it out of her hands wasn't fine, though. He'd had no right to make all those unilateral decisions. He'd thought he was setting her free, but she'd felt exiled.

Then he'd had the balls to beg her to come back home.

He'd been reeling. Lost in grief and righteously angry, but his demand that she give up everything hurt even more than his decision to let her go. She couldn't keep getting bounced around, so she'd walked away—no matter how much it had ripped her apart to do so.

She'd known their breakup had hurt him, too, but she'd

still been taken aback by the pain in his voice last night. The bitterness.

She'd felt exiled, but he'd felt abandoned. The worst part of it all was that he wasn't even wrong.

Then again, neither was she.

Which was more or less how they'd left it. No matter what they did, they were stuck in this pattern. They'd both hurt each other, and they were both hurting. In the end, though, they wanted different things. There was no way to bridge the divide.

So here she was. Instead of waking up in his arms after one last night of passion, celebrating his incredible victory at Taste of Blue Cedar Falls, she was here, listening to June drone on and on.

May cut a glance to the side. Her only consolation was that Elizabeth appeared to be in roughly the same mood she was, except with the benefit of a pretty heinous hangover, too.

As if she could feel her gaze, her younger sister looked up. May raised her brows, quickly checking in that Elizabeth was all right. Elizabeth shrugged and turned back to her coffee and dry toast.

"Enough," their mother said out of the blue.

"Mom?" June asked.

Their mother shook her head. "Not you." She pulled her mouth to one side. "Though, maybe enough from you, too." She patted June's hand to show she didn't mean that in a bad way. She redirected her attention to May and Elizabeth. "You. And you."

May and Elizabeth glanced at each other, then back at their mom.

"Uh-uh." Their mother made a tutting sound. "No innocent looks. What happened last night?"

"Nothing," Elizabeth said.

Their mom only narrowed her eyes. "I've heard that before."

Ugh, she really had. Elizabeth had gotten into a lot of trouble over the years, and as far as May could tell, she still hadn't lived most of it down. She'd been keeping her applications to various artist residencies a secret to this point, and the idea of her having to talk about them only in the context of a bunch of rejections was too cruel.

"Han and I had a fight," May blurted out.

All eyes turned to her.

Oy. Then again, putting herself under the spotlight like this was pretty cruel, too.

But the truth of the matter was that she was itching to talk about it. She'd been stewing all night, and Ruby was at work, and her next-best choices were…

Well, her family.

With shock, she realized that really was true. She'd spent most of her time working or hanging out with Han while she'd been home, but she'd also gone for mani-pedis with her mom and sisters, gone out for ice cream and lunches and drinks, sat around the dinner table and yes, the corner booth of the Sweetbriar Inn's breakfast room. Spilling her heart out to them didn't feel weird. It felt… normal. Like the kind of thing a sister or a daughter might do, and oh no. She'd thought she was all cried out, but fresh tears formed at the corners of her eyes.

She'd missed her mom. June, Elizabeth. Ned, too. Growing close with them again these past few weeks had been one of the best things about getting to spend some real time here, overshadowed only by reforging her relationship with Han, but well. Everybody knew how that had gone.

Or at least they were about to.

"What happened?" Elizabeth asked carefully. Genuine care shone in her eyes—as well as maybe a little relief about having the spotlight directed away from her.

In fits and starts, she recounted their argument. Elizabeth looked ready to go punch Han in the face, while her mom kept shaking her head, her eyes as damp as May's. June's mouth set itself into a grim line.

May turned to her. "You knew, huh?"

June flicked her gaze to Elizabeth. "About Jenny?"

"Yeah."

Elizabeth nodded. "We both did."

"It didn't last long," June added.

"And it was ages ago."

May looked from one of them to the other. "And you didn't think to tell me?"

"At the time, it seemed kinder not to," June said carefully.

"How about now? When you knew we were hanging out again?"

"Uh," Elizabeth said, "you didn't exactly put a sign up saying you wanted to talk about it."

Their mother shrugged. "I only knew you and Han were together again because you never came home at night anymore. Figured you'd talk about it in your own time."

For crying out loud, how had May created this situation where literally no one in her family felt like they could bring things up with her?

She had a momentary flashback to running into Han her first night home and telling him to his face she wasn't having any emotional reunions.

Maybe it really wasn't such a wonder.

She blinked rapidly and swiped the back of her wrist across her eyes. "I just feel like— I hate that this is how we're going to leave things. It's such a mess."

Tentatively, June reached across the table for May's hand. May placed her palm in her sister's and braced herself. She didn't need some lecture about how living hundreds of miles away meant things would always be messy with the people she cared about back home.

But instead, June just gave her fingers a soft squeeze. "It sucks."

"It does," May agreed.

"Like, a lot," Elizabeth said.

Their mother did a few suspicious blinks of her own. Despite the mistiness in her eyes, her voice was clear and steady as she raised a brow at May. "But you're still going back to New York tonight."

"I have to." She didn't have any more vacation time, and she had seven meetings in the office tomorrow, not to mention a two-day trip to some fancy ice sculpture "experience" some other billionaire was hosting at a resort in Chile for the weekend. She was pretty sure Zahra had booked it for her as an apology after the harshness of their last call.

Then there was the small issue of the story she still had to write about Blue Cedar Falls. She had no idea how she was going to sit back and make it sound like she'd had a fabulous time—she had, of course. But it was intertwined with such bittersweet feelings about everything she was leaving behind.

Her mother nodded, as if she could hear all of that. "Then you make your peace with it being a mess." She shrugged.

"I don't know how to do that," May admitted.

Her mom reached for her coffee cup with her stronger

hand and brought it to her lips. "It's your choice. But you either live with a mess..." Lifting a shoulder, she took a sip. Her gaze was supportive but unflinching. "...Or you find a way to clean it up."

———

A few hours later, it was time to leave for the airport, and May hadn't even come close to figuring out how to clean up the mess she and Han had made. It wasn't for lack of trying, though. She'd nominally spent the entire afternoon hanging out with her family, and she'd tried to enjoy it, even. But mostly, she'd been moping.

As she stood up from the table, leaving behind two-thirds of a jigsaw puzzle she, her mom, and her sisters had been overly ambitious enough to try to start—and which Sunny the cat had been eyeing up like a tasty mouse all afternoon—her mother fixed her with a somber look. May shook her head, and her mom offered a sad smile.

"Is it that time?" June asked, standing as well.

"Afraid so."

Elizabeth pouted. "Bummer." She got up and wrapped her arms around May. "Was awesome having you in town."

May hugged her back. She didn't hesitate to agree. "Yeah, it was."

"And thanks." Her sister pulled back by a fraction. "You know. For everything."

Glancing at June and their mom, May nodded. To Elizabeth alone, she said, "I'm sure it'll all work out."

Elizabeth rolled her eyes. "I'm not." She let go and stepped away. "But that's okay. I'm good at rolling with the punches."

"You really are."

Her mom wedged her way forward next. "You call more often, you hear?"

May enveloped her mom in a big hug. It was hard to believe that a few short weeks ago she'd been so concerned about her mother's health. She might be a little worse for the wear after her stroke, and her hand and smile might never be quite as strong, but she was just as fierce as ever. "I will."

"And visit more often, too."

"Definitely." And she always promised that. This time, though, she really meant it. She couldn't imagine going more than a year again.

The door to the apartment creaked open, and Ned popped in his head. "I hear a tearful goodbye going on in here?"

May swabbed at her damp eyes. "No tears here."

"That's my girl." He claimed the next hug. "Take care of yourself up there, sweetie."

"Will do."

Finally, it was just June left to go. May turned to her big sister with a heart that was somehow both heavy and full. In a sign of how much had changed between them these past few weeks, June greeted her with a smile.

"Thanks for everything," she said, tugging her in. "You helping out these past couple weeks was huge."

"I'm sorry I can't do more."

"We've got it under control." June gave her a strong squeeze. "Maybe this'll be the kick in the pants I need to finally hire some help again."

"What are we?" Elizabeth complained. "Chopped liver?"

Their mother playfully swatted at her. "Shh. They're having a moment."

"It's a good question," Ned chimed in.

Tossing her gaze skyward, June pulled back. "I appreciate you all."

"That's better," Elizabeth said, crossing her arms.

"But seriously." May looked around the room. "I'm going to come home more."

"We'll hold you to it," June said.

For the first time in her life, May really hoped she would.

With that, there were no more goodbyes to say. Her bag stood ready by the door.

As she headed for the exit, she cast a glance over her shoulder. Ned had wrapped an arm around Elizabeth and their mom. June moved to stand on their mother's other side, completing the picture, and already, it felt like May was on the other side of the world, looking at a photo of them on her phone.

"Have a safe trip," her mother called.

"I will."

She made it all the way to the car before she let a little hiccup escape her lips. She brushed away the couple of tears that had fallen. This wasn't goodbye. It was so long for now—or something like that. But especially after the painful way she and Han had ended things last night, the difference felt hard to hold on to.

As she drove down Main Street, every storefront and restaurant brought back a different memory—some from these weeks together and some from what felt like a lifetime ago. The Junebug was packed full of them, of course, but so was Dottie Gallagher's florist shop, where Han had bought her corsage before prom. Groovy Tunes Records, where they used to hang out sometimes after school. The bookshop where he took her on their first date, because even then he knew her well enough to understand that was what she would enjoy the most.

The Jade Garden. Where he was probably working right now, figuring out his next move for starting his own place.

More tears stung the corners of her eyes, but she was *not* going to cry anymore. How on earth was she not a dried-up, shriveled husk at this point?

White-knuckling the wheel, she made it to the outskirts of town before she gave up and pulled over at a gas station. Her tank was low anyway—probably for the best to fill up now. It definitely wasn't about how her vision was so blurry she wasn't sure she could safely keep her eyes on the road.

She pulled up at a pump and gave herself one minute to let the rest of her feelings pour out of her eyeballs. When that was done, she mopped her face with a tissue, feeling no clearer, but less...well, damp.

She got out to deal with the gas, except of course the stupid credit card slot wasn't working. She managed to restrain herself from kicking the thing. She let out a low growl of frustration and turned to head into the station.

Just as she was reaching for the handle of the door, it swung outward. She jerked backward, narrowly missing getting hit by the door itself.

She wasn't so lucky when the person inside didn't notice her and practically walked into her. A splash of coffee flew out of its cup, landing on May's shirt, and she let out a little yelp.

"Watch where you're—" the person started.

May flinched, her gaze darting up.

To find Jenny freaking Sullivan standing there in front of her.

All the usual awful reactions started happening in

May's body and brain, but she'd had enough. "Watch where *you're* going."

Blinking, Jenny stared at her in confusion. "Sorry, I—"

"Save it." May went to brush past her and into the station, her heart pounding, but Jenny stopped her.

"Hey."

May ignored her and kept going.

"Hey, May," Jenny tried again.

May's face was on fire, but for once, she squashed the instinct to run. The instinct to take a swing was way stronger. She whirled around. "What?"

"Just…" Jenny huffed out a sigh, like this was taking all her will power. "Look. Tori pointed out that I was kind of a b-word last night."

Which part was worse? "Kind of" or "last night"?

Stepping back into the sun, May let the door to the gas station swing closed. No need to waste all their AC—or force the attendant to be an audience.

"Rubbing that thing about Han in your face was mean." And—was Jenny actually squirming?

May took a couple of deep breaths, really looking at the woman.

The past decade or so hadn't been unkind to Jenny. She was as pretty and skinny and blond as ever. But there was a sharpness to her that didn't used to be there. Like maybe things hadn't exactly been on the easy street for her.

Considering what Han had told May about Jenny and her mom, maybe they never had been. Back in high school, she'd acted like a queen and treated everybody else like garbage. Was that her uniquely crappy way of deflecting from her own pain?

Did it matter? She could have the best reasons for being awful, but in the end, she'd still been awful.

May exhaled long and hard. Jenny's apology was inadequate in the extreme, and it was for all the wrong things, but it still softened something inside May that had been clenched for all these years.

"Look," May said, "yeah. It was not cool. But in the end it kind of helped me have a conversation I needed to have. So don't sweat it."

Jenny visibly relaxed.

But that wasn't what May was going for, either.

She wasn't sure what came over her. She lifted her chin. Had she ever noticed she was the same height as Jenny? Back in high school, the girl had always seemed a foot taller. Probably because May had her head down, her shoulders hunched.

Not anymore.

"What you should be apologizing for is all the crap you pulled thirteen years ago."

Jenny startled, her eyes flying wide. May wanted to be annoyed at that, but she was mostly annoyed at herself. No, she'd never fought back before. She hadn't been strong enough.

That wasn't the problem anymore. "You made me feel like I was worthless, and like I didn't belong."

"Look, that was ages ago—"

"For you. For me, it's every day." Or at least it had been. The subtle twinge of doubt about whether or not she fit in any space had followed her around her entire life, but it was suddenly starting to fade. Coming home had healed something inside May. "So let me answer all those questions you used to ask me." Flashes of Jenny's taunts came to her, but she swatted every one away with aplomb. "Do I wear a kimono at home? No, and that's Japanese anyway. What is China like? Amazing, crowded, full of history and pride—you should be so lucky as to go there someday."

May advanced, and Jenny took a step back, and she had never retreated before. Not once.

"Tell me to go back where I came from," May said, and there was a growl in her voice she barely recognized.

Jenny shook her head, her eyes wide. "I'm sorry. Jeez— I didn't mean—"

"Yes. You did." May stopped, her pulse echoing in her ears. Something in her chest went silent and still, clarity eclipsing her thoughts. "You know where I come from?" She didn't wait for an answer. "Here." She pointed at the ground, and her vision threatened to mist over again, but for once it wasn't out of sadness or outrage or shame. "I come from right here. And I'll come back whenever I like."

This wasn't Jenny's town anymore. It was May's.

And she was never going to be scared away from it again.

———

Taking the train into the city from the airport, May kept looking around her. The buzz of life and activity on public transportation usually excited her. People-watching or just sitting there in quiet communion, reading alongside folks from all walks of life, was one of her greatest simple pleasures.

It didn't seem so fun today.

The smells and the jostling motion of the train, the constant chatter, the guy in the back playing music through headphones too loud—none of it set her at ease. She'd only spent a few weeks in Blue Cedar Falls, but its quiet rhythms had seeped into her. She'd gotten accustomed to running into people she knew wherever she went, to casual greetings outside every shop and everyone knowing her name.

Back at her apartment, she drew in a deep sigh. Only her relief didn't last. The Manhattan streets were too loud, but in here, the silence pressed in on her. How many times had she wished she could get some time alone while she was suffering constant interruptions at her mother's dining room table? Now the isolation felt like it could smother her.

A text from Ruby pulled her out of her spiraling thoughts. She seized on the picture of Todd the tortoise—this time with what looked like a crocheted set of dinosaur spikes arranged on his shell—and the caption that said simply, *RAWR*.

*Be there in 5*, she replied.

She was out the door and down the block in four. She pressed the button for Ruby's apartment, holding it down too long. The second the door released, she dashed inside and up the stairs.

Ruby stood just inside her apartment, Todd in her hands. May grabbed the tortoise and clutched the little guy to her chest, but there was a reason reptiles made lousy pets. He was no comfort at all.

Ruby took one look at her and frowned. "What happened?"

"So much," May said, her eyes leaking *again*, and holy cow, if she didn't stop spontaneously bursting into tears soon, she was going to lose it. "I just—"

Ruby reeled her in. May clutched Todd harder and sagged into her friend's arms. "There, there," Ruby said, only sort of ironically.

"For the first time in my life," May murmured, sniffling into Ruby's hair, "I don't know what I want."

Ruby laughed fondly and hugged her tight. "Welcome to what life is like for us mere mortals." She let go, looking into May's eyes and squeezing her upper arms. "Come on. Let me make you about fifteen cocktails, and you can tell me all about it."

May sniffed again and nodded, grateful to have someone in this city she could turn to.

When everybody else she wanted to talk to in this world were hundreds of miles away.

# CHAPTER NINETEEN

✿ ✿ ✿ ✿ ✿ ✿ ✿ ✿ ✿ ✿ ✿ ✿

P enny for your thoughts?"

Han looked up from the mostly empty bottle of Tsingtao he'd been contemplating for probably way too long. All around the Moore family's backyard, folks were having fun, celebrating Bobbi and Caitlin's wedding. The bride and bride were out there on the dance floor, looking radiant. Han had tried his best to be cheery, too, but sometime around the third slow song Caitlin's brother—the aspirational DJ—had put on, he'd given up.

Passing Han a fresh beer, Clay plunked himself down into the seat next to his, groaning as he stretched his bum leg.

"You're not on duty." Han dismissed him. "No need to play bartender tonight."

"Ha-ha," Clay said humorlessly.

Devin pulled out the chair to Han's other side, and Han resisted the urge to bang his head on the table.

Yay. Gang up on Han time again.

"Shrimp are awesome," Devin said, his mouth full and his plate even fuller.

"Of course they are; I made them."

"Just saying. No need to be all cranky pants."

"Pretty sure he's forgotten how to be anything else." His sister Zoe patted him on the back before kissing the top of Devin's head. Devin smiled up at her, touching her arm affectionately, which was their right. They were together.

Clay and June were together, his sister and his best friend were together, Bobbi and Caitlin were together *forever* now.

All the romance in the air was making Han sick.

"I'm not cranky," he lied.

"Uh-huh." Zoe cast him a concerned look before walking away to join June by the cake.

"You're really, really cranky," Clay told him.

"Like you're one to talk."

"He's right," Devin said.

Devin had slightly more room to talk, but Han still didn't want to hear.

Han gulped down the last of his old beer and picked up the fresh one, sliding his chair back from the table. "I should go check on Naomi."

Devin hooked his ankle behind the front leg of Han's chair and pulled him back. "Pretty sure Naomi's doing fine." He tipped his head toward where she was loading up Bobbi's dad's plate with yet more shrimp. As if on cue, she glanced over at them and gave Han a thumbs-up.

Traitor.

Darn good assistant chef/server. But still a traitor.

Clay reached past Han to grab a shrimp off Devin's plate. "These are really good, you know."

"I hear."

All evening, people had been complimenting him on the food. Normally, that would have put him on cloud nine. But any thoughts he'd had of branching out on his own—with or without his mother's blessing—had been squashed. He'd been too busy being miserable.

But not cranky.

"Seriously, man." Devin kicked his chair. "Spill."

"There's nothing to talk about." Han looked over at his best friend with a glower. "Especially not to you." His chest panged. "Last thing I need is you blabbering about 'I told you so.'"

"I won't." Devin wiped his fingers on a napkin before making an X over his tie. "Cross my heart."

Han snickered. "Yeah, right. Go ahead, tell me I had this coming."

"Nope. Not gonna happen."

"You love rubbing crap in my face."

"I do not." Devin rolled his eyes. "I just take my responsibility to rub crap in your face very seriously." He nudged Han's elbow with his own. "Someone has to look out for you, you know."

Clay nodded, and Han's throat got a little tight. He might be doomed to spend his life alone except for the company of his mother and his dog, but at least he had these guys.

He regarded his beer bottle intensely. "I just miss her, you know?"

"May?" Clay asked.

Han nodded. Who else?

May had left. She'd taken the crushed remnants of his heart with her, along with his ambitions for his restaurant, his muse, his hope for his life ever changing at all.

And he knew that was pathetic. He shouldn't be dependent on any one person like that. He wouldn't be— not forever.

But for now, while the wound was still fresh, all he could think about was how she'd supported him, believed in him, inspired him. He hadn't cooked so creatively in years as he had when she'd been by his side. All his dreams had felt fresh, new and—most dangerous of all— possible.

Then she'd left, exactly like he'd always known she would.

And now here he was. The sad guy at his friends' wedding.

Even his mom—the patron saint of spoilsports—was having a good time out there. He stared at her morosely. She'd worn a new dress and everything. Goaded on by Zoe, she'd even done the chicken dance. Half of him was happy to see her having fun.

The other half just kept compounding his misery.

The two of them had hardly talked this week. If she felt bad for squashing his dreams, she hadn't had any- thing to say about it. If she'd overheard him and May finally hashing out thirteen years' worth of resentment, well...she hadn't mentioned that, either. As for him, he'd kept his thoughts to himself, as well.

Like usual, they were a pair.

"That sucks, man," Devin said. Han had to give him credit. He kept his voice carefully neutral.

Han turned to look at him. Bitterness coated the back of his tongue. "Not like I didn't know what I was getting myself into, right?"

"Don't put words in my mouth." Devin sat up straighter in his chair. "Was I worried? Yeah. Did I want you to get hurt again? Of course not."

Clay took a swig of his beer. "You guys seemed really happy together."

They had been. Not that it mattered.

Devin clapped him on the shoulder. "Wish you could have found a way to make it work this time."

"Yeah." Han couldn't keep talking about this or he was going to be the *really* sad guy in the corner, and that was just embarrassing. "Me, too." He made sure Devin's leg was clear of his chair before pushing it back. "Now seriously, I gotta check on the food. I'm working here."

"Fine, fine." Devin held up his hands. "Don't say we didn't try, though."

"Hang out tomorrow?" Clay asked.

Han glanced back at his friends. "Yeah. That'd be good."

"Bring some tissues." Devin smirked. "We'll put on *The Notebook* or something."

"You guys are the worst," Han said fondly. He liked the movie, and they knew it.

"Darn right we are," Devin agreed, giving him a salute and an empathetic smile. Clay held up his bottle, and the two clinked.

Shaking his head at them both, Han wandered over to where Naomi was starting to clean up. The last of the shrimp had been disposed of, and the happy couple was almost ready to cut the cake, so their job was basically complete. He thanked Naomi profusely. She'd done great, handling most of the serving while he'd been celebrating with friends. And maybe moping, but whatever.

Bobbi accosted him just as he was finishing packing the final couple of trays. Launching herself at him, she wrapped her arms around him, and he caught her the best he could, trying to keep from messing up her white linen dress.

"Thank you," she babbled. Tears beaded at the corners

of her eyes. "It was so perfect, you have no idea. Exactly what I wanted."

Caitlin hustled over in her matching white vest, slacks, tie and collared shirt, and tugged at Bobbi's arm. "Let him breathe, babe."

"Seriously, Han, you did so great."

"It was really good," Caitlin agreed. "We owe you."

"I'm just—I'm just so happy," Bobbi bawled.

"Oh-*kay*, let's go find you some water," Caitlin said, but she was smiling the whole time.

Han shook his head. Bobbi had been hitting the champagne pretty hard. She had every right to celebrate, though. Less than a year ago, she'd been stressing coming out to her parents; now here she was, newly married in their backyard. "Good call."

"Come on." Caitlin led her away, and Han wished them both well.

He helped Naomi finish packing up and sent her back to the Jade Garden with the truck and a hefty bonus. "You sure, boss?" she asked.

"You earned it."

She grinned. "Thanks."

He ambled back toward the party still going hard in the yard. Caitlin's brother had put on *another* nineties getting-it-on love song, and Devin and Clay had rejoined their girlfriends on the dance floor. Bobbi and Caitlin were out there, too, Bobbi leaning heavily on Caitlin, and Caitlin looking like she'd won the jackpot as her new wife sagged into her.

Han's smile faded. Back to being the seventh wheel, he supposed, as he hit up the cooler for another beer. As he popped its top, he turned, figuring he'd find himself a new corner to be sad in.

What he found instead was his mom.

She cocked her head to the side as she regarded him. "You haven't danced all night."

"Rub it in, would you?"

"Humor me." She held out her arm.

He shook his head, holding up a hand to the sky to indicate the sultry music. "Nope, no way I am dancing with my mom to *this*."

She chuckled. As if on cue, the current song faded out, and an ancient seventies folk song came on. One she used to hum to him when he was a kid. He felt it like a— loving—punch to the gut.

Casting him a sly smile, she held out her arm again. "Slipped a little something extra in the tip jar."

He glanced around. Bobbi's dad had wandered out to the dance floor and gently cut in. Caitlin's father did the same to her. Devin and Zoe and June and Clay gracefully exited, and a few other older couples took their place. He could say no and go join his friends, but it'd be a pretty jerk thing to do. And after a week of near silence, it wasn't as if he didn't appreciate his mom finally offering an olive branch. Even if it was a really, really awkward one.

With a put-upon sigh, he set down his beer and led her to the edge of the dance floor. He took her hand in his and put his other on her back. They swayed, stiff and awkward, and with room for about three Holy Ghosts between them.

"Beautiful ceremony," his mom said after a minute.

"Yeah, it was."

In a careful tone, she added, "Food was pretty all right, too."

He glanced down, his brows pinching. "Uh, thanks?"

"I never had a chance to try any of it last week," she reminded him.

Yeah, he'd noticed.

"You mean before you told me it wasn't good enough?"

She tightened her grip on his hand. "That is *not* what I said."

"I mean—"

"I said your math was no good. Never your food."

"Does it matter?"

"Of course it matters." She stopped moving and pulled away so they were looking at each other more directly. A fire blazed in her eyes that he hadn't seen in a long, long time. "You matter to me, *hǔ zǐ.*"

Tiger son. His mom's rough equivalent of "baby boy."

Forget a gut punch. This was reaching into his insides and squeezing.

"Look, Mom—"

"I said a lot of things the other night. When I say I depend on you, I mean that like a good thing." For the first time, a bit of doubt entered her gaze. "But maybe, I depend on you too much."

"You're my mom. You can always depend on me."

"You're my son. You should always be able to depend on *me.*" Her voice wavered for a second. "Ever since your father died, it's been the other way around."

Han didn't quite know what was going on here. They never talked about this kind of stuff. They were still standing at the edge of the dance floor. People were looking at them. He glanced around. "Mom..."

She took his hand again, resting her other palm on his shoulder. They started to sway again, but it was different now.

"You were a good boy. Always. Did what you were told. Sometimes even when we didn't tell you."

"Okay…"

"I know you gave up everything, after."

His chest was too tight. "It's fine."

"It's not fine," she said sharply. She made a *tch*ing sound behind her teeth. "You were always there for me, for your sisters, for this family. But until the other night, you never fought for yourself." She looked him square in the eye, a new conviction in her gaze. "It was about damn time."

He scrunched up his brow. "Wait—"

He'd promised himself he wouldn't apologize for speaking his mind, but he'd been wholly unprepared for her to not just let him off the hook but to actually be…proud of him for going toe to toe with her?

"Your food is good. Your restaurant plan—maybe needs work. Your math, definitely."

"Look—"

She pinched his arm, hard. "Listen to your mother."

"I thought I was supposed to be fighting you."

"Stand up to me. Tell me what you want. Tell me when I'm wrong, or not giving you a fair shot."

He swallowed hard. "You didn't give me a fair shot. My restaurant could work. I have so many ideas."

"Then you'll find a way." One corner of her mouth curled up, and she patted his chest. "What is it American parents always say?" Her eyes twinkled. "'I believe in you.'"

He rolled his eyes and tugged her in, giving her a hug right there in the middle of this stupid dance floor. "You're an American parent."

Always had been. Always would.

The song ended, and Caitlin's freaking brother transitioned right into "Y.M.C.A." Han groaned.

His mother took his hand and pulled him toward the grass. "Quick, run—before Zoe sees us."

His sister let out a whoop as she dragged Devin and June—who dragged Clay, in turn—out to dance. "Come on, losers," she called at Han and their mom. Letting go of Devin's hand now that he was stuck there, she reached for Han's.

His mom held on tightly, though. "I mean it, Han," she said quietly.

"Okay, Mom."

She squeezed his palm hard. "The restaurant is not the only thing you should be fighting for, either, you know."

His first instinct was to put his hands over his ears and shout, "La, la, la, la." That was generally how he used to react to his parents making any comments about his relationship.

But the frank nature of her advice had him squashing that impulse.

Before he could think of an appropriate response, Zoe yanked harder on his other hand. His mom let go.

"Think about it," she said, giving him a little wave.

"Wait—how am I getting dragged into this and you're not?" he called as he was hauled onto the floor.

His mother shrugged and retreated to go stand by Bobbi's father, who had also escaped.

"What was that all about?" Zoe asked him as she danced.

The chorus of the song hit, and despite himself, he threw his arms in the air. "Just how I should stand up for myself when people try to get me to do things I don't want to do."

"You mean like this?"

"Definitely." He kept dancing anyway, laughing at Clay

making an absolute mess of the steps and June burying her face in her hands.

Dancing with his friends wasn't exactly a hardship, though. Without any additional protest, he allowed himself to be pulled into the scrum. Devin even shot him a smile. "'Bout time," he mouthed, and yeah, okay. Maybe being the sad guy in the corner was overrated—especially when he had friends who wanted to include him.

As he got his dorky, dorky groove on, he couldn't help but think about what his mother had said. The way she'd basically praised him for standing up to her. For standing up for himself.

All this time, he'd been putting off his own ambitions, trying to live up to the silent expectations his parents had placed on his shoulders. His duty to his family had been the be-all and end-all for him for—well, pretty much forever. He didn't regret that. They were his foundation, and no sacrifice was too big where they were concerned. Whatever they needed, he would always be there for them.

But how much of the expectations he'd been laboring under had his mother laid on his back?

And how much had he put there all on his own?

As he looked at his little sister busting a move with her boyfriend—at his mom socializing with her friends—it struck him, though. Did they need him?

Or had he been hiding behind them as an excuse?

If he pushed his duty out of his mind—and that was a herculean task, but he could do it, for brief stretches at least... If he was going to fight for himself... What would he even want?

A restaurant of his own. Definitely. But that wasn't it.

If the sky were the limit, he'd be running it with May by his side. She could have her freedom. He didn't care if she traveled half the time or if she was obsessed with her career. She'd always had big dreams, and she'd never hesitated to follow them.

If she was his dream... If being with her was what he truly wanted in his life...

Then what would he sacrifice to be able to make a future with her?

It was like the sky opened up and dropped a ten-ton piano on his head.

All the fantasies he'd concocted and discarded came back to him in force. The idea of chasing after May had occurred to him enough times by now, but never once had he taken it seriously.

Suddenly, for the life of him, he couldn't understand why.

He'd let her go half a dozen times now, it felt like. He'd done it by telling her what he wanted without listening to her. He'd done it by lying, too. This last time, they'd both said goodbye with brutal honesty.

The one thing he'd never done, though—the one route he'd never tried—

It was the one his mother had just accused him of shying away from.

The only answer left was that he had to put his heart—and maybe his entire conception of his life—on the line.

If he wanted to be with May, he had to make the decision and commit.

Quite simply, he had to fight.

# CHAPTER TWENTY

* * * * * * * * * * * * *

Trudging through the door to her apartment, May let her bag slip off her arm and down to the floor. Her wheeled carry-on followed it, landing with a clatter. She locked up behind herself and sagged.

Well, that had happened.

Two days in the mountains of southern Chile had been as cold as she would have expected them to be, in terms of the temperature. What she hadn't expected was how cold her reaction to them had been. The new Patagonian winter "experience" she'd been sent to cover had been...fine. Ice carvings were neat, and they got even neater when you put colored LEDs in them and served obscene amounts of pisco—a sour cocktail made from grape brandy that was usually one of her favorites. Unique as the trip had been, it had somehow failed to faze her, though. The entire time, she'd stood there making small talk with obscenely wealthy jet-setters, and she'd just been *bored*.

No one had said anything interesting the entire time. No one had challenged her. No one had known her.

A year ago, she would have considered that to be a good thing. Now, she couldn't help longing for simple food, good conversation with close friends in a small, unpretentious setting. Her family.

Han.

Huffing out a breath, she shook her head at herself. She hauled herself across the space, drained and desperate for a shower.

But even as she turned on the tap and got in, disappointment tugged at her. This entire apartment was set up to be her refuge from the world. She'd chosen every fixture and decoration. The shower head had a thousand five-star reviews, but the pulsating jets couldn't soothe her. She let out a wet, sad hiccup of a laugh beneath the spray. Her parents' shower was absolute crap. The tiles were old, and there was still the shadow of a cartoon her sister Elizabeth had drawn on the wall in Sharpie back when she was twelve.

Gazing at the natural slate and sea glass she'd picked when she'd redone her own bathroom, she found herself longing for that stupid drawing.

She longed for the plain, off-white, built-in shelves of Han's shower. She longed for his hot body behind hers, his arms and scent surrounding her as he kissed her deep and slow.

With a growl, she turned the shower to pure cold. Two seconds later, icy water poured over her. Shuddering, she flipped off the tap. She put her hands over her face and dug the heels of her palms into her eyes.

One week. It'd been one week since she left Blue Cedar Falls. Since her big, final, blowout fight with Han where they'd laid all their cards on the table.

It still hurt like it had happened yesterday.

She missed him so much it felt like it had been a year.

Numb, she dried off and padded to her dresser to put

on her raggediest, most comfortable pajamas, but even they didn't help. The whole place was too quiet. The decor she loved suddenly felt stark and cold. Her refuge felt like a cage.

Maybe the frayed shorts and holey T-shirt hadn't been the right answer. If she gave Ruby a call, her friend would probably be up for a night out.

Only that wasn't what she wanted, either. Ruby had been great this past week. After May had vomited her entire sob story at her, she'd let her stay over and fed her ice cream and cocktails. Ever since, her friend had kept checking up on her. It'd been nice, knowing she had someone in her corner.

But she really was tired. The trip had taken a lot out of her. She didn't have the energy to head right back out the door.

Thinking of Ruby, she wandered over to Todd's terrarium. The tortoise was sunning himself on a rock under a heat lamp, and she shifted the top off to reach in and pet his shell. She got him some food and refilled his water.

"Whadaya say?" she asked him. "Quiet night in?"

He blinked at her, emotionless as ever.

Then he turned his head toward her desk.

The guy didn't know what he was doing, but she followed his gaze and groaned.

He was right.

Usually, she was pretty good at getting writing work done on planes and in hotel rooms, but she'd hadn't managed a single word this trip.

She glanced at the calendar above her desk. Her one act of productivity since she'd returned had been flipping it to the correct month and circling the due date for her article about Blue Cedar Falls. She had two days to bang the thing out and absolutely no idea what it was going to say.

"You're the worst," she mumbled at Todd. She imagined he shrugged, but he was a freaking tortoise. Did tortoises even have shoulders?

With a sigh, she put the top back on his enclosure. She washed her hands and fixed a cup of coffee before grabbing her laptop and plunking it down on her desk. She settled herself in her chair, fired up a new document, and...

Stared at the blinking cursor.

She cracked her knuckles. Okay, no big deal. A basic travel piece about a buzzy, off-the-beaten-track destination. She wrote these in her sleep.

*Nestled in the western Carolina mountains, Blue Cedar Falls is...*

What? An idyllic small town with perfect spring weather, and quirky independently owned businesses.

Ugh, it all sounded so trite.

She deleted her first half of a sentence and tried again.

*If you've been on the internet recently, you've no doubt spotted a three-legged calico cat judging you in memes that range from hilarious to pointed.*

She deleted it all again.

Yes, her mother's cat had been the star that had put Blue Cedar Falls on Zahra's radar, but the article wasn't about Sunny.

What was it about?

She tried again, doing her best to push past the first line. These kinds of overviews usually wrote themselves. They were all the same. *Passage* had a winning formula, and her mastery of it had driven her career. She just had to bang it out.

Over and over, she wrote and erased and wrote and erased. With every iteration, her frustration only grew, and by the time she trashed her tenth stab at it, she was reaching a boiling point.

All her tricks—more coffee, a snack, a few stretches, even more coffee—*none* of them worked. Her anxiety ratcheted up. This should be a piece of cake. Was she broken?

Or was writing about the best and most painful week of her life not the usual piece-of-cake assignment? She'd never tried to put together an article about anything so intensely personal before. In her notes, she'd tried to reduce her entire trip to the Carolina mountains down to the easiest, breeziest morsels. *Passage* readers liked to keep it light and aspirational.

Maybe that was the problem.

Nothing about her trip had been light. It had been the heaviest assignment of her career, weighed down by family drama and relationship baggage at every turn.

It hadn't exactly been "aspirational," either. Blue Cedar Falls didn't have any of the luxury amenities that had started to make other destinations blur together in her mind. It hadn't needed them. The town and its surroundings had charm, instead. Friendly people, perfect spring weather, quirky independently owned businesses...

Those adjectives didn't seem so cheesy anymore, once she matched them with her stepfather's pancakes, her sister's meticulous landscaping. Bobbi's bakery. The new cottages Devin's construction company had been putting up. The Junebug.

The Jade Garden.

She'd headed home with every intention of hating it there, but despite her prejudices, Blue Cedar Falls had won her over. She hadn't been bored for one second. The town had character. Soul—when so many of the places she'd visited of late felt soulless.

And maybe that was her way in.

With a sudden flash of inspiration, she erased the contents of her document again.

*At first glance, Blue Cedar Falls, North Carolina, is not the kind of place you might imagine as a* Passage *destination. I certainly didn't when I first got off the plane. Or out of my rental car. A solid two hours from civilization, connected to the world only by back roads, this little hamlet is the definition of "off the beaten track."*

*But spend one day there—or better yet, a week—and I dare you not to be won over.*

Her fingers took over, typing away at speeds she rarely reached. In a smooth flow, she described the quaint attractions of Main Street, the way it married the traditional small-town vibe with fresh, youthful energy. She snuck in a few mentions of her mother's cat, of course, and segued into a quick overview of the surrounding areas, which had merits of their own.

But she kept coming back to Blue Cedar Falls itself. Its restaurants, its wildlife, its inn, its antique shops, and its anachronistic record store. Its people. Its overwhelming sense of community.

Which led her to the way that community had come together at Taste of Blue Cedar Falls. The array of local dining options could have given any major metro a run for its money, but somehow it transcended the sum of its parts. Instead of seasoned, classically trained chefs cranking out gastronomic delights, the entire event had been held together by raw talents cooking with their hearts.

And wasn't that just the crux of it all?

Blue Cedar Falls didn't offer the kind of anonymous, interchangeable opulence that had slowly dulled her senses over the past few years.

It had offered home-cooked meals. Imagination. People who engaged her—and not just because she was some sort of prodigal daughter. She'd seen other travelers welcomed with the same energy.

She'd found a peace there she'd thought she'd lost.

She looked up from her screen, shocked to find tears running down her face. She swiped them away, but as she did, her gaze caught on her surroundings. Her four square walls that she'd imagined were her home. Her view out over the East Village which she'd imagined was her city, only it wasn't. She knew—really knew—like, six people here. Her life might be out in the wider world.

But her home…The place where she'd felt most welcomed, most safe, and most secure…

The most loved…

Was Blue Cedar Falls.

Surrounded by her family and by the people she'd left behind but who had become as good of friends to her in a few short weeks as anyone else had in literal years. Sure, she had Ruby here, but they'd known each other since college. Was there anyone else she felt as connected to as her mom and sisters?

Was there anyone she'd ever, in her entire life, loved as much as Han?

"What am I *doing* here?"

She rose from her desk with a lurch.

All this time she'd wasted, running from her home and running from the man she was in love with. She'd been chasing a dream, but what was left for her to achieve? She'd lived in New York. She'd traveled the globe. She'd risen to the top of her field and become a master of her craft, and all she wanted was to go back home. To Han.

She wanted to go to bed with him every night and wake up with him every morning. She didn't want to have to worry what his mom or his best friend was going to think. She wanted to test out his recipes and cook by his side.

And she still wanted to write. Of course she did.

But she wanted to write pieces like this. Ones that made her think and feel, about places that meant something to her.

She didn't know how she was going to cobble together a career from that, but she also didn't care. She had a nest egg and a great network of professional contacts. The cost of living in Blue Cedar Falls was so low, she could freelance and work at the inn, and it would be fine.

It would be amazing.

She couldn't wait.

Her exhaustion of a couple of hours ago disappeared in a puff of smoke. Fresh energy—or maybe that third cup of coffee—kicked in, and she grabbed her laptop. She threw it and its cord back into her bag. Everything in her carry-on was dirty, but it didn't matter. They had laundry machines in Blue Cedar Falls. She might not be able to get a direct flight to Asheville tonight, but she could almost definitely get to Charlotte. It'd be a slightly longer drive, but that was fine. She pulled up the app for her preferred airline on her phone and started searching for the next available flight. As she waited for the results to load, she spotted poor Todd in his terrarium, though. Crap. If she had it her way, she wouldn't be back for a while. She should bring him to Ruby's—or maybe just haul him along with her. Could you even take a tortoise through airport security? No, Ruby's was the way to go. She should really say goodbye to her best friend in New York anyway; if she didn't, she'd never hear the end of it.

Resolved, she scooped Todd up and put him into his little carrier. "Sorry, buddy," she murmured to him.

Tortoise, carry-on, computer bag, check, check, and check. She turned toward the door, grasped the handle.

And pulled it open, only to have a minor heart attack.

Because there, standing on her welcome mat, his own duffel bag slung over his shoulder, creepy garden gnome in hand...

Was Han.

———

Han still had his hand in the air, ready to knock, when the door to May's apartment swung open, revealing none other than the girl he'd traveled across half a dozen state lines to see.

She was so beautiful, he could hardly keep his feet.

Every emotion possible rushed through him as he stood there, drinking her in. Relief—it had only been a little over a week since he'd seen her, but it felt like months. Elation and excitement, nerves and terror.

Dismay.

She had her laptop bag slung over her shoulder, a weird blue plastic tackle box in one hand, and the handle of a wheeled carry-on in the other. His stomach sank. Where was she going?

What would have happened if he'd gotten here five minutes later?

The past twenty-four hours had been so impulsive. He'd been in such a rush, he'd scarcely stopped to think things through.

One minute, his mom was telling him that he should fight harder for what he wanted in his life, the next he was waking up at the crack of dawn, packing a bag and booking a flight. He hadn't called or texted May to ask if she'd actually be here.

Only sheer luck had brought him to her door in time. Once, he might have looked at that as a strike against him.

Today, he was choosing to view it as the universe smiling down on him.

May opened her mouth to speak, finally breaking the shocked moment, but he cut her off.

He'd been rehearsing what he would say all day, driving to the airport and through two flights and a layover and what felt like hours of circling LaGuardia, waiting to land.

It all flew out of his head.

"I need to go back home at least twice a year," he told her. "Maybe more if Mom needs me, or if she has health problems." He sucked in a breath, trying to keep up with himself. "I know that'll be an issue, especially depending on what kind of job I can get."

Opening his own place in Blue Cedar Falls was one thing, but opening one in New York City was going to be another. He'd have to work his way up in other people's kitchens. Having zero creative control after being co-owner of the Jade Garden was going to suck, but he didn't care.

It didn't matter what he was doing—or where. So long as he was doing it with May.

That didn't mean he didn't have conditions.

"And we'll have to get a place that allows pets." Who knew how Ling-Ling would react to the city, but with any luck, she'd get used to it. He heard the dog parks around here were really nice. Maybe she'd even make new friends.

"Wait—" May started.

"They have them." He'd done that research during his layover. "They're more expensive, and sometimes you need insurance—"

"Wait," she tried again.

"But I'm sure we can—"

"What on *earth* are you talking about?" May finally flung out there.

A record skipped in Han's brain. He scrunched up his brow. Hadn't he said that part?

"How we'll deal with things when I move here." Wasn't that obvious?

Apparently not. May threw her head back and laughed.

Okay, forget a record skipping. An entire shelf of them got swept to the ground, shattering on impact.

Oh, hell. He'd just assumed and he knew better than to assume—with May, things never worked out the way he thought they would, and he'd already apologized once for taking away her right to decide her own future.

He'd just thought...

"You don't want me to move here?" His rib cage crushed in.

Her laughter suddenly cut off. She gazed at him with wonder. "Han. Han— I was just..." She scrambled to set down her laptop bag and the tackle box and pulled her phone out of her pocket. She unlocked it and held it in front of his face.

He struggled to focus enough to read the small print— reading was hard when your heart was so smashed in you couldn't breathe. But he registered the logo for the same airline he'd just ridden on his way up here. The airport code for Asheville Regional.

He jerked his gaze up to her face. Her big, beautiful brown eyes gleamed, a watery smile curling her lips, and for the first time since he'd gotten in his car this morning, real hope inflated his lungs.

"Han, I was on my way back to Blue Cedar Falls."

"You were?"

She nodded wildly. "I've been miserable without you."

"Not as miserable as I've been without you."

Just like that, his feet came unstuck from the hallway carpet. He surged forward. She took a step back to let him in. The instant the door swung closed behind him, he dropped his duffel bag and the stolen garden gnome with it. They both thudded on the ground, but he paid them no mind. He reached for her, and she reached for him.

They met in the middle, their mouths crashing together. He clutched at her, scarcely able to believe the miracle of having her in his arms again.

"Missed you so much," he murmured against her lips.

"Me too."

Unbearable lightness expanded inside his chest, pushing his heart back into the right shape. How had he ever thought he could let this woman go?

"I don't care where we live," he gasped, unwilling to stop kissing her. He wasn't going to make any more mistakes with her—no more ultimatums, no more taking choices out of her hands, no more putting his foot down or drawing lines in the sand. "I'll go anywhere with you. I won't tie you down."

"I know, I know . . ."

"I won't ever stand in your way again. I'll follow you anywhere. I'll support you—your dreams, your career— whatever you want."

"I just want you." She kissed him harder, and he lost his mind for a minute there, sinking into the feeling of being connected to her like this.

They'd both been so stubborn, so set in their ways. But nothing worked without her. Whatever their future held, they'd figure it out together.

He finally pulled away, breathless from her kiss. "Wherever you go, it's fine." He held her tight. "Just so long as you come home to me."

"I will. Always. And Han—"

"Yeah."

"I want our home to be in Blue Cedar Falls."

It was like Christmas, his birthday, and a day at the beach all rolled into one. Still... "You don't have to."

"I want to." The shine to her eyes brightened further. "Being back there made me realize I've been running away for all this time. But the people I love most in the world are all there. My family..." Her voice cracked. "You."

"I love you so much." He tugged her into another deep kiss. When he came up for air, he shook his head, though. "But we don't have to stay there if you don't want. New York was your dream."

"Not anymore. It was great, being here the last ten years, but it's not where I want to be anymore. I've never been so happy or so comfortable as I was back in our hometown. With you."

"Only if you're sure."

"I'm sure." She swabbed at her eyes. Then she drew back, releasing her grasp on him to point toward the floor. "Just so we're clear, though, I'm not living with that thing, though."

He laughed, loud and unguarded, as he followed

her gaze to the creepy gnome. "You're the one who stole him."

"For you—not for us."

"Maybe you should have thought of that earlier."

"Yeah." She bit her lip, and the softness in her eyes squeezed his heart all over again. "Maybe I should have." She blinked. "Seriously, though—I'm not so sure about living with your mom, either, but—"

"Then we won't. We'll get our own place. Just for us."

There were going to be so many things to sort out, logistically, but somehow, they'd make it work. The only obstacle left that he could think of was...

"Your job..." he started.

She shook her head. "Can deal with me being remote. I'm never here anyway. And if they refuse, I can free-lance." She clasped his hand. "I still care about my work. I always will. But it's not the most important thing to me. Not anymore."

His throat tightened. He cupped her cheek, brushing his thumb beneath her eye. "Nothing in the world is more important to me than you."

"Then come on." She tilted her head toward the door. "Take me home."

From the bottom of his heart, he laughed. "I thought you'd never ask."

# CHAPTER TWENTY-ONE

❀ ❀ ❀ ❀ ❀ ❀ ❀ ❀ ❀ ❀ ❀

*Four months later...*

Pretty sure that's the last of it." Wiping her brow, Elizabeth added one more box to the teetering stack.

May set hers down beside it and stepped back.

June sat cross-legged on the floor, poring over the assembly instructions for what currently looked like a medieval torture device, but which Elizabeth had assured them was eventually going to be an easel. May wasn't sure how much she'd paid for it at the wacky discount art supply store she liked to order from, but it had definitely been too much.

"Good thing," June said, looking around. "Not a whole lot of room left."

Elizabeth smiled and patted another box from the dubious supply store. It claimed to contain a storage cabinet, but who knew? "No worries. Once we get this bad boy put together, I'll be able to fit so much more stuff in it."

"Aha!" Graham called out. He'd been sitting at Elizabeth's drafting table for a while now, fiddling with an electric drill. He held it up and pulled the trigger, and it spun like... well, like a drill.

"Uh..." May frowned, not really sure what she was looking at.

"I turned an Allen key into a drill bit," he announced, looking incredibly proud of himself.

"Okay..."

"Trust me." He gave the trigger another quick pulse. "This is going to make this all so much easier."

As he spoke, the portion of the easel June had managed to assemble so far collapsed.

"Perfect timing, bud." Elizabeth clapped him on the shoulder—and was it just May, or did Graham flinch? "Looks like we're going to need all the help we can get."

Graham's weird reaction aside, May couldn't argue with her about that.

After receiving rejection after rejection for all the artist residencies she'd applied for, Elizabeth had gotten pretty low for a while, but May had to give her credit. She picked herself back up with aplomb. Finally deciding those kinds of programs were too snooty for her anyway, she'd shifted gears. She'd taken the money she'd earmarked for the residency and put it toward renting a vacant in-law cottage from one of Ned's friends to turn into a studio of her own. The place needed a lot of work, but Elizabeth saw potential in it, and that was all that mattered. She'd keep reaching for the stars, but she'd do it here—feet firmly planted on the ground.

It was a sentiment May could relate to.

As if to underscore the point, her phone chose that moment to buzz. She pulled it out of her pocket and grinned to see Han's name on the screen.

*Thinking of taking Ling for a hike before the dinner crowd. Wanna come with?*

She didn't hesitate. *Absolutely. Meet you at JGA?*

He texted back a thumbs-up, and her grin grew. She pocketed her phone. "Sorry, guys. Gotta take off for a bit."

Elizabeth pouted. "But there's so much stuff to do."

"Say hi to Han for me." June smiled knowingly.

"Will do." To Elizabeth, May said, "I'll be back in an hour. Two, tops."

"Ugh, fine."

May gave her little sister a quick hug, then waved at June and Graham. "Try not to finish everything before I get back."

Graham shook his head. "Pretty sure there's no risk of that."

Outside, the late summer sun beat down on her, and she drank it up. She'd never imagined she would miss the heat of this place, but there was something about it that comforted her. Reminded her that she was home.

That didn't mean she was a complete martyr, of course. In her car, she put down the windows and cranked the AC. She drove through the residential neighborhood and south toward Main Street.

On the way, she was pretty sure she passed Jenny sitting at Gracie's Café with a couple of her friends, but she didn't care. They were still chilly to each other when they happened to cross paths, but May didn't go deer in the headlights around her anymore. This was her hometown, and she belonged here as much as anyone.

Minutes later, she parked in front of a very familiar storefront at the north end of the strip. What wasn't familiar was the new marquee.

Right next to the big, lit sign for the Jade Garden hung a new one. It was small, the font more modern. But it was all Han's.

She got out of her car and strode toward the second entrance.

The Jade Garden Annex's brick-and-mortar location

had officially opened its doors a month ago. It had required some tense negotiations, but Han and his mother had come up with a solution that they both could live with. The Jade Garden carried on with its tried-and-true menu of standard Chinese takeout. Meanwhile, in a newly converted dining room, the Jade Garden Annex served casual but still upscale, modern takes on beloved classics. Han had complete creative control, and he'd run with it, in the best possible way. Out were the dishes his mother ragged on him for being too fussy. In were recipes he'd developed with his whole heart and soul, including the most successful hits that had earned him acclaim at Taste of Blue Cedar Falls.

Business was booming at both restaurants—helped along just a smidge by a feature May had written about them in her article for *Passage*, which had hit newsstands just as the Jade Garden Annex was opening for business. From there, Han's creations and top-notch service had spoken for themselves.

As she entered, she passed Mrs. Leung, who was paging through a magazine as she waited by the phone at the counter of the original Jade Garden.

"Afternoon," May called.

Mrs. Leung waved absently. "Afternoon, May."

May smiled. Mrs. Leung had reacted to May's return with the same reserved welcome she'd shown the last time May had turned up out of the blue. She seemed glad to have May here, but not particularly surprised by it.

Really, it seemed like the only people who were surprised were May and Han themselves.

Speaking of which...

"There you are." Han strode out from the back recesses of the kitchen shared by the two restaurants.

Even now, May's heart did a little dance in her chest at the sight of him. She felt like she floated, crossing the distance, and he caught her up in his arms.

He pressed a firm kiss to her lips, and shivers of happiness flowed through her. "Hey."

"Hey, yourself." He looked down at her with warm, dark eyes.

Things over the last few months hadn't been completely simple. There had been a lot of details to work out.

*Passage* had declined to keep her on once she declared her change in zip code. They'd been in the middle of a round of layoffs anyway, so she probably shouldn't have been surprised. The news had hurt, but she'd been undeterred.

Especially when Zahra slipped into her DMs to tell her she was moving to a new publishing house, and would May like to come on board as a freelancer? Zahra kept her jumping at the new magazine just as thoroughly as she had at the old one, only now May could pick and choose which assignments she wanted to take. She supplemented her income writing articles for Tori at the tourism bureau, plus she'd started working on a book, all about the Carolina mountains. When she was in town, she worked two shifts a week at the family inn. She still traveled about fifty percent of the time—usually to boring resorts.

But that was all right.

At the end of the day, after every trip, she had a spring in her step. Coming home meant something new to her.

Instead of a sad, lonely apartment, home meant the Leung house. Home meant Han.

And yes—home also meant a lot of costly and time-intensive remodeling. To both their surprise, when they'd broached the subject of their living arrangements with her, Mrs. Leung had been delighted to move out. She'd apparently been secretly plotting with her brother, Han's uncle Arthur, to move into a senior complex together on the other side of town. The only reason she hadn't yet was Han's protest that he'd never let her waste away in a place like that.

"Waste away?" she'd scoffed. "They have pickle ball league and a pool."

With his objection removed, she'd packed her bags the instant there'd been an available apartment. That left May and Han with a giant house to turn into a place of their own.

Slowly but surely, they were doing precisely that. It didn't matter that it was a continual work in progress, or that Han's dog was deeply suspicious of her tortoise, or that Han kept moving the stolen garden gnome around their yard to freak her out.

She and Han could live in a tent in the middle of the woods, and she'd be good. So long as it was here.

"You ready?" she asked, pulling away.

"For you?" His eyes twinkled, and her pulse raced. "Always."

Taking her hand, he led her out to the parking lot and toward her car. She slipped into the driver's seat, and he got in beside her.

She looked to him as she put the car in gear. "Where to?"

Smiling, he said, simply, "Home."

# ABOUT THE AUTHOR

**Jeannie Chin** writes contemporary small-town romances. She draws on her experiences as a biracial Asian and white American to craft heartfelt stories that speak to a uniquely American experience.

She is a former high school science teacher, wife to a geeky engineer, and mom to an extremely talkative kindergartener. Her hobbies include crafting, reading, and hiking.

You can learn more at:
Website: JeannieChin.com
Twitter @JeannieCWrites
Facebook.com/JeannieCWrites
Instagram @JeannieCWrites

Don't miss *The House on Mulberry Street*, the next book in the Blue Cedar Falls series.

Coming Winter 2023

*Fall in love with these small-town romances full of tight-knit communities and heartwarming charm!*

### THE BEACHSIDE BED AND BREAKFAST
**by Hope Ramsay**

Ashley Howland Scott has no time for romance while grieving for her husband, caring for her son, and running Magnolia Harbor's only bed and breakfast. But slowly, Rev. Micah St. Pierre has become a friend…and maybe something more. Micah cannot date a member of his congregation, so there's no point in sharing his feelings with Ashley, no matter how much he yearns to. But the more time they spend together, the more Micah wonders whether Ashley is his match made in heaven.

### THE SUMMER SISTERS
**by Sara Richardson**

The Buchanan sisters share everything—even ownership of their beloved Juniper Inn. As children, they spent every holiday there, until a feud between their mother, Lillian, and Aunt Sassy kept them away. When the grand reopening of the inn coincides with Sassy's seventieth birthday, Rose, the youngest sister, decides it's time for a family reunion. Only she'll need help from a certain handsome hardware-store owner to pull off the celebration…

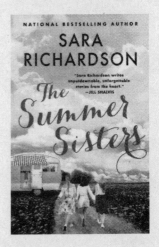

*Find more great reads on Instagram with*
*@ReadForeverPub*

**SOMETHING BLUE**
**by Heather McGovern**

Wedding planner Beth Shipley has seen it all: bridezillas, monster-in-laws, and last-minute jitters at the altar. But this wedding is different—and the stakes are much, *much* higher. Not only is her best friend the bride, but bookings at her family's inn have been in free fall. Beth knows she can save her family's business—as long as she doesn't let best man Sawyer Silva's good looks and overprotective, overbearing, older-brother act distract her. Includes a bonus story by Annie Rains!

**HOW SWEET IT IS**
**by Dylan Newton**

Event planner Kate Sweet is famous for creating happily-ever-after moments for dream weddings. So how is it that her best friend has roped her into planning a best-selling horror writer's book launch extravaganza in a small town? The second Kate meets the drop-dead-hot Knight of Nightmares, Drake Matthews, her well-ordered life quickly transforms into an absolute nightmare. But neither are prepared for the sweet sting of attraction they feel for each other. Will the queen of romance fall for the king of horror?

## Connect with us at
## Facebook.com/ReadForeverPub

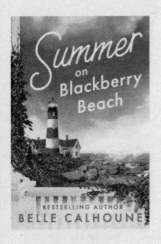

### SUMMER ON BLACKBERRY BEACH
by Belle Calhoune

Navy SEAL Luke Keegan is back in his hometown for the summer, and the rumor mill can't stop whispering about him and teacher Stella Marshall. He never thought he'd propose a fake relationship, but it's the only way to stop the runaway speculation about their love lives. Pretending to date a woman as stunning as Stella is easy. Not falling for her is the hard part, especially with the real attraction buzzing between them. Could their faux summer romance lead to true love?

### FALLING FOR YOU
by Barb Curtis

Just when recently evicted yoga instructor Faith Rotolo thinks her luck has run out, she inherits a historic mansion in quaint Sapphire Springs. But her new home needs fixing up and the handsome local contractor, Rob Milan, is spoiling her daydreams with the realities of the project...and his grouchy personality. While they work together, their spirited clashes wind up sparking a powerful attraction. As work nears completion, will she and Rob realize that they deserve a fresh start too?

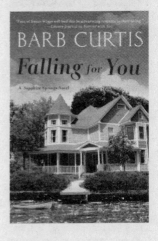

## Discover bonus content and more on
## read-forever.com

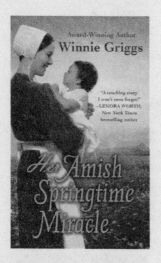

### HER AMISH
### SPRINGTIME MIRACLE
**by Winnie Griggs**

Amish baker Hannah Eicher has always wanted a *familye* of her own, so finding sweet baby Grace in her barn seems like an answer to her prayers. Until *Englischer* paramedic Mike Colder shows up in Hope's Haven, hoping to find his late sister's baby. As Hannah and Mike contemplate what's best for Grace, they spend more and more time together while enjoying the warm community and simple life. Despite their wildly different worlds, will Mike and Hannah find the true meaning of "family"?

### THE AMISH FARMER'S
### PROPOSAL
**by Barbara Cameron**

When Amish dairy farmer Abe Stoltzfus tumbles from his roof, he's lucky his longtime friend Lavinia Fisher is there to help. He secretly hoped to propose to her, but now, with his injuries, his dairy farm in danger, and his harvest at stake, Abe worries he'll only be a burden. Yet, as he heals with Lavinia's gentle support and unflagging optimism, the two grow even closer. But will she be able to convince him that real love doesn't need perfect timing?

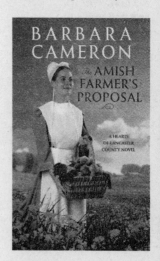